LIBRARY

D0032047

"An ol... ... ... wes
story th... ...
Dunlap'... ...
—Johnny D. Boggs, four-time Spur Award–winning author

"A rip-roaring yarn that realizes the best traditions of the
Western genre: strong, well-defined characters, the color of
the West vivid and perfectly researched, and the writing
entertaining and quick as a bronc set free to run wild. A sure-
fire read for Western fiction fans."
—Larry D. Sweazy, Spur Award–winning author

"There's nothing unusual about page-turning action in a
paperback Western, and you'll find plenty of it in *Cotton's War*.
What separates this novel from the pack is layer upon layer
of intriguing subplots, parallel storylines and a cast of characters that diverges from the norm." —*Roundup Magazine*

Praise for the novels of Phil Dunlap

"With a raft of well-drawn, even indelible, characters, the
novel also offers a compellingly involved, quite plausible, and
tightly woven plot." —*Booklist*

"Dunlap uses his passion for history and the Old West to
paint a realistic setting for his work. . . . For those who share
his love affair with gamblers, scalawags, and claim-jumpers
with gold fever, this fun novel will keep you guessing."
—*The Indianapolis Star*

"Phil Dunlap is a writer to fog the sage with! Flesh and blood
characters, compelling plots, and cinematic action—Western
writing doesn't get any better than this. I've become a big fan!"
—Peter Brandvold, author of *The Last Lawman*

Berkley titles by Phil Dunlap

COTTON'S WAR
COTTON'S LAW
COTTON'S DEVIL

COTTON'S DEVIL

A Sheriff Cotton Burke Western

Phil Dunlap

Thompson-Nicola Regional District
Library System
300 - 465 VICTORIA STREET
KAMLOOPS, B.C.   V2C 2A9

BERKLEY BOOKS, NEW YORK

THE BERKLEY PUBLISHING GROUP
Published by the Penguin Group
Penguin Group (USA) Inc.
375 Hudson Street, New York, New York 10014, USA

Penguin Group (Canada), 90 Eglinton Avenue East, Suite 700, Toronto, Ontario M4P 2Y3, Canada (a division of Pearson Penguin Canada Inc.) • Penguin Books Ltd., 80 Strand, London WC2R 0RL, England • Penguin Group Ireland, 25 St. Stephen's Green, Dublin 2, Ireland (a division of Penguin Books Ltd.) • Penguin Group (Australia), 250 Camberwell Road, Camberwell, Victoria 3124, Australia (a division of Pearson Australia Group Pty. Ltd.) • Penguin Books India Pvt. Ltd., 11 Community Centre, Panchsheel Park, New Delhi—110 017, India • Penguin Group (NZ), 67 Apollo Drive, Rosedale, Auckland 0632, New Zealand (a division of Pearson New Zealand Ltd.) • Penguin Books (South Africa) (Pty.) Ltd., 24 Sturdee Avenue, Rosebank, Johannesburg 2196, South Africa

Penguin Books Ltd., Registered Offices: 80 Strand, London WC2R 0RL, England

This is a work of fiction. Names, characters, places, and incidents either are the product of the author's imagination or are used fictitiously, and any resemblance to actual persons, living or dead, business establishments, events, or locales is entirely coincidental. The publisher does not have any control over and does not assume any responsibility for author or third-party websites or their content.

COTTON'S DEVIL

A Berkley Book / published by arrangement with the author

PUBLISHING HISTORY
Berkley edition / January 2013

Copyright © 2012 by Phil Dunlap.
Cover illustration by Dennis Lyall.
Cover design by Diana Kolsky.
Interior text design by Tiffany Estreicher.

All rights reserved.
No part of this book may be reproduced, scanned, or distributed in any printed or electronic form without permission. Please do not participate in or encourage piracy of copyrighted materials in violation of the author's rights. Purchase only authorized editions.
For information, address: The Berkley Publishing Group,
a division of Penguin Group (USA) Inc.,
375 Hudson Street, New York, New York 10014.

ISBN: 978-0-425-25062-4

BERKLEY®
Berkley Books are published by The Berkley Publishing Group,
a division of Penguin Group (USA) Inc.,
375 Hudson Street, New York, New York 10014.
BERKLEY® is a registered trademark of Penguin Group (USA) Inc.
The "B" design is a trademark of Penguin Group (USA) Inc.

PRINTED IN THE UNITED STATES OF AMERICA

10 9 8 7 6 5 4 3 2 1

If you purchased this book without a cover, you should be aware that this book is stolen property. It was reported as "unsold and destroyed" to the publisher, and neither the author nor the publisher has received any payment for this "stripped book."

ALWAYS LEARNING   **PEARSON**

3 5444 00048309 8

Acknowledgments

This book would not have been possible without the help of many good friends, family, and a terrific publisher. First, my thanks to my critique partner, author Tony Perona, who makes certain the plot doesn't wander off to the hinterland; to my wife, Judy, who is relentless in keeping me from making embarrassing mistakes with characters and storyline; and to my untiring editor at Berkley, Faith Black, to whom I owe everything. Of course, I cannot fail to thank the many faithful Western readers who live for the sound of gunfire rising off the pages. My undying gratitude to you all.

Chapter 1

New Mexico Territory–1880

The telegram read simply:

COME TO SILVER CITY. NEED HELP. GOING
TO HANG.
THORN MCCANN

That was all. But it was enough.

"I'm not sure why you feel the need to ride all the way to Silver City to try saving the worthless scoundrel that rode into town pretending to be a common gunslinger looking to add you to his list of kills. You know he nearly scared me to death. Remember how long it took for him to tell *you* who he really was? You said yourself you weren't sure he could be trusted. And you *know* he probably shot and killed Bart Havens, so what makes the man worth saving?" Emily Wagner held out a cup of coffee to Sheriff Cotton Burke. "Even though killing Havens was certainly in *your* best interest."

Cotton was stuffing a couple of freshly boiled shirts and

some socks into one side of a saddlebag. The other side was filled with coffee, some beef jerky, flour, beans, and extra ammunition. Emily leaned on the door frame watching him prepare for his trip to Silver City, to see for himself what bounty hunter Thorn McCann had done to earn him a date with the hangman's noose. Her expression was a mixture of skepticism and disdain. Whether Cotton believed Thorn deserved to pay the ultimate price for his misdeeds was something else entirely. He was neither judge nor jury, except when faced with the choice to kill or be killed by another's hand.

"Didn't say anything about savin' his, uh, butt." He brushed a shock of brown hair back from his forehead, took the cup, and raised it to his lips. "Thanks."

From the perspective of recent events, Thorn had probably been guilty of many crimes, although Cotton couldn't put his finger on exactly what those crimes were. He had been asked to come to Silver City and see what could be done to save a man's life, and Cotton Burke was the type of person to honor such a request. Besides, he still had a lot of unanswered questions for McCann concerning the death of Bart Havens. So he'd assigned his deputy, Memphis Jack Stump, the task of keeping Apache Springs safe until he returned. It was a decision he hadn't made lightly, especially since Jack had a tendency to drink a little too much and spend a little too much time in the bed of a prostitute named Melody, with whom he lived. Other than a touch of irresponsibility from time to time, Jack was a generally dependable friend and a damned good man with a gun. Still, a lot was riding on his ability to take being a deputy as seriously as was needed.

"You still haven't answered my question: Why are you going?" Emily said, again.

"I'm not sure I got it all worked out in my own mind, but I know I need to go before whatever it is they're plannin' on stringin' him up for puts him in the ground before I get to ask him some questions of my own. I reckon the thing that puzzles me most is why he called on *me* for help. Especially considerin' the circumstances which brought him here in the first place."

"I know you want to do right by him, but I'm not convinced he's an honorable man, nor one deserving of your friendship," she said with a frown.

"I've got plenty of reservations about him, and I'm not goin' out of anything near to friendship. I figure any man's due the benefit of the doubt, though. And I'm not entirely satisfied with his story on how Bart Havens died. This could be my last chance to get some answers. I plan to be back in about a week or so. Keep the coffee hot," he said, handing her back the empty cup and leaning over to kiss her. She followed him out the door of his tiny house, to where she had tied her buckboard. The little house was the one extra accommodation the town of Apache Springs afforded its sheriff, even though he chose to spend his nights at Emily Wagner's ranch whenever possible. His house was too small, too confining, and far too lonely. And besides, being away from Emily too long made him damned difficult to be around.

Emily gave him a weak wave and tentative smile as he mounted his mare and rode slowly down the south road out of town. He hadn't felt the need to wake Jack. They'd spoken at length the evening before. Jack had waved off the responsibility handed him, as if being the sole lawman in a town that had seen more than its share of gunplay over the past three months was merely an everyday event. As Cotton passed the jail on his way through town, he glanced over to see his deputy at the desk. The sheriff was shocked, it being barely nine o'clock in the morning, an hour that usually found Memphis Jack still snoring away.

Jack didn't look up as Cotton rode by.

Cotton wasn't making very good time. The day was hot and the terrain difficult. He dared not push his mare too hard lest she fail him at a time and place where help was nonexistent. A few months earlier, a band of renegade Chiricahua Apaches from across the Arizona Territory border had tried to raid a small village and stockade called Fort Tularosa, not far from the trail he now rode. They'd been driven off by a small detachment of buffalo soldiers led by a brave sergeant. But even then the locals were understandably nervous about the possibility of the Indians returning, since the leader of the Apaches was a notorious warrior named Victorio, who was not known to take defeat lightly. This incident weighed on the sheriff's mind, too. One man alone would stand little chance of survival if caught in the open by a band of Indians bent on killing anyone with white skin.

Small raids on local ranches were a reality most endured, though fearfully. Few lives were lost, but the same couldn't be said for any cattle or horses straying from the herds. Some of the renegades raided simply because they were hungry. Most of the ranchers didn't begrudge them a few missing cattle if it staved off open warfare. But Victorio's attacks were an attempt to convince the white settlers they should go back east and leave the Indian lands alone.

Cotton urged his horse down a rocky slope, toward some trees and the likelihood of finding water. He decided to camp by a stream close to where he and the Silver City blacksmith, Bear Hollow Wilson, had once sought shelter from two opposing bunches of men bent on taking Cotton's prisoner from him over three months back. That occasion had given Cotton a new appreciation for mob rule. Well-armed and cautious, he and Wilson had thought they were fully prepared to safely transport and protect their prisoner. Their preparations had proven inadequate, for by happenstance they'd lost him, only not in a way Cotton and his temporary deputy could have ever contemplated. Their prisoner, a man named McMasters, had murdered the town marshal of Silver City. Since Cotton had been desperate to get back to Apache Springs to do whatever he could to free Emily Wagner from a gang of ruthless outlaws holding her hostage, and the town had been left without a lawman, he'd volunteered to take the killer to his own jurisdiction for trial. He and Wilson were faced with townsfolk who wanted the killer brought to justice without any trial and the man's own men who wanted him freed. Or so everyone assumed.

After a brief standoff amid volleys of gunfire, McMasters managed to break his bonds and make a dash for freedom toward his own men. But, without warning, one of those men rose up from behind a boulder and blew him into the next century with a twelve-gauge shotgun. The man later explained that no one wanted there to be any chance that McMasters might escape justice and return to the mines, where he regularly inflicted harsh punishments for minor infractions of his rules, especially when he had been drinking heavily, which was often. Now, camped nearby, the whole incident came back to Cotton as if it were an unsettling nightmare.

When Cotton reined in at the hotel in Silver City, he looked around to see if he could remember where the blacksmith's shop was located. And because his last time in town had been a while ago, he needed to get reacquainted with his surroundings. And he also hoped to say hello to the man who'd volunteered to help haul the killer to Apache Springs for trial: Bear Hollow Wilson. But first, he needed to locate the marshal's office. Since he didn't remember where the law hung out in Silver City, and didn't immediately see any sign to indicate a location, he figured to ask one of the locals for whoever had been elected to fill the shoes of the murdered marshal.

He hefted his saddlebags onto his shoulder and strode into the hotel and up to the desk. The same young man he remembered from his last visit was behind the counter, only this time he seemed to be gazing off into nothingness. Cotton figured his distraction meant he must be in love.

"Excuse me, young man, do you know where I can find the law in this town?"

"Uh-huh," the fellow mumbled with his chin in his hands, a distant look in his eyes.

"I wonder if it would be too much trouble for you to tell me, then."

"No trouble at all," said the desk clerk, barely above a whisper, his gaze still locked on some distant visage.

Yep, this kid's in love, Cotton thought. But, since waiting for the smitten youth to awaken from daydreaming of his beloved was not part of Cotton's agenda, he felt it time to make a statement that might be responded to properly. He slammed his fist on the counter. The young man's eyes came open in shock. He began to stammer, clearly flustered by Cotton's action.

"Oh, yes, sir, uh, what was it you wanted? I only have two rooms left and you can have whichever one you want, and if you want dinner the dining room is off to the left, and if—"

"Hold on, sonny, I just asked where I could find the law in this town."

When the kid noticed the sheriff's badge pinned to Cotton's shirt, he became more disoriented than before.

"Oh! Why, yes, the county sheriff is off somewhere chasing rustlers. And the town marshal is, uh, probably in his office, er, the jail, unless he isn't, in which case I'd suggest you try the restaurant next door to the—"

"Son, just direct me to the marshal's office. I really don't have all day to listen to your blathering. Okay?"

"Uh-huh. It's down the street, one block, on the other side. Above the door it says—"

" 'Marshal's Office'?"

"Why, er, yessir, how'd you know?"

"I don't have my head up my butt over some female; that's how I was able to figure it out. Thanks."

Cotton left the lad stammering and fidgeting behind the counter, still trying to gather his wits about him. *Oh, to be seventeen, again*, Cotton thought to himself. As he walked out into the sun-splashed street, one glance and he saw his objective. *Maybe I should have looked around more thoroughly before making it harder on myself*, he thought. Exactly where the boy had indicated, a small, barely visible wooden sign stuck out at ninety degrees from the front of a clapboard-sided building next to a restaurant. As he approached the jail, the door opened and a massive shadow emerged. He broke into a smile as he recognized the man with the Sharps rifle dangling from his hand.

"Bear Hollow Wilson! Good to see you're still here." Cotton stuck out his hand and was momentarily taken aback as the sun struck the silver badge on the man's chest.

"Sheriff Burke! What brings you to Silver City?"

"Couple of things, actually. But first, tell me what convinced you to take up a badge."

"Short and simple: No one else would take it. Scared, I suppose. They offered, I accepted. Besides, I needed the money."

"I can't think of a better man for the job. Congratulations."

"Thanks. Now, what brought you . . . ?"

"Oh, yeah. Well I got a telegram from a fellow named Thorn McCann. Said you had him locked up. Said he was going to get his neck stretched. I wanted to talk to him before that happened."

"Hmm. Sorry you made the trip for nothin', Sheriff. You're a tad bit late."

"Oh? Pretty quick trial, wasn't it?"

"Didn't ever get to a trial. Judge wasn't due for another week. Some of the townsfolk was kinda gettin' impatient waitin around, so . . ."

"So, where is he?"

"He's gone."

Chapter 2

———◆———

"You already strung him up? Without a trial?"

"Nope. Didn't hang him. The vigilantes didn't get to him, either," Bear Hollow said.

"So where is he?"

"Now that's a puzzlement. Wish I knew. I came in with his dinner late yesterday evenin', sometime after dark, and his cell was empty. Musta happened while I was out checkin' the streets."

"Someone busted him out?"

"I reckon you couldn't actually call it 'busted.' More like they just sauntered in, unlocked the cell, and he walked out. Took his gun with him, too. Right outta my desk drawer. Looks like he got his horse from the stable and rode out of town pretty as you please. No one saw him, so they couldn't stop him. Don't imagine anyone was that inclined to tangle with a gunslinger like him even if they had spotted him."

"Did you get up a posse?"

"Nope. While the folks hereabouts were damned upset

with what he'd done, they weren't all that interested in chasin' him to hell and gone. So it was up to me, or nobody. The town is my jurisdiction, period. And the county sheriff is, as usual, out of town. I'm sure you see my predicament."

"I reckon. But, tell me, what was it that McCann did that brought on his arrest?"

"He was livin' high, him and that beautiful gal he took up with right after he arrived. Gamblin', buyin' new clothes for the both of them, a new gun, ammunition, finest rooms at the hotel, and meals for himself and the lady. Wasn't until some of the merchants took the money their newfound benefactor had paid their bills with and tried to deposit it in the bank. That's when all hell broke loose."

A wry smile came over Cotton's face. "Let me guess. Every last cent of it was counterfeit."

"Right down to what he paid the liveryman for takin' care of his horse."

"I reckon I see why everyone was thinkin' of a necktie party. But unless it could be proven that *he* did the counterfeiting and that he'd spread it around *knowing* it was worthless, what he did wasn't a hangin' offense. That's where trials come in handy."

"True enough. But it was hard to make folks understand the finer points of the law when they'd been taken in by a charlatan. Hard on a man's pride, if you know what I mean."

"I do, at that. Do you know where I can find the lady? What was her name?"

"Called herself, uh, Eve Smith, as I recollect. And a real looker she was, too."

"Eve Smith? Black hair, brown eyes, well dressed?"

"That's the one. She cut a right smart figure."

"If I was to want a word with the lady, where would I find her?"

"Same boardin' house you and that other feller stayed in last time you was here. End of the street."

"Thank you, Marshal Wilson. I'll be stoppin' by before I leave town. Still got a couple of things puzzlin' me."

* * *

When he got to the end of the street, he saw the lady who owned the boardinghouse out front sweeping the porch of dirt and debris brought by the night winds. Along the front of the porch grew a row of sunflowers. He took off his Stetson as he approached.

"Good day, ma'am. Do you remember me? I stayed with you some months back."

Without looking up from her task, she said, "Of course I do. I don't never forget a voice. Don't need to see a face, neither. But if you're lookin' to stay a night or two, I'm afraid I'm all full up. Some cattlemen just arrived expecting a herd they're lookin' to buy. Fellers from Santa Fe, as I recall."

"No, I'll not be needin' a room, but I *would* like to talk to a young lady you have stayin' with you, Miss Eve Smith?"

"Was," she said, leaning the broom against the wall.

"Was?"

"Was here, ain't no more."

"Do you have any idea where I can find her? It's important."

"Nope. Can't say I care, either. Took me for a pretty penny, she did. Her and that scoundrel McCann. She stayed with me only two nights before she moved down to the hotel. Took them, too, as I understand it."

"I take it the money she paid for her room with was bogus."

"Yep. Good thing she didn't stay longer or I'da had to haul out my dead husband's twelve-gauge . . . Oh, never mind. I'm a softhearted old fool. Truth is I wouldn'ta done no such thing."

Cotton had to grin at the old lady's admission of what she figured was a flaw in her personality. He didn't see it that way, however. He put his Stetson back on and turned to walk away.

"What is it you were wantin' to see her about, anyway? I see you've a badge on your vest, so it must be something havin' to do with the law."

"I'm not all that sure, myself. Kinda hopin' she could give me somethin' to go on that might help with findin' Thorn McCann."

"Can't tell you nothin' other than he slipped the noose just in time and made tracks for the freedom trail."

"Freedom trail?"

"That's what my old pappy always said meant 'gettin' shed of the law.' "

Cotton laughed. "Reckon that's just what he did, at that. Thank you, ma'am."

He headed back down the dusty street to find Marshal Bear Hollow Wilson.

Chapter 3

———⬥◆⬥———

Marshal Wilson was at his desk, struggling as he attempted to bite off a piece of jerky. The expression on his face suggested he would just as soon be eating an old shoe.

"Hope that's not your lunch, Marshal."

"Yep. Got a *real* tight budget here in Silver City. The council don't keep marshals around long that can't stay to a budget. As you can see by my size, that ain't always easy. I'm already a tad over for the month, so . . ."

"Too bad. I was goin' to offer to take you to the hotel and buy you a steak, but . . ."

The marshal stood suddenly, grabbed his floppy-brimmed hat, and tossed the jerky in the wastebasket next to the desk. He grinned broadly as he put his beefy hand on Cotton's shoulder.

"Best damned offer I've had today, Sheriff. Lead the way, my friend."

Cotton couldn't resist a chuckle as they wandered out into the street.

"Bet you're buyin' me lunch so's you can try to wheedle some information outta this old blacksmith. Am I right?"

"You couldn't have hit the target better if you were two feet away."

It was Bear Hollow's turn to chuckle. "Well, fire away. I'm yours all the way through dessert."

After finishing off a thick steak, beans, fried potatoes, fresh bread slathered with butter, and three cups of coffee, they continued their conversation as they awaited two pieces of apple pie.

"Sounds like this Thorn McCann character has been doin' some pretty fancy dancin' for quite a spell. Likeable sort, I noticed, though," Bear Hollow said.

"I think tellin' a lie where the truth would just get in the way has become a way of life for him. I really don't know how to figure him. He say anything to you about Apache Springs?"

"No. Just went on and on about how the bad money wasn't his fault. Didn't even spot it as phony. Said it was given him by a banker somewhere or other. Don't remember him sayin' anything about your town or county for that matter." Bear's eyes lit up at seeing the pie that was placed in front of him. A big grin crossed his face as he wasted no time attacking it with his fork.

"So, he didn't mention his line of work?"

"Well, he did say somethin' about him bein' a lawman, but he offered no proof of any such thing. Figured it was a lie aimed at gettin' him some sympathy and a free pass out of the hoosegow."

"You called it right. He's likely the biggest truth twister I've ever met."

"That what he told you, too? That lawman part?"

"Started out sayin' he was a deputy U.S. marshal, then, when I caught him in that lie, he admitted to bein' a bounty hunter."

"So what was it brung him to Apache Springs in the first place?"

"Huntin' down some poor soul."

"Did he ever tell you who?"
"Yep. Me."
Bear stopped mid-bite with a wide-eyed look of surprise.

Ten miles outside of Silver City, a man on horseback sat beside the road watching the Butterfield stagecoach as it left a dusty cloud coming toward him. As the stage approached, the rider sat easy, making certain the driver and shotgun guard didn't take him for a highwayman. He kept his hands well away from his gun. He removed his hat, ran his forearm across his forehead, then replaced his hat. He held up his hand. As the stagecoach drew up, the guard, a kid who looked like he couldn't be more than seventeen, pointed the coach gun at him. The horses came to a halt, showering gravel and dirt and raising a dust cloud.

"You got a problem, mister?" the driver said.

"It's awful hot out here for a man on horseback. I got the fare if you could see your way clear to lettin' me tie my mount on the back and ride inside the rest of the way to Apache Springs. That is where you're headed, isn't it?"

"Only got two passengers, so there's plenty of room. Climb aboard, but be quick about it. I got a schedule to maintain."

The man thanked the driver, dismounted, and slipped the horse's reins through one of the straps on the luggage boot. He then opened the door and climbed inside, after being nearly tossed off the step as the driver, true to his word about being in a hurry, slapped the reins of the team and the coach lurched ahead.

The man removed his hat when he found himself in the company of a woman, a strikingly beautiful, dark-haired woman, at that. He made no attempt to announce that he already knew her. The other passenger was a slight, mousy gent in a wool suit that looked uncomfortable for the heat. He sported a thin mustache and wore glasses. In one hand he held a handkerchief with which he mopped at his brow often and also covered his nose and mouth during the times dust swirled through from wind gusts, which were often. On his lap he carried a small, highly polished wooden case with brass fittings. The way he gripped it, the case obviously held something of value. At least to him.

"Good day to you both. Travelin' together?"

The man in the suit shook his head and looked at the floor, as if he was embarrassed at the suggestion of him being in a lady's company.

The lady smiled and said, "My name is Eve Smith. And your name, sir?"

"Why, uh, I'm John Thorn. From Tucson."

"Nice to meet you, Mr. Thorn. Lucky the stage came along when it did. You could have been overcome by a heat-stroke riding in that blistering sun."

"Yes, ma'am, mighty lucky."

The man in the suit said nothing, just turned his head and began staring out the side window. Eve dropped her eyes and looked away, covering a smirk with a dainty, gloved hand.

The coach rumbled on for two hours with no one saying a word. Occasional glances from John Thorn into the face of Eve Smith, while obvious to any casual observer, raised no flags to the man in the suit. Dust from the coach's wheels continued to fill the cramped interior. Eve rode with a hand-kerchief covering her mouth much of the time. The men coughed and cleared their throats often. If ever there were a time to imbibe a cool glass of beer, that time was now, thought Thorn. But that was before the driver called out with a panicked voice.

"Injuns! Anyone with a gun, get it out now! We're about to be attacked!"

Thorn drew his .45 and turned to get a view of where the Indians were and how many there might be. He clearly didn't like what he saw. A dozen yelping braves astride paint ponies were taking up the chase even as the driver whipped the team into a run.

In this heat, our team won't last long, Thorn thought.

Better we get out and try to make it to cover. We'll have a much better chance of picking some of them off that way than from a rocking, bouncing coach.

Just then a yell came from atop the coach when it took a sudden lurch to the left, careened off the road, and tilted to one side as one of the rear wheels slid into a deep rut, still drawn furiously by the frightened team of six horses. The coach's tenuous hold on remaining upright finally gave way to a sudden drop into a hole from which it could not recover. One front wheel's spokes shattered as the stage tipped onto its side, dragged through cactus, rocks and brush by frantic horses for a hundred feet before the scraping and grinding came to a halt. Thorn was the first one out the door, which now faced skyward, grabbing Eve's hand as he went. The battered stagecoach lay on its side, the driver's seat sheared from the frame. The mailbag had burst open, strewing letters everywhere. Baggage had likewise been tossed hither and yon. One wheel had splintered its axle from where it hit a large rock before coming to rest. The whole side of the coach had been stripped away by the impact and from being dragged along through a proliferation of desert debris.

"C'mon, you two, get to some cover in those rocks up there before we're overrun," Thorn hollered.

He then jumped to the ground, reaching up to pull Eve to safety. The man in the suit scrambled out as best he could, caught his foot on the door, and tumbled into the ditch. From the front of the coach, Thorn heard a groan. He looked up to see the marauding Apaches racing to reach the stricken stage. He threw a couple of hasty shots their way to slow them down.

"Get up that hill! Mister, help the lady up the incline and both of you drop behind anything that looks substantial enough to stop a bullet. Do it now!" Thorn yelled. He turned to see if he could do anything about the driver and the guard.

The young shotgun guard struggled to free himself from beneath the crumpled forward boot. Thorn grabbed his arm and yanked so hard the boy yelped.

"Sorry, son, but we got to get up that hill before they hit us."

The two of them began a scrambling, stumbling race to the top of the rise. The kid still had a firm grip on the scattergun, but by the way he limped, he was obviously hurt. Thorn had a hold on the kid's shirt and was pulling him nearly every step of the way. As they reached the top, Thorn felt a sharp pain as he took a bullet in the shoulder. He let out an anguished groan and fell forward. He'd nearly made it to the top. It was the kid's turn to try dragging *him* to safety. It was only by the grace of God that they made it to cover before the Indians overran the coach and descended on it like vultures.

Chapter 4

Since McCann wasn't here long enough for you to get anything useful out of him, at least nothin' you can pass on, I reckon I'd best get back to Apache Springs. No sense lollygaggin' around this burg," Cotton said, half-smiling. "Besides, eatin' like this would just make me fat."

"Don't blame you none, Sheriff. I'd do the same, too, if I wasn't gettin' paid to keep myself available to stop the unruly element from gettin' the upper hand. Reckon I'd as soon go back to makin' horseshoes and mendin' tools, truth be told." Bear gave a big, satisfied smile. He was about to say thanks for the meal when a huge man rushed in, panting, gasping for breath. He stopped a couple feet from the marshal, leaned over to put his hands on his knees for support, and struggled to get his words out.

"Marshal, y-you . . . gotta come . . . quick . . . or, or they's . . ." His big head drooped as his words came with more difficulty.

"What is it, Casper? You're too durn fat to be runnin' around hollerin' like that. Now, what's the problem?"

"Th-the saloon. They's two of 'em. Gonna be a real dustup . . ."

Bear Hollow pushed his chair back with such force it scooted halfway across the room. He grabbed the Sharps rifle from where he'd leaned it against the wall and stomped through the dining room doors toward the lobby. Cotton was close behind.

"What's your plan, Marshal?"

"Wha-what do you mean?"

"You can't go bursting into the saloon without knowin' who's in there, whether there might be more than two, how well armed they are, and what their intentions are," Cotton said.

Bear Hollow slowed down before getting to the batwing doors of the saloon. He stopped and turned to the sheriff. "You're right. You got a lot more experience than me in this kind of situation. What do you suggest?"

Cotton took his badge from his shirt and put it in his pocket. "How about you go around back and come in the rear door. Make sure that cannon is ready to use, just in case. I'll saunter in the front like I'm just off a trail drive, lookin' for a drink and some female company. I can assess the situation better without them knowin' I carry a badge, even if it don't mean spit here in Silver City."

Bear Hollow grunted in agreement as he began to lope down the alley to the back of the building. Cotton gave him a minute and then continued up the steps and through the swinging doors. He looked around inside to see if he could identify the source of the trouble. It didn't take him long. There were two of them, just as the big man had said. One was an old man, scruffy and dirty, with a scraggly beard. The other, young but feisty, was waving a Smith & Wesson .45 around, variously pointing it first at the bartender and then at any of a number of cowboys sitting around the room. The youngster seemed to take particular interest in a man seated at the nearest table, wearing a wide print scarf, with a bowler hat pushed back on his head, and sporting a thick mustache that all but hid his mouth. The man's face said he wasn't afraid. The kid was yelling as if he were angry at every living thing. When Cotton came in, the kid turned the gun his direction.

"What the hell do you want, mister? Can't you see we're doin' business here? Move on."

Cotton held both hands in the air in mock surrender, a look of puzzlement on his face.

"Sorry, son. Didn't know you were even here. I'm lookin' for a drink to parch a powerful thirst from a long drive. I don't mean to interfere. You can go on about your business."

The kid stared at him for a moment, then jabbed his .45 in Cotton's direction.

"Get your damned drink, then get on your way. I got no patience with interruptions," the kid snapped. He turned his attention back to the bartender and the man in the bowler.

The old man held a Winchester Yellow Boy in both hands, cocked and pointed at the floor, but unmistakably at the ready. The look on his dirty, heavily lined face seemed to find complete agreement in the youth's actions. A toothless grin wrinkled his chapped and sunburned lips.

"Thank you, son," Cotton said, turning to the bartender and pointing toward a bottle of whiskey sitting on the bar top. "Pour me one of those, bartender, if you please."

The bartender, lean and lank, was sweating profusely. His hand shook as he tried in vain to pour whiskey into the small glass without spilling half of it. Cotton remained calm, slowly sipping the amber liquid, hoping to catch a bit of what the fuss was all about. While obviously full of piss and vinegar, the younger of the two men was not a gunslinger. His nervous demeanor also suggested that the last thing he wanted to do was kill someone. His main weapon was his anger and his willingness to demonstrate it. Cotton hoped someone would mention what the problem might be, though. The mouthy kid didn't disappoint him.

Directing his rapidly building anger toward the man with the bowler hat, the kid said, "What the hell made you figure you and your men could just up and steal our horses? You got no right, and we want to be paid for 'em."

"Son, those horses weren't yours in the first place. They had the Campbell brand on 'em plain as day. You shoulda knowed that."

"They had no such brand, and they was on our land, that makes 'em ours. And that's that. Now, fork over a hunnert dollars apiece for all ten, or I'm goin' to put a bullet in you." The kid jabbed his .45 toward the man a couple times for emphasis.

Cotton could see this wasn't going to end well. Whose horses they were wouldn't make a bit of difference if a man died defending his position. The seated man was beginning to get nervous. Sweat ran down his forehead. His hand slid slowly toward his own revolver.

"I wouldn't go for that hogleg if'n I was you, mister," hollered the kid. That's when Cotton decided it was now or never to make his move.

"Son, the gent's got a point. But if you can prove the horses are yours, he *has* to give 'em back or pay you for them, don't he?" Cotton kept one hand on the bar and the other holding his whiskey glass.

"You stay out of this, whoever the hell you are. It ain't none of your business. Now, drink up and move on."

By looking past the old man, Cotton could see Bear Hollow slip silently in the back way. He was carrying his ever-present Sharps carbine. They had the two in a cross fire if it came to that. He hoped it wouldn't.

"I didn't come lookin' for trouble, just a little sip to settle my stomach. But it sounds like you got yourself a hornet's nest. I'd like to help you out if you'd let me. I got some experience in situations like this," Cotton said to the kid.

"How? How the hell you gonna help me? You don't even know me or my pa." He waved the Smith & Wesson in Cotton's general direction once more.

Cotton turned to the man at the table. Out of the corner of his eye he spotted several other men scattered around the room placing their hands on their guns. *One false move by this kid and there's gonna be another Shiloh in here*, he thought.

"Sir, are the horses in question nearby? Might be we could solve this whole problem real quick if they were. We can easily check those brands."

"Like the kid says, it ain't none of your business. Now, shove off. Me and my boys can handle this little shit and his old man." The man in the bowler stood up slowly, scooting his chair back with his legs. His hand fell to his six-gun. But before he could even clear leather, Cotton's Colt .45 was in his hand, cocked and aiming at the man's head. They were less than ten feet apart. The man stopped his draw, tossing Cotton a cold, narrow-eyed stare.

"What's your stake in this, mister?"

"I like to have peace and quiet when I come to a town. You're spoiling it for me. Now, *answer* my question." Cotton's voice had quickly changed from casual observer to the man in charge. This turnabout in attitude didn't elude the other cowboys that had apparently been behind the man claiming ownership of the remuda.

The man in the bowler looked around at several of the other men. None still had his hand hovering over a six-shooter. Two had sat back down. The man seemed to be getting more and more nervous. He removed his hand from the butt of his gun and wiped at his forehead.

"No, they ain't nearby. I-I sold 'em . . . to the army. A-ain't got 'em no more."

"So, I'm guessin' there wasn't a Campbell brand on 'em, and they likely *did* belong to these fellows. Did I guess right?" Cotton's eyes narrowed as the man nodded.

"It's possible . . ."

Just then Bear Hollow, who had heard every word, spoke up.

"Sounds like you just admitted to horse stealin', friend. That's a neck-stretchin' offense around here." He pointed his Sharps at the man, who had now begun to rock back and forth. "I'm thinkin' you best cough up a hundred dollars apiece for them horses or plan on meetin' up with the meanest judge these parts ever saw. He sure does love a hangin'."

"But, I . . ."

"And you best unbuckle that gun belt, too, 'cause you're goin' to visit my jail until you can find it in your heart to pay what you owe these folks," Bear Hollow said. He thrust the business end of the Sharps at the man, just to make sure there were no doubts as to his intentions.

Cotton fished out his own badge and pinned it on his shirt. He looked back at the other cowboys, who gave every impression they were preparing to leave town while they still could.

Chapter 5

———◆———

"Pretty clever the way you buffaloed that fella. What was it made you think the fool kid wouldn't plug you?"

"He wasn't a killer, and I had my doubts whether that old gun would even shoot. It was rusty and he hadn't cocked it, either. He was bluffing. Now, the old man was a different matter altogether. He looked near to the breakin' point. He was the one that worried me."

"Well, by gosh it turned out right and proper. The old fellow and his boy got paid for their horses, and I doubt we'll ever see that horse-stealin' scoundrel in these parts again," Bear said with a gleam in his eye. "Thanks to you, Sheriff."

"Just returnin' a favor."

"Just so's you know, I'm obliged. I learned something about gettin' myself out of a tight spot, thanks to you."

Cotton started out into the street to reclaim his mare. He patted the horse on her neck, took the reins, and swung into the saddle. Bear Hollow had followed him outside.

"You plannin' on goin' after that Thorn McCann fella, Sheriff?"

"Only if his tracks lead back in the general direction of Apache Springs. Got no hankerin' to traipse all over the countryside to find a man I don't know for sure did anything wrong. A hunch says so, but . . ."

"I know what you mean. It's only a hunch. Some fellas got a knack for swayin' folks with an easy way about 'em, real likable sort. He's one of them. Hope you'll drop in next time you're in the area. I think I owe you a meal. Or if you're feelin' generous again, I'll gladly join you in one on you." The marshal gave a gleeful snicker and went back inside to get out of the sun.

Before he left town, Cotton decided to stop at the stage depot. As he strolled down the street, he couldn't help thinking that the description of 'Eve Smith' closely matched Delilah Jones. He began to search his memory for some sense that Thorn and Delilah Jones had been more than casually involved during the Bart Havens affair. She had been employed by Havens, but he'd not noticed any particular alliance with McCann. Had there been a conscious effort to keep it secret? Was it a coincidence or was it planned all along? And how long *had* they known each other? He had no intention of leaving Silver City with questions hanging over his head. He tied the mare to the railing and went inside, ducking under the Butterfield Stage Line sign that had begun to droop on one side from a broken chain.

A short, balding man stood up from behind a counter at his arrival.

"Good day to you, sir. Where is it you're lookin' to travel to? The next stage will be arrivin' in three hours from Las Cruces."

"I'd like a couple of answers, rather than needin' a ticket. When was the last stage out? And where was it headed?"

The man thumbed down the last page in his ledger and, looking over half-frame glasses, said, "Well, sir, the last one left here at six o'clock this morning, going to Albuquerque by way of Apache Springs. Two paid passengers, a man and a woman."

"Can you remember what the man looked like?"

"Businessman, as I recall. Short, rumpled suit, carryin' a wooden case of some sort. Had brass hinges like a gun case."

"And the woman?"

"Hard to forget her. Right smart-lookin' lady. Dark hair and a smile that could, er–"

"I got the picture. Only the two of them, you say?"

"That's all. Only sold two tickets."

"Thanks," Cotton said over his shoulder as he rejoined his horse.

He was several hours late for any chance of catching up to the coach, and it made little sense to try, especially during the heat of the day such as it was. Best he casually head on back to Apache Springs. Maybe the coach got there and had a layover. *Reckon I'll just have to wait to find out if the mysterious dark-haired woman is anyone other than Delilah Jones, but I'd stake my reputation it's her.*

He had a wry smile on his lips as he rode out of town.

The road out of Silver City was an easy ride, at least until he reached the foothills several miles north. A slight breeze kept the day's heat down to a bearable temperature, and clouds had begun to move in, heralding the possibility of a few drops of rain, but well before it reached the ground the dryness of the desert usually sucked up any moisture that didn't come in the form of a thunderstorm. This day was no different. Cotton felt not a drop of anything other than perhaps some slight perspiration on his forehead.

He reached down and pulled one of his canteens from around the saddle horn, unscrewed the cap, and sipped some of the warm water. Unlikely as it was, Cotton didn't feel alone. All around him were the calls of birds and the howls of coyotes. A family of Gambel's quail sauntered in front of him, then, taking notice of him just for a moment, hurried on their way into the brush on the other side. A grunt from a javelina, or peccary as they were sometimes known, emanated from off to his right, although he never caught sight of it. He did catch a brief glimpse of a couple of mule deer making their way up a rocky slope in the distance.

With nothing of particular importance to concentrate on, the sudden mental image of Emily popping into his head almost startled him. He'd been away only a short while, not long enough to start missing her any more than he normally did. But somehow he was surprised by his vision of her, almost as if she were in trouble. It was a very strange feeling. He tried to shake it off as nothing. But he couldn't. A tinge of fear came over him and he urged the mare to increase her pace.

She's all right; I know she is. Although, I do have a powerful feeling *someone* is in serious trouble. And it feels like it's not far off. He gave his horse a knee to her sides to add a little incentive to pick up the pace even more.

He'd gone no more than another mile when his fears were realized. Up ahead, lying on its side in a ditch was the stagecoach. And a man was lying in the road. He wasn't moving. Cotton kicked the mare into a run. As they approached the stricken coach, he reined the horse to a dusty stop. He jumped from the saddle and ran to the man. Dead. A bullet had torn much of his head off. Cotton spun around to check on the stage, or what was left of it, yanked open the door, and peered inside. Empty.

It was obvious that someone had presented a threat to the coach and given chase when the driver tried to elude whatever danger had been thrust upon him. When the racing stage had come to a sharp curve in the road, it appeared to have lost its balance and slid sideways, dropped into the ditch, then turned over on its side, ripping a wheel off and shredding one side. Baggage was scattered everywhere, bags and valises ripped open, not by the force of the crash, but by deliberate intent from whoever had precipitated the attack.

Indians! Damn! And Apaches at that!

He looked around to see if he could pick out where the passengers might have gotten off to, or if they had been

taken hostage. He found tracks of four people where it
appeared they had made a hasty retreat up a slight incline,
but were not followed by the Indian ponies. At least not
immediately. The team of horses pulling the stage had been
taken, cut from their traces and led away. *That must have
been what gave the passengers time to make their escape*,
Cotton thought, or hoped anyway.

Just as he was thinking he should get the body of the
dead man into the ground, he was drawn to something that
gave solid evidence of his greatest fear. The passengers
were *not* out of danger. Gunshots could be heard coming
from the other side of the foothills just ahead, foothills that
led up the side of a mountain. He swung into the saddle to
seek the exact location of the roar of the rifles. It didn't take
long to spot smoke from the Indians' weapons being fired
into the air, a dead giveaway that they had their quarry
trapped and were preparing to go in for the kill.

Chapter 6

———◆———

Cotton saw his only option placed by fate right in front of him.

He rode like the devil himself was hot on his trail, pushing him straight into a battle he was woefully outgunned for. He dared not ride straight for the Indians, but instead he circled to the east to follow a ridgeline toward where the ground dipped into some trees. As he spotted a small rise, he headed for it, and reined in at its base.

Cotton dismounted, with the intention of climbing the rest of the way up the ridge on foot. He didn't want whoever was on the other side doing all the shooting to spot his silhouette astride a horse. With the sun at such an angle as to make that likely, he hunched over, keeping himself as insignificant as possible against the terrain, slipping and sliding up the tricky incline. When he reached the top, he dropped to one knee, keeping as close as possible to the larger of the boulders around him. He had pulled his field glasses from his saddlebags when he dismounted. He raised them to his eyes, focused the ring, and shook his head at what he saw.

Below were about a dozen screaming Apaches firing at some people who had obviously sought shelter in a slight ravine in a copse of cottonwoods. They were protected by several large boulders that had at some ancient time broken from their brethren at the top of the mountain on the other side of the ravine. The huge hunks of granite and sandstone had come crashing down to land near a stream, thus giving the hapless souls trapped by the marauding Indians almost a fortlike cover from which to defend themselves. It took no more than one quick glance to know that the four people hunkered down were sadly outgunned and outmanned. *More'n likely those folks are from the stage*, Cotton thought.

Cursing under his breath as he returned to his mare, he mounted up and began to follow a narrow trail that he hoped would lead to a position to make a flanking maneuver on the renegades. While the trail did get him to a spot slightly behind the Indians, he could see he would also have to ride like hell straight through their ranks to make it to those trapped in the ravine.

"Nothin's ever easy. I hate situations like this," he muttered, thankful no one could hear him but the mare. He had almost a hundred yards of rocky, cactus-laden ground to cover, and six shots weren't going to give much protection for that great a distance. Racing through a bunch of Apache warriors while trying to shoot would be even more difficult. He urged the horse to a run, hoping to gain as much ground as possible before he was noticed. He had his Colt in his hand, cocked and ready. When one of the renegades saw him and shouted an alert, he began firing at any painted savage within range. He leaned over the mare's neck to make himself a small target, as if, considering the odds, that made any difference. He began yelling, making as much noise as he could in hopes of confusing the enemy, although he didn't hold out a lot of hope of that having much effect.

When he found that fate had allowed him to reach the creek unscathed—for which he was both grateful and surprised—he splashed through the water across to the other side, whirled the mare around, and jumped off, dropping the reins as he raced to the cover of the cottonwoods. He dove behind some tree trunks as several bullets careened off the rocks straight ahead, thwacking off small limbs from the trees behind him. He looked around to get his bearings just as another volley of shots tore through the trees, clipping more branches and thudding into the soft trunks. Realizing his position was untenable, he dove for the dirt, then half-crawled, half-scooted to reach the relative safety of the boulders where the others were huddled together like puppies.

What he found wasn't encouraging. A boy no more than a teenager wielded a twelve-gauge coach gun with no sign of any ammunition other than the dozen shells left in his cartridge belt. A man in a sack suit and a bowler hat, holding tightly to a flat wooden box with brass fittings like it was a newborn baby, hunkered behind the others. He appeared to have no weapon and was obviously scared out of his wits. Thorn McCann was sitting propped up against a boulder, a scarlet stain seeping from beneath and through a wad of white cloth being held to a wound in his shoulder to stem the flow of blood. From the looks of it, the wound was damned serious. He was white as a newly washed sheet hanging on the clothesline. And the mystery of the dark-haired woman had been solved, too. The one holding the cloth was definitely Delilah Jones. Cotton figured she had ripped the cloth from one of her own petticoats. Thorn loosely held his revolver, the barrel of which dangled in the sandy soil. Delilah cradled a .41-caliber Remington double-derringer in her lap.

Somewhat out of breath, Cotton managed a snide greeting. "You folks new to the area? Looking for a guide to show you around? Hmm, Thorn McCann. Didn't expect to see you here."

"Didn't . . . exactly seek out . . . the opportunity, myself," he gasped.

"You're not lookin' too good. Could you use a hand?"

"Mighty nice of you . . . to ask, Sheriff. Wouldn't mind a taste of brandy . . . if you have any," Thorn said, managing a weak smile.

"Fresh out, pard. Got a canteen we can dip in that stream behind you, if you've a hankerin' for some liquid refreshment."

"Couldn't turn down such a mag-magnanimous offer," Thorn said, then started coughing.

"Any of you sharpshooters manage to hit anything out there?"

Thorn stared at him like he was a raving lunatic. "With a short-barrel shotgun, a near empty forty-five, and a pea-shooter?"

"You folks *do* seem a little short of firepower. I'll go get you some water . . . and a Winchester. May make the odds closer to even, at least until those redskins decide to quit playing with us."

Cotton scurried back to where he'd left his horse. The mare was nonchalantly drinking from the stream. Fortunately, the spot where he'd chosen to leave the mare was completely hidden from the view of the renegades. He took one of two canteens he'd brought along from around the saddle horn, unscrewed the cap, and dipped it into the cool water, watching it bubble as it filled. Then he grabbed his saddlebags and withdrew the Winchester from the scabbard. By the time he had crawled back to the safety of the rocks, the Indians were preparing for another frontal attack. He dropped the canteen in front of Delilah and began loading bullets into the Winchester. He levered a round to await the charge. He looked over at the kid with a questioning look.

"You ever been in a situation like this before, son? What's your name?"

"N-no, sir. This is my first trip on the stage. They hired me because I needed a job and didn't care how little the pay was. Reckon I know why there weren't no one else standin' in line for the opportunity. Name's J-Jimmy. Jimmy Culp, sir."

"You know how to use that twelve-gauge?"

"Yessir, I-I grew up on a farm and went huntin' for wild turkeys and such."

"Ever shoot at a man before?"

"Just today, and I don't think I've hit anything but the dirt."

Cotton turned to the gent in the sack suit. "And you, sir, got a gun or know how to use one?"

"D-Denby Biddle's the name. I, uh, don't carry a gun. I'm only a simple printer."

"Any chance you could hit anything if I gave you one?"

"I-I c-could try."

"Get yourself up here and take this." Cotton took Thorn's revolver from him and handed it to the man. "Sorry, Thorn, but I don't see you as bein' much use at this crossroads."

Thorn grunted something unintelligible as Delilah wiped perspiration off his forehead. Having been wounded himself more than once, Cotton could tell at a glance how serious Thorn's condition was. He'd lost a lot of blood and was in great pain. Cotton looked into the beautiful but worried eyes of Delilah. She answered his silent question with eyes beginning to flood with tears.

He silently willed Delilah to hold on to herself. The last thing they needed was a sobbing woman to make the situation worse.

"Looks like they're gettin' ready to come at us. Jimmy, you come here beside me. Only fire that shotgun when I say to, understand?"

"Yessir, I do at that. You want me to make my shots count. I understand right well."

"Good. Now, Denby, you scrunch down between those two boulders over there. That'll make you a tough target to hit. You can still fire easy enough, though. But don't squeeze off a shot unless you are certain of a hit, man or horse. We can't afford to waste ammunition."

He'd no more than finished giving orders to his tiny army of less-than-eager volunteers than five Apaches came racing toward their position. Cotton waited until they were at most fifty feet away before he rose up and began firing his Winchester as fast as he could lever the next cartridge. The lead rider flew over the back of his pony and was trampled by the one right behind him. As one rider yanked his pony to skirt the makeshift fortress, Cotton shouted to the boy.

"There! Jimmy, to your right. Now!"

The kid jumped up and pulled both triggers. The twelve-gauge spit out smoke and flame with a mighty roar. The Apache grabbed at his chest as he was hurled off his mount into a sea of cactus. He didn't feel any of the flesh-piercing barbs, however. Any pain he'd experienced during his young life had abruptly come to an end.

As much as he hated shooting any horse, Cotton squeezed off one more shot that brought down a pony, throwing its rider and leaving him afoot and limping back to the safety of the arroyo where the other Apaches had gathered for their initial attack. The lot of them retreated to regroup out of range of the sheriff's deadly rifle. If the Indians had figured they'd have an easy time picking off three men and a woman, they'd been sorely mistaken. Cotton was hoping the eight or nine that were left might consider retreating to fight again another day. He didn't really care, though; it was as good a day as any to kill some renegade Indians bent on his destruction.

Chapter 7

———◆◆◆———

"I-I don't think I hit anything, sir," Denby said. He'd only pulled the trigger once and closed his eyes when he did it.

Pondering his next move, Cotton noticed Delilah staring intently at Denby.

"Have we met before, Mr. Biddle? You look real familiar," she said.

"Nope. We never met."

"You're certain? I never forget a face. Since the stage was so dusty, I didn't get a good look at you before."

"Dead certain. I woulda remembered," Denby said with almost angry conviction. Delilah gave up further inquiry to return to helping Thorn.

Thorn groaned and tried to scoot to a sitting position. "Let me have my six-shooter back, Cotton. Then drag me over to where you got Denby. I'll not be much good, but at least I can *hit* what I'm aimin' at."

Cotton thought about that for a moment. Thorn was right; Denby wasn't much good in a life-and-death situation. The sheriff glanced at Delilah, who was very subtly shaking her head. She obviously didn't think Thorn could sit up long enough to be any help. She must also have been concerned about his loss of blood. Her compresses had slowed the flow some, but not entirely. Cotton knew he had to make short work of the bloodthirsty Indians or Thorn would be dead before long. He decided on a long shot. He pushed cartridge after cartridge into his Winchester, levered one into the chamber, then made sure his Colt had all six cylinders full.

"If I don't make it back, folks, reckon you'll have to get yourselves out the best you can. If I don't shake those redskins up real good, I fear Thorn will be breathin' his last right here."

"Me 'n' the kid will do our best to keep the one or two you miss at bay. Good luck, Cotton," Thorn said, struggling to eke out a weak smile.

Delilah put a hand on his arm and wished him luck. Denby huddled as far back into the rocks as he could, shivering like a frightened rabbit facing a rattlesnake.

Cotton made a scrambling, sliding dash for his horse. When he got to where he'd left her nibbling on some short grass along the stream, he grabbed the reins, vaulted into the saddle, and spurred the mare to a thundering race around the largest of the boulders. Following the stream downhill below the rim of the ravine would, he prayed, keep him hidden from the Apaches' view until he could outflank them, before they could gather in readiness for their next try at their prey.

His plan seemed to be working until a bullet ricocheted off a rock five feet from his head. He yanked the mare's reins to the left to gain a better place from which to observe where the shot might have come from and avoid the next one being even closer. But before he could get complete control of the mare to get a look, the question was answered for him. Suddenly, a young brave jumped from between some boulders and raised a Spencer rifle at him. *Looks like the one whose horse I shot*, Cotton thought. He didn't have time to get to the Winchester, so he yanked his Colt and sent two quick shots at the Apache. The first one grazed the man's rifle butt and ruined his shot. Cotton's second bullet found its mark, and the Indian tumbled backward, rolling down the embankment, gathering spiny cacti as he went. The element of surprise now lost, Cotton's only choice was to charge into the midst of the howling and whooping warriors, firing as he went. His hope was that at least a few of the shots would find flesh.

He spurred the mare from behind a mix of piñon and sagebrush, into a stretch of desert grasses and chaparral. Ahead, several renegades were bunching up for the kill, raising their rifles above their heads and whooping for the spirits to give them a glorious victory over the white-eyes. That was Cotton's call to action. As the mare raced directly into the middle of the suddenly surprised Apaches, his Colt was blazing away, taking two Indians with it and scattering the others. The Indians were now down to six by Cotton's count, and with the Apaches trying to regroup sufficiently to drive off or kill this madman who'd dared take on a superior force, the sheriff had time to pull his Winchester from its scabbard, cock it, and urge the mare on toward the rock sanctuary where his comrades were holed up. He fired left and right, yanking the horse's reins back and forth to come as close to the Indian ponies as he could, in an attempt to frighten the animals sufficiently to make shooting back at him all but impossible. He took down at least two more renegades as they clambered to evade the crazy white-eyes. His horse thundered on in a dusty cloud as his more powerful mount broke from the remaining four Indians and drove downhill toward the safety of the boulder fortress he'd left only a few minutes before.

One renegade took up the chase, but as they neared the makeshift fort, Jimmy Culp cut loose with a load of buckshot that knocked the Indian from his mount with a dusty thump. He didn't move.

Cotton reined up only after he was sure he'd eluded what was left of his followers. Sporadic gunfire erupted from his little band of ill-equipped defenders. As he dove for cover, Jimmy Culp hollered a victorious, distinctly Confederate yell. Thorn was trying mightily to sit up but tottering and obviously in great pain. The look on Delilah's face told Cotton much about the condition of the bounty hunter, and it wasn't positive.

"Boy, oh, boy, Sheriff, you sure scattered them redskins. Looks like you got a bunch of 'em, too. I count only three left that ain't hunched over tryin' to keep sittin' their ponies," Jimmy said with a wide grin.

"That last shot of yours looked like it might have sealed their fate, Jimmy. Good shootin'."

"Thank you, sir. Does it look like they plan on another try?"

"Hard to tell, but if I was a bettin' man, I'd say they're finished for the day."

Barely above a whisper, Thorn muttered, "Damned good shootin', Sheriff. Glad I never made it a point to go up against you."

"Uh-huh."

Cotton pulled his field glasses from the saddlebag and tried to take his own accounting of the damage done or imagined. "Looks like you've made an accurate count, Jimmy. And from the looks of things, I'd say they're gettin' set to withdraw. At least, I hope that's what their thinkin' is. We'll wait for a spell, just to make sure before we go venturing out, though."

"Sheriff, I-I don't know how we're going to get Thorn to a place where he can get patched up. He sure can't walk, and he's damned sure too heavy to carry," Delilah said, eyes misty.

"Yeah, and I don't see any tree limbs strong enough to make a travois, either. Don't worry, ma'am, we'll come up with somethin'. Jimmy, where's the next stage station?"

"Hard to tell from here, but figurin' from where we left the coach, I'd say about four miles to the Hardins' place."

Cotton just grunted. He went back to his horse and pulled the other canteen from the saddle horn. He brought it back, unscrewed the top, and handed it to Delilah. She took only a sip before holding it to Thorn's dry, blistered lips. He guzzled like he hadn't had a drink in weeks.

Cotton sat back against a boulder, chewing his lip as he pondered his best chance at getting out of here with everyone still alive. For the moment, at least, prospects were looking dim, for Thorn at least. As Cotton sank deeper and deeper in contemplating their predicament, his eyes suddenly lit up. He turned to the kid with the shotgun.

"Jimmy, doesn't the Hardin ranch have a stream that cuts though it right behind the corral?"

"Why, yessir, now that you mention it, I believe so."

"Any chance it might be the same stream that's dribbling down the hill behind us?"

"Could be. Can't be certain, but the direction is right," Jimmy said.

"If it *is* the same stream, and if I'm right, we could follow that water right to the place we want to go. And it should cut about a mile or so off the trip. What d'ya think?"

"I'd say it's a good plan."

"All right, here's what we'll do. I'll load Thorn on my mare. The rest of us will have to hoof it, but with water always at the ready, shouldn't be too bad."

"If there ain't any Indians figurin' the same damned thing," Thorn muttered.

"You better pray there aren't, McCann, because your future depends on it goin' the way I hope for."

Thorn's head rolled and settled on his chest. Delilah had dark circles around her eyes from fear and worry, Cotton assumed. He had a feeling she'd bear up all right once they got moving, but he didn't say so, for fear it might push her to tears, and he didn't need that right now.

Nearly an hour had passed before Cotton decided it was safe to venture out. He and Jimmy hoisted Thorn into the mare's saddle. The horse nickered as if she knew she was the only chance the wounded man had of surviving. Cotton led the mare into the middle of the swiftly running stream. The others followed, with Jimmy and his shotgun bringing up the rear. He'd been told to keep a keen eye out for any sign of danger from the remaining renegades seeking to revenge their fallen comrades. Cotton had given Thorn's revolver to Delilah, figuring it was safer in her hands than Denby's. At least she knew which end to point at the enemy. By the time twilight was upon them and a full moon began its rise over the mountains, the shadowy outline of the corral where the Hardins kept fresh teams of horses for the stage line came into view. When they got to within earshot of the house, Cotton called out, "Hello, the house!"

He was greeted by a rifle shot that struck the dirt ten feet in front of them.

Chapter 8

———◆◆◆———

S orry to put a scare into you, Sheriff. These old eyes don't see as well as they used to. 'Specially when it's gettin' dark," Mrs. Hardin said as Cotton and his band walked up to the house.

"It's all right, Miz Hardin, no harm done. Sorry to be comin' up on the house from the back way, but we ran into a bit of Indian trouble and we got a wounded man with us. Could use some help."

Mrs. Hardin yelled for her husband to get his lazy butt outside and lend a hand. It was no more than ten seconds later when a scrawny, balding man appeared at the door, tugging up his suspenders with one hand and dabbing at his mouth with a napkin in the other.

"What's all the commotion?"

"Got a man shot. Don't just stand there, lend a hand gettin' him inside," she said.

Mr. Hardin reached up to steady Thorn as Cotton eased him from the saddle. Thorn groaned, but tried to get his legs under himself when they got him to the ground. Cotton knew he didn't dare let loose of McCann's one good arm or he'd collapse like a squeezebox. They got Thorn inside and placed him on a bed. Mrs. Hardin said she'd fetch something to get the bullet out, but Cotton allowed as how that wouldn't be necessary.

"I haven't looked real close, but considering the blood on both the front and back of his shirt, and two distinct holes, I'd have to say it went all the way through."

"That'd be a blessing," Mrs. Hardin said. "We can clean and sew up the holes. Why, he'll be good as new in short order."

"That might be a tad optimistic. He's lost a lot of blood."

"Get his shirt off and let's take a look. He won't be the first hombre with holes I've had to stitch up."

Delilah helped get the bloody shirt unbuttoned. Cotton tugged it off as Thorn's eyes rolled back and his head lolled from side to side. Mrs. Hardin brought a bowl of water and placed it on the bedside table. She clucked her tongue at the sight of the two holes, one fairly small going in, but a larger one where the bullet exited. She said, "Looks like the bullet might have nicked a bone on its way through," as she reached for a cloth and dipped it in the water. She washed the wounds, but it didn't stop the bleeding.

"You folks got any alcohol around?" Cotton asked.

"Got some whiskey, just for medicinal purposes, mind you," Mr. Hardin said.

"Well, don't just stand there jawin' about it, Jeremiah, get the bottle down from the cupboard," Mrs. Hardin said with a frown. Her husband hurried off to do her bidding. "We'll give him a good slug of it, then pour some over the hole. I'll get some thread and a needle. If I can sew him up tight enough, that might stop the gushin'. Gotta get it done a'fore it starts festerin'."

"Yup." Cotton looked over at Delilah as she grimaced at Mrs. Hardin's description.

When Jeremiah Hardin returned with the nearly full bottle of whiskey, his expression suggested he'd rather not part with even a drop of it. Cotton figured that was his refuge from Mrs. Hardin's ordering him around. He did seem a little henpecked.

Jeremiah had twisted the cork from the bottle and was about to dribble some on the wound when his wife grabbed it from his hand.

"You idjit, don't you ever listen? I said we give him a good guzzle of the stuff before we pour it on. It's goin' to burn like hell, and then I'm goin' to poke holes in him with a needle. Ya durn fool, it's gonna smart somethin' awful. He needs to be drunk before I go to it."

Jeremiah's face tuned red from the dressing down. He slunk over to a chair near the door and sat in silence. Delilah looked as if she was going to get sick. Cotton led her outside for some fresh air. *He* wasn't all that interested in watching the old lady demonstrate her sewing skills, either.

Delilah crossed her arms and stared off into the dark. Cotton started to say something, but her pensiveness gave him pause. He'd wanted to ask her about Bart Havens, her relationship with him, and some further explanation about her claim to have been the one who killed him. His curiosity about her relationship with Jack was also on his mind. The light from several lanterns inside glowed through the open door like a shaft of sunlight when it peeks through holes in dark clouds. Her features were accentuated by the warm radiance on her cheeks and her raven hair. He had no trouble understanding why Thorn had taken such a liking to her. But exactly who *was* this beautiful but mysterious woman? He needed to know, but for the moment at least, he had no sense of how to go about penetrating her facade.

She looked over at him after several silent minutes. "You have questions, don't you?"

Cotton was stunned by her perception of what had been going through his mind. "Yup, reckon I do, at that."

"First, you can't understand how a woman like me could have tied up with Havens in the first place. Right?"

"Uh-huh."

"It was never what you thought, not what anyone thought. Havens paid me to act as his eyes and ears in town. He never bedded me, nor did he ask to. He did, however, demand complete allegiance to him and his scheme."

"I assume you went along with him out of a need for a livelihood. Right?"

"I was broke. Destitute. My husband had just been hanged for absconding with some horses and cattle that belonged to someone else. Never made it to a trial. Vigilantes took justice into their own hands. Bastards."

"I don't hold with vigilantes, but then I also don't hold with folks taking things that don't belong to them. Havens was an old hand at that."

Delilah looked away briefly. "I know. But when you're in desperate need of money, you don't always have a firm grip on the difference between right and wrong."

"How did Havens dealing in counterfeit money play into your moral dilemma?"

"I-I never knew he was using counterfeit money. I couldn't tell the difference. It never occurred to me to even ask. Thorn didn't know either."

Cotton stroked his chin, puzzling over her claim of innocence. He wasn't quite ready to be taken in by a beautiful woman, although it would have been easy to do.

"When did you figure it out?"

"When those folks in Silver City raised a ruckus. We realized we had to get out of there before someone started talking about a necktie party. As it was, the marshal arrested Thorn before we could leave. The citizenry was madder than a coop of wet hens."

"Can you blame them?"

"Well, no, I suppose not."

"Back in Apache Springs, you didn't question why Havens was putting the town's money in valises separate from his money?"

"No, Sheriff, I did not. It was only after the marshal in Silver City told Thorn we'd been spreading fake bills all over town that I figured it out."

"Havens musta figured he needed to keep the monies separate so he could pull the same scheme again in some other unsuspecting community," Cotton said.

"I imagine so."

Cotton began to stare at his boots as if he was thinking of something else. Delilah picked up on his pensiveness.

"Is there something else you wanted to ask?"

"When you said that fellow Denby looked familiar, where is it you figured to have met him?"

"I don't know, but for some strange reason when I saw him, Bart Havens came to mind."

"You think there might be a tie between them?"

Before Delilah could answer, they were interrupted.

"Sheriff, you best come inside now," Mrs. Hardin called out. "Your man is sound asleep. Actually, he's drunker'n a skunk."

Delilah led the way back inside. Thorn McCann was snoring loudly, spread out naked to the waist, wrapped mummy-like in long strips of white cloth. Delilah walked over and sat beside the bed. She put her hand on his arm. Cotton gave Mrs. Hardin a questioning glance.

"Can't say for certain, mind you, but I got him sewed up real nice and tight. Got the bleeding stopped and the wounds good and cleaned out. If no infection comes on him, he'll survive. Hope that's the answer you was lookin' for, Sheriff."

"It was, indeed, ma'am. You think he'll be able to travel tomorrow?"

"If 'twas up to me, I'd say let him rest up for a couple more days. Oughta let them holes sorta grow together some on their own. If you're in a hurry to get on with your own business, he's welcome to stay for a spell."

"That's kind of you, Mrs. Hardin. I may take the rest of these folks out tomorrow and head on to Apache Springs. Hopefully we won't run into any more Apaches. Word is these hills are full of 'em. You better keep a keen eye out yourself."

"Jeremiah and I have been drivin' them red rascals off every whipstitch for over ten years now. They don't come around much anymore. They never did take a liking to Jeremiah's ten-gauge," she said with a crooked grin.

"Since the stage is out of business for a couple more days, how's about loanin' me three horses to transport Mr. Denby, Miss Delilah, and Jimmy back with me? The county will reimburse you for their use."

"Reckon that'd be all right. You plannin' on leavin' in the mornin'?"

"That's my plan."

Mrs. Hardin hollered for Jeremiah to have three extra horses saddled and ready at first light.

"Yes, Ma," Jeremiah answered, somewhat bitterly.

Cotton marveled at the way she got things accomplished with just the two of them, and, of course, Jeremiah's complete acquiescence to everything she demanded of him.

Chapter 9

In a dust-blown town on the East Texas prairie, weeks before Sheriff Cotton Burke departed on his quest to save Thorn McCann from the hangman's noose, the devil's own plans were being set in motion, which would change Apache Springs forever.

A large, rough-looking man with a scowl that seemed to say, "keep the hell out of my way," tied his dun-colored mare to a railing in front of a narrow storefront with peeling paint and filthy windows. He looked around before entering through the door, almost instantly coming face-to-face with the man he was there to see. The man motioned for him to take a seat across from him.

A thin, shriveled old man sat behind a huge oak desk littered with scraps of newspaper stories, clipped and tossed randomly about. Paper nearly covered the entire top of the desk. The balding gent wore a wrinkled shirt that might have been white at one time but was now a sad, badly worn and faded gray. A wooden gavel sat next to a hunk of stained walnut that was dented from too many abuses from the old man's rulings. A lightly stained, hand-carved wedge of wood at the front edge of the desk proclaimed the man who sat behind it was Judge Arthur Sanborn.

Across from Sanborn sat a grizzled, Kentucky-born, self-styled gunslinger with a flat-brimmed hat tilted back on his head. He wore two guns: one a .44 Remington and the other a .38 Smith & Wesson with a spur trigger that rested in a shoulder holster. He went by the name his daddy had bestowed upon him at birth: James Lee Hogg. He hung his duster on a peg behind him. The office—or what Sanborn referred to as his courtroom—was tiny, dusty, and cluttered. No trials had been held there for a very long time.

"Hogg, I sent for you to do a job for me, a serious job. So let's get down to business."

"That's what I'm here for, Mr. Sanborn."

"Judge! That's *Judge* Sanborn! And don't you forget it!" Sanborn slammed his hand on the desktop.

"I heard a rumor that the county commissioners fired your scrawny ass two years ago, and that you ain't a judge no more. Ain't that right?"

"Never you mind about whether I am or am not currently a judge. This is but a temporary setback. So it don't affect our association. Got that?"

"Yeah, sure, whatever you say. Go ahead and lay it out for me."

"You must listen carefully and do just as I say," Sanborn said.

"Just as long as the deal is for cash on delivery."

"That's the deal. What I want you to do is make nothing but trouble for a certain Sheriff Burke in Apache Springs. You ever heard of him?"

"We've met and it weren't all that friendly."

"Well, I want him pushed to the limit. He has to be angry enough to call you out."

"And then I'm supposed to take him down?"

"Not exactly. I'll be taking care of that end of things."

"What's in it for me?"

"Two thousand dollars cash money."

"We goin' there together?"

"No. I've some business to finish before I get there. You'll have to use your own judgment as to how much pain you bring to the sheriff. Just don't shoot him."

"How're you gonna know I've done what you're askin' if you aren't there?"

"I'll know, all right. I got eyes and ears taking note of every move you make. I don't want you trying to kill him until I get there. I just want him to have plenty of reason to want you dead." Sanborn shook a bony fist at Hogg. His nod sealed the deal.

"I've heard tell Burke ain't too easy to kill. Didn't you send another bounty hunter after him? He never came back, did he?" James Lee Hogg lifted one eyebrow and gave the judge a wry grin. "You likely got a story on his demise in one of them clippin's spread all over your desk."

"I have no idea whether he's dead or alive. Ain't important now, anyway. Never felt Thorn McCann was all that reliable, but, at the time, I was forced to rely on him," Sanborn said.

"What if I come up against resistance from Burke's family?"

"He doesn't have any family. Believe me, I've looked high and low for some relative—a brother, cousin, uncle— anyone I could kill in retribution for Burke shooting my only son, Billy."

"And the well came up dry? There's no one?"

"Not that I can find. Now, that don't mean he hasn't taken up with some woman of recent. If he has, kill her. I'm none too particular who falls to your gun, Hogg. Just as long as it has a devastating impact on that murdering badge-toter."

"How come I have to wait for you to get to town?"

"I *must* be there to see it! *Absolutely must!* And as many men can attest, I'm not a good man to cross."

"That's plain enough for me. I'm goin' to need some

travelin' money, though, and enough for a hotel room when I get there. You say he's in Apache Springs, New Mexico Territory?"

Sanborn reached down into a lower desk drawer and drew out a tin box. He opened it and pulled a stack of bills from it. One of the two hinges was rusted through, nearly causing the top to break free. He pulled off several bills and handed them across the desk to Hogg.

"That's right, Apache Springs. Here's fifty dollars. That ought to get you food, room and board, and ammunition sufficient for your journey."

Hogg took the money with a greedy grin on his scarred and deeply lined face.

"Should be. Well, then, I reckon I'll be off to do the job McCann couldn't. I'll send you a telegram when I got him good and riled. That way, it'll give you time to come up with every penny of my money so I don't have to wait around after you give me the go-ahead to kill him."

"One more thing, Mr. Hogg. You'll not be working entirely alone when things get serious," Sanborn said.

"I don't need no help. I can take that sheriff."

"You'll take the help and be glad for it. I guarantee."

"Who is this so-called helper?"

"You'll be given that information at the proper time."

"What's the matter with now?" Hogg growled.

The old man said nothing as he drilled the gunslinger with a glare that could have killed a rattler.

Feeling unfairly chastised, Hogg scooted his chair back, stood with a frown, grabbed his duster from a peg, and left his dusty surroundings in favor of some sunshine. He stood for a moment to acquaint himself with the small, dirty, ramshackle cluster of buildings, hoping to find a general store where he could buy supplies. Finally he saw a narrow whipsaw-sided building with a sign that proclaimed it as having EVERYTHING A BODY MIGHT NEED FOR TRAVEL OR SETTLING DOWN.

"Looks like a perfect place to spend some of the old man's money," he mumbled bitterly.

* * *

Hogg chewed on a stick of hard candy as he slowly made his way across the Texas prairie and into the mountains to the west. He'd been in the saddle for two and a half days now and was growing impatient to reach New Mexico, even though he knew Apache Springs was all the way across the territory to the southwest. Another three, maybe four days should bring him face-to-face with his quarry and a show-down between him and the sheriff with a reputation for being too tough to kill. He laughed to himself at the thought. While it wasn't something he was willing to share with the grizzled old judge, James Lee Hogg already had a little history with the sheriff of Apache Springs.

When he came to a stream where he could climb down off his saddle, rest awhile, and water his horse, he marveled at the number of cattle grazing everywhere. As he leaned over to fill his canteen, he heard hoofbeats. He stood up to find several tough-looking cowboys at a dead run, racing for the very place he was standing. When they came upon him, they circled around as if they were expecting trouble. Lots of it.

"What're you doin' here?" said the one who'd led the approaching riders.

"Just waterin' my horse. What's it to you?" Hogg was angered by the man's stern questioning of what he had felt was his right to be there.

"You ever heard of Charlie Goodnight?"

"The cattle baron? Why, sure, who hasn't?"

"Well, you're on the JA Ranch, which, in case you're too ignorant to know, is Charlie's ranch. He don't like fellas wanderin' around in the middle of his cattle. Lots of rus-tlers in these parts. You one of 'em?"

"Do I look like a rustler?"

"You look more like an idjit who don't know his head from his ass."

That kind of talk had gotten more than one man killed. But with more men than he could hope to cut down, even

with both revolvers blazing away, Hogg decided he'd better
try a friendlier approach.

"I'm sorry, gents, but in fact I didn't know I was on Goodnight land. Just stopped to water my mare. I'll be moseyin'
along, then."

"Where you headed?" the cowboy asked, with eyes
squinted like he was waiting to catch Hogg in a lie of some
sort. The way the cowboys stared at him, glancing to one
another as if a hanging might be appropriate, was beginning
to rattle Hogg.

"I'm goin' to Apache Springs. That's in New Mexico, in
case you don't know."

"No, I didn't know. What's in them saddlebags?"

"Food. It's a long trip to where I'm goin'. I don't intend
to starve on the way."

The leader turned to one of the others and said, "Joe
Bob, check out his story. Make damned sure there ain't no
runnin' iron in there. If you find one, he hangs. If not, well,
we make sure he gets on his way, pronto."

The one called Joe Bob dropped to the ground and
grabbed Hogg's saddlebags from behind his cantle. He
wasn't gentle in his approach, either. He nearly tore one of
the leather straps off before he was able to ram a beefy
hand down inside and feel around for anything that
remotely resembled a running iron, a makeshift piece of
iron that could be used to alter brands. Many a man had
been judged and hanged for just having such a piece of
equipment in his possession. Joe Bob shrugged and shook
his head.

"Sorry, Boss, no iron in there. Guess he's tellin' the
truth."

"Then you have just one hour to clear the JA," the leader
growled at Hogg, then yanked his reins and spun his roan
around in the direction they'd come.

Hogg wiped sweat from his forehead as he watched the
riders disappear in a cloud of dust. Looking after them, he
grumbled, "If there'd been no more'n four of 'em, they'd all

be lyin' in the dirt, deader than a stick." He mounted up and headed west, angry, and eager to pick a fight with someone, just not a dozen rough-looking, armed-to-the-teeth cowboys, all at once.

Chapter 10

———⋙•⋘———

The day was shaping up to become a real summer blow. No rain, but plenty of wind. And wind meant clouds of dust and dirt swirling up and down the streets of Apache Springs hard enough to find their way through loose-fitting siding, windows not closed tightly, and doors propped open to keep the stifling heat from driving folks gasping to get their breath. From the law's standpoint, things were quiet, so Jack had closed the jail up tight to partake of his daily libation—a shot of whiskey followed by a glass of beer— across the street. It didn't *really* make any difference in which order they came because, after about three rounds, he could no longer keep count anyway. No one had created a stir worthy of being given a free night on a wooden bench in the jail since Cotton Burke left town more than a week before. Therefore, Jack was left to his own devices, or in his case, vices. He was leaning on the bar at Melody's Golden Palace of Pleasure, the combination saloon and brothel recently bought and revamped into a burgeoning money-maker by his lady friend and sleeping companion, Melody Wakefield, the town's only madam.

"When do you figure Cotton will get back?" Arlo, the saloon's bartender, asked as Jack downed his second whiskey/beer interlude.

"He'll get back when he gets back, Arlo. That's the way it is with our sheriff. He has his own schedule. I have no idea where he is right at this moment. Probably got himself in some tight spot and is figuring a way out," Jack said with snort. Arlo gave him an understanding grin and moved down the bar to serve a new customer.

Melody glided down the stairway, one hand on the polished railing, slowly surveying everything that was happening below. A couple of tables were surrounded by consummate cardplayers deeply ensconced in their games of chance, while two of her girls were trying to entice cowboys to let go of their dollars for a visit upstairs instead of blowing it on watered-down whiskey, and one rangy man in coveralls could be seen leaning on the bar sucking the foamy head off a glass of warm beer. One of the girls found her efforts successful and had latched on to a young, scrawny wrangler and was directing him toward the stairs. The kid kept glancing around, appearing shy and embarrassed, unsure of what he was about to get himself into.

Melody walked up to Jack and slipped her arm through his. The top of her dress was open far enough to reveal more than most men could tolerate and control themselves. Jack, on the other hand, knew every inch of her body and was less moved to a public reaction than another might be. A satin ribbon that usually tied at the bodice was undone and dangling free, adding to the enticement. She smelled like wildflowers, and not one person in the house let it go unnoticed as she strolled by. Jack liked the idea of being kept by a real head turner.

"Melody." Jack acknowledged her arrival and squeezed her arm. She smiled a coquettish smile and moved her head in a way that suggested they retire to their upstairs hideaway. Before he could respond, a tall, mean-looking hombre pushed open the swinging doors and limped inside, getting everyone's attention by his noisy arrival. Melody showed her immediate disdain for the man with a grunt of disapproval.

The man, wearing a Remington .44, a flat-brimmed hat, and a large red scarf draped around his neck, headed straight for the bar, paying no attention to the other patrons. He seemed to have a singularity of purpose as he slammed his fist on the bar and demanded a whiskey. "A double, and leave the bottle," he growled in a most unfriendly manner. His face was sunburned and dirty. A long, thin nose had a bump in the middle, making him look not unlike a buzzard.

"Comin' up," Arlo said as he slid a bottle in front of the man and placed a large glass beside it. "That'll be fifty cents."

The man dug into his dusty coat pocket and pulled out two coins, tossing them on the bar so hard they bounced across and onto the floor. Arlo frowned as he bent over to pick them up. The man snorted at Arlo's discomfort. But, gentleman that he was, the bartender seemed to take no offense and went back to doing what he'd been doing prior to the man's rude appearance.

The man turned to notice the badge on Jack's shirt.

"Say, Deputy, can you tell me where I might find a feller named Burke?"

"You mean Sheriff Cotton Burke?"

"Hell yes, the sheriff. I doubt you got more than one Cotton Burke in this pitiful town." His sneer was anything but the kind you'd expect from a friend. That wasn't lost on Jack, as an instant dislike of this rude oaf welled up in him. "So where can I find this 'sheriff'?"

"Can't rightly say. He could be here or he could be there. He hasn't been around for a spell. What'd you want with him?" Jack asked.

"Just a little unfinished business for Judge Arthur Sanborn. And it ain't none of yours."

"I'll tell him when he gets back to town. Who shall I say was lookin' for him?"

"Ain't important. I'll just hang around and wait. No hurry." The man poured himself another glass of whiskey and strolled over to watch a table of serious-looking card-players with a pot that really didn't amount to much, but which had certainly captured the imagination of those involved. The stranger stood, drink in one hand, the other hand hanging on his gun belt, with a thumb stuck through a loop. He said nothing.

"What do you suppose he wants with Cotton?" Melody whispered.

"I have no idea, but whatever it is, I have a sneaky suspicion Cotton isn't goin' to like it."

"I don't like men like that hangin' around. Why don't you shoo him off?"

"He hasn't bit nobody yet. *Seems* bent on keepin' the peace. So, until he strays from the herd, I'm obliged to keep hands off." Jack took Melody's arm, with the intention of leading her toward the stairs. She pulled away and walked over to stand beside the rough-looking man. He gave her a quick glance.

"I ain't interested, lady. Maybe some other time," he said out of the corner of his mouth.

"I'm not offerin', mister, but you said something about wantin' to find the sheriff."

"Yeah. You know where he is?"

"Maybe. Sometimes he stays out at the Wagner ranch with his lady friend, straight up Old Hill Road about five miles to the north. You can't miss it."

The man grumbled something unintelligible, then limped away and pushed through the doors, taking his bottle with him. Melody returned to Jack's side and took his arm, with the clear intention of continuing their liaison upstairs.

"What'd you say to get him to leave?"

"Nothin'. Just said he might be out at the Wagner ranch," she said with a smirk.

Jack stopped mid-step. "Melody, I swear sometimes you do the dumbest things."

"I didn't want him in here. Seemed like a good way to get rid of some trash."

He pulled away from her and left the saloon, shaking his head and muttering to himself.

After leaving the saloon and getting mounted, the man in the red scarf stopped at the livery before venturing into a countryside he didn't know his way around in. He asked the stable boy how to get to Old Hill Road. The young boy leaned on his pitchfork and looked at him as if he were stupid.

"You makin' fun of me just because I'm muckin' out horse shit?"

"I'm not makin' fun of you at all. Just want to know where the damned road is, that's all. If you don't want to tell me, I'll be on my way."

"You're on it, mister. Don't you know nothin'?"

The man's first impulse was to draw his Remington and put a hole straight through the scrawny smart-mouthed kid, but he decided instead to ride on, erasing his anger by sucking on the whiskey bottle as he went.

As soon as I find that sheriff's lady friend, he thought, *I reckon that's when my job begins.*

Chapter 11

———◆———

Emily had come out on the porch when Henry Coyote called to her about an approaching rider. As she took a step closer to Henry, the rider pulled up just in front of the steps. He did not offer the courtesy of tipping his hat to a lady but instead leaned forward, dark, brooding eyes searching about as if he expected to find someone else.

"What can I do for you, mister?" Emily said.

"I'm lookin' for a gent I was told would likely be here."

"What gent would that be?"

"A man named Cotton Burke. Where is he?"

"Why would you figure him to be here?"

"I was told in town that if he wasn't there, this is where I could find him. Spoke like you was his woman. You sayin' that ain't true?"

"I reckon you've been led astray. I'm nobody's woman, and he isn't here. Now it's time for you to move on," she said, and turned to go back inside. "And don't come back or I'll have you thrown off the ranch."

"Don't believe a word you're sayin'. I can see it in your

eyes. And don't you show your backside to me, lady. I won't stand for dismissal from no damned bitch. Now tell me where I can find this Cotton Burke. And be quick about it. I ain't a patient man. Got a message for him."

"What message would that be?"

"I been on the road a spell, and I'm plumb tuckered, so tell me what I want to know, or else you ain't gonna like what comes next."

The man in the dusty black flat-brimmed hat clenched his teeth as he drew a nickel-plated .38 from a shoulder holster beneath his duster. He thrust it out straight, pointing directly at her. Emily froze in place, her eyes wide in a mixture of surprise and fear. No one had *ever* pointed a gun in her direction before.

"I told you once and I'm not going to tell you again, he isn't—"

Before she could finish her sentence, the man followed her with the little spur-trigger .38, a couple inches to the right in the direction she'd moved, keeping it aimed directly at her as he cocked the hammer and placed his finger on the trigger.

"Last chance," he hissed through gritted teeth.

Emily stood her ground with a defiant jut of her chin, arms crossed.

"Go to hell," she spat, with a venomous scowl.

That's when he made his move, but Henry moved quicker. He shoved Emily out of the way, taking the full force of the explosion himself. He fell on top of the surprised woman. As the stranger raised the gun to shoot again, one of the ranch hands came around the corner of the house, six-shooter drawn. He pulled off a quick shot that hit nothing but air. It did, however, serve its purpose. The man yanked hard on his reins and wheeled his horse about, then spurred the mare to a dead run toward the gate.

Struggling to free herself from beneath Henry, Emily felt something wet as she gripped his arm. Blood dripped onto her shirt and onto the porch. Henry had been shot. She felt a jolt of panic as she looked into his wandering, questioning eyes. She scrambled to untangle herself from beneath the Apache, finally managing to roll him over just as the ranch hand rushed up the steps to help.

"Oh, my god, Henry's been shot! Teddy, go get some men, hitch up a team, and bring the buckboard around. We have to get him to the doctor before he bleeds to death. Scoot!"

Teddy Olander, a twenty-year-old kid from Arkansas she'd hired only a week before, and the one who'd scared the shooter away, nearly tripped over his own feet as he lit a shuck for the bunkhouse, shouting as he went. Three cowboys tumbled out of their bunks and scrambled to see what all the yelling was about.

"Henry's been gunned down by some scoundrel that tried to shoot Miss Emily. Get the buckboard hitched up and be damned quick about it!"

For a brief moment, as the seriousness of the situation slowly sank into the suddenly awakened cowhands, they stood in stunned silence, trying to rub the sleep from their eyes. Then, one must have caught on, and he broke ranks, pulled his suspenders up, and stumbled toward the corral. That was sufficient for the others to scatter in search of their part in the job at hand.

Emily carried several blankets from the house and placed them in the bed of the buckboard. She rolled a couple up to place on either side so the Indian wouldn't be jolted so badly that the bleeding would increase, cutting his chances for survival even further. They all helped lift the old Apache onto the blankets as gently as rough, calloused cowhands could be expected to do.

"Teddy, you drive. I'll stay back here with Henry and try to stop as much bleeding as I can."

Teddy slapped the reins like a hardened teamster as the horses strained at their traces, thundering through the front gate and out onto the road toward Apache Springs. Emily held Henry's head up, while attempting to stop the blood from flowing by pressing a wetted compress against the wound as best she could. She prayed Henry would live as the buckboard bounced and rattled along the rutted road. *Cotton, I need you. Please come home.*

As the straining, heavily lathered team thundered down the Old Hill Road and slid around a corner onto the main street of town, Emily was already screaming for the doctor. Teddy yanked the reins back and pushed as hard as he could on the foot brake to stop the buckboard. It shuddered to its final last few skidding feet right outside the Dr. John Winters's office porch.

"What in tarnation is all the fuss about, woman? Oh, it's you, Miss Emily, sorry."

Doc Winters was wearing his usual baggy, wrinkled pants held up with suspenders. Along with the top to his long johns, which appeared to have been washed less than regularly. In his hand was a half-empty bottle of whiskey, which he tried to move behind him but failed. Emily's eyes immediately shot to the bottle then to the doctor, whose stance was unsteady at best.

"Whatever's in that bottle better be medicinal, Doc, or you're about to wish it was. I've got a badly wounded man here and he needs tendin' to. And not by some drunk. You up to it or do I have to hold a gun to your head?"

Doc Winters was at once embarrassed at the dressing down he'd just received. He could find no words to rebut her condemnation. He was a drunk. Had been for years. Truth be known, he'd never made an attempt to change, either.

"Get your man inside, Miss Emily. I'll be just fine. You can keep your gun tucked in that holster. Who's been shot?"

"Henry Coyote."

"The Injun?"

"Yeah. That gonna be a problem?"

"Uh, well, uh, no, I reckon not. Never operated on no Injun before, though."

"Don't worry none about that, Doc. He is no different than any other man. He bleeds when he's wounded, and he dies when he isn't tended to properly. I'd surely hate for something like that to happen to one of the best men I've ever known. You *do* understand, don't you?"

Emily's hand slowly dropped to the butt of her revolver, holstered and drooping on a belt that dangled loosely around her small waist.

"I, uh, understand, ma'am. I'll do my best. You can bet on it."

"Teddy, help me get Henry inside." The two of them lifted the Apache as gently as they could and, draping one of his arms over each of their shoulders, half-carried, half-dragged him up the steps and across the threshold into the doctor's office. The doctor waved his hand to direct them to heft him onto a table in a room that brought back bad memories for Emily. It was where she first saw Cotton after hearing he was still alive, dangling his legs over the edge of the table, and trying to shrug into his bloody shirt. Only hours before, he'd been shot and nearly killed by one of the Cruz gang. That terrible moment brought relief only after Cotton refused to be denied the destiny he'd sworn to keep with the vicious outlaw. That destiny was finally served as Virgil Cruz lay dying from Cotton's deadly aim in the very cabin where Emily had suffered humiliation at the hands of a degenerate gunman.

As Henry lay on the table, the doctor began fumbling around on another table, this one laden with instruments—shiny, sharp, and unfriendly. Emily prayed that somewhere in that jumble was the one that would save Henry's life.

Teddy leaned on the back of a pressed-pine chair across the room. His stomach had been full of butterflies ever since he first saw Henry lying across Emily, blood flowing over her dress. When the doctor finally selected a long, thin pair of tweezers and started probing around in the wound, Teddy's stomach began to grumble its disdain. The sight of blood was nothing new to the boy, but when it was someone he worked with and the possibility of death loomed large, he was sorely tempted to make a beeline for the door and some much-needed fresh air.

But his feet would not move. No matter how badly he wished to be somewhere else, he felt as though his boots had been nailed to the floor. Watching the old Indian's complete control over what Teddy could only imagine had to be insufferable pain astonished him. The Apache held perfectly still and made no sound, neither groan nor curse. Henry's black eyes were open, fixed on the ceiling above, intensely focused, drilling through the beams, the roof, and beyond. The boy was transfixed by the man's capacity for pain and an apparent ability to be at peace with all that had happened. Henry had waved off the doctor's attempt at sedation with laudanum. He wouldn't even accept a drink of whiskey. The doctor merely shrugged and went to work.

Teddy was instantly roused from his trance by the sharp sound of a hunk of lead being dropped into a metal cup. A small bottle of powder sat nearby and the doctor sprinkled a bit of it over the wound. Teddy watched as the man, who'd been stumbling, presumably from too much libation prior to their arrival, wiped his hands on a white cloth, quickly threaded a curved needle, and began the job of sewing up the crimson hole in Henry's shoulder, with the deft hand of an accomplished seamstress.

After he clipped the thread and tied it off, the doctor reached for the whiskey and, after pouring a healthy amount of it over the wound, lifted it to his lips and guzzled the rest of the bottle's contents.

"Keep him quiet for a few days. If he gets up and wanders around, he could open the sutures. If he starts bleeding again, get him back here as quickly as possible. Do as I say and he'll live." The doctor walked from the room, out into the sunlight, and lit a cigar. He leaned on the porch railing and took a deep breath.

Emily followed him.

"I'm sorry I was a bit disagreeable with you, Doc. I reckon I wasn't myself. Henry is very important to me. He

saved my life for the second time by jumping in front of a
bullet that had been intended for me. Please accept my
apologies."

"No apology necessary, Miss Emily. I had it comin'." He
sighed deeply and took another draw on the cigar. "Your
Indian's going to survive, Miss Emily, but he'll need rest for
a few days. He's too weak to travel just yet, however."

"Since Cotton is away, I'll ask his deputy to help me take
him down to the sheriff's house. Maybe he can rest up there
until I can get him back to the ranch."

The doctor nodded, turned back inside, and began to
gather up the bloody instruments and carry them over to a
large copper tub full of water. He tossed them in, lifted the
tub, and placed it on the stove. Emily watched for a moment,
then turned to go find Cotton's deputy, Memphis Jack Stump.

Chapter 12

All saddled and ready to go at dawn, Cotton and the three others prepared to mount up and get on their way. Delilah had gone back inside, presumably to say good-bye to Thorn. Cotton hadn't bothered. He'd told Mrs. Hardin of his plans to return in three days and bring back her horses. He figured she would pass the word on to McCann. He was hoping by then Thorn would have healed up sufficiently to be able to travel, even if it was lying flat on his back in a buckboard.

Seeming hesitant, Delilah started to come out on the porch, then stopped in the doorway to glance back over her shoulder. The sour look on her face suggested indecision. Cotton saw she was having a problem.

"What's the matter, Delilah? We best get goin' if we aim to get back to Apache Springs in the daylight."

"I-I'm staying here with Thorn. He may need me. I'm sorry, I just can't leave him."

Damn, Cotton thought, *Thorn McCann's gone and got*

himself all tangled up in a woman's skirts. Wonder what she'll say when he tells her he figured all along to return to the life of a bounty hunter.

"I'd advise against it, but you're free to do as you please. I plan to return in about three days to take you both outta here. I doubt Thorn will be in any shape to ride a horse, so I figure to bring a buckboard."

"Thank you for understanding," Delilah said, as she gave him a halfhearted smile and a nod and stepped back inside.

Mrs. Hardin looked up at the sheriff. "Don't blame her, son, she's likely in love. It's just one of those silly things women do now and again." She gave a sigh and followed Delilah, closing the heavy door behind her.

"Keep those rifles loaded at all times!" Cotton shouted after the lady. He wasn't certain if she heard or not, but for now his job was to get the other two to safety in Apache Springs. He motioned for them to fall in behind as he led the way.

Emily didn't have to look far for Jack. He was just coming out of the sheriff's office. He paused for a moment to allow his eyes to adjust to the brightness of the afternoon sun. When he looked up, he saw Emily Wagner rushing toward him from the direction of Doc Winters's office.

"Jack, thank heavens I found you. I have a favor to ask of you."

"Why, of course, ma'am, what is it?"

"A man showed up at the ranch a few hours ago. He tried to shoot me, but Henry took the bullet instead. The one intended for me. Doc's got him patched up, but I can't take him back to the ranch, at least not yet. Since Cotton's out of town, do you think we could take Henry to his place, just long enough for him to get some of his strength back?"

"I'm certain ol' Cotton wouldn't mind. C'mon, I'll lend a hand gettin' him settled. Who did you say shot him?"

"I didn't say, mainly because I don't know who he was. Just a tall, rangy fellow, with a flat-brimmed hat and a bright red bandana around his neck."

Jack swallowed hard. He knew more of the story than he dared let on at the moment. His anger at Melody's loose tongue boiled up in him. *She's always been a bitch*, he thought, *but I've tolerated it because she's so damned good in bed. Now she's risked someone's life with her mouth. And I have to live with the consequences.*

"You don't know something you're not telling me, do you, Jack?"

That shook Jack out of his woolgathering. "Uh, no, no, nothing at all. We, uh, best get Henry down to Cotton's place. The sooner he has a place to lie down that's more comfortable than Doc Winters's table, the sooner he can get on with the job of healin' up."

"Yes, let's do that. I see no reason why we can't carry him out and put him in the buckboard. Teddy will help."

"Teddy?"

"Teddy Olander. He's a new hire out at the ranch. I needed some extra help and he came along at just the right time." She looked around to see if she could see where the young wrangler had disappeared. About that time, the young man came through the doors of the saloon with a wide smile on his face and sauntered across the street. "Where'd you get off to, Teddy?"

"I was, uh, just needin' a little somethin' to ease my nerves after seein' Henry all bloody and all. I only had one beer. Was that okay, Miss Emily?"

"Uh-huh. But now we need you to help get Henry in the back of the buckboard. We'll take him to the sheriff's house down the street."

"Yes, ma'am."

As Teddy approached, Jack stuck out his hand. "Name's Memphis Jack, Teddy. I'm the deputy. Pleased to meet'cha." Teddy shook hands, and they both followed Emily Wagner up the steps to the porch of the doctor's office.

When the three of them got inside, Henry was stretched

out on his back, staring at the ceiling. His eyes told a story of much pain, but he made no sound to indicate any discomfort whatsoever. Jack just shook his head. He and others had long thought Henry Coyote was the toughest hombre they'd ever known.

Jack carefully lifted Henry by the shoulders and Teddy took his feet. The doctor admonished Jack to take care not to jostle the patient or the stitches could open and the wound begin bleeding all over again. Jack nodded his understanding. He was getting to be an old hand at helping wounded men get needed medical attention. He still couldn't get the mental picture out of his head of old Hank Brennan's battered body lying on a ledge halfway down a sheer cliff after Virgil Cruz had tried to murder him by pushing him over the edge. When Cotton was shot down in the streets of Apache Springs by one of the Cruz gang, Jack had the unenviable task of getting *him* to the doctor's, too. Yeah, Jack knew the meaning of *take it easy*.

Emily had rearranged the blankets in the bed of the wagon to get the lumps out of them for the short ride down the street. Jack then led the horse-drawn buckboard down the side of the street to miss the ruts left by heavy wagons using mainly the center of the road. When they got to the house, the three of them gently lifted Henry from the bed of the buckboard and carried him inside. The door was never locked. Cotton didn't see the need. After all, what idiot would break into the sheriff's house?

When they laid the old Indian on Cotton's feather mattress, Jack was sure he saw the corners of Henry's mouth form a slight smile. He couldn't be certain, but when he heard a slight sigh, he got the impression things were going to turn out okay for Henry. Jack watched as Emily scurried about straightening things up, clucking her tongue, probably at the messiness of a bachelor, keeping herself busy. Doing something, anything, was as good a way as any to ward off the fear and anger that obviously followed such a dastardly deed.

"What will you do, now, Miss Emily? Are you planning to go back out to the ranch tonight?"

"No. I'll stay with Henry until he's able to get around on his own. Teddy can pick up a horse at the livery and go back alone. I'll write out some instructions for him and the others."

"I'll tell him," Jack said as he went outside to find the kid.

Chapter 13

———⊶◦⊷———

Cotton, Denby Biddle, and Jimmy Culp had been on the road for no more than three hours when they heard riders approaching from the west. *More damned Indians*, Cotton thought and swore under his breath. He pulled his rifle as he signaled for the other two to take cover in some trees off the road in a ravine, and the riders came into view. There were about twenty-five of them, buffalo soldiers from Fort Tularosa. Cotton let out a sigh of relief and awaited their arrival. The column reined in, and the leader, a black sergeant, held up his hand to the others to take a rest.

"Sergeant, good to see you fellas takin' care of business. Seen any Indians?"

"No, suh, only the problems they done left behind. A couple ranches was hit and some cattle were stolen 'bout three miles over yonder."

"Chiricahua?"

"Uh-huh. Mangas or Victorio, or one o' them other wild'uns."

"Well, if you continue on this road, you'll come across a wrecked stagecoach and a body lyin' in the dirt. Then, just over the hill, down in a cut where a stream goes through, you'll likely find a few of them Indians' bodies, unless their friends already hauled them off to the happy huntin' ground."

"Y'all look to be in one piece."

"Left a woman and a badly wounded man down at the Hardin place."

The sergeant shook his head, then made a circling motion to his troops and, as he put a foot in a stirrup, said, "We'll see if we can follow their tracks. Mebbe we'll give what's left of 'em a dandy what fer. Y'all be watchful for signs yer bein' follered."

"We will. Thanks, Sergeant. Good luck." Cotton watched the cavalry troop disappear in a cloud of dust over the hill, toward where the stagecoach lay overturned and broken. He stood watching for a minute or two, thinking he should have gone back and buried the stage driver before starting for Apache Springs. He had a look that suggested disappointment in himself as he turned to the other two.

Denby had a sour expression that wrinkled his already disagreeable face.

"Now, can you tell me what's the army coming to? Having black men as soldiers. Nonsense, that's what it is, nonsense," Denby said as he shook his head in disgust.

Cotton was instantly incensed.

"Well let me tell *you* somethin', *Mr.* Denby. If you ever find yourself in a tight spot with Indians all around, you'd best pray some of those buffalo soldiers come to your rescue. They're the best there are. Someday I'll tell you about the battle for Fort Tularosa. You'll be a believer in what I'm tellin' you, then."

"I, uh, didn't mean no—"

"Let's get movin', gents. If we *do* run into more redskins, I'd prefer doin' it in the daylight."

"I'd prefer not doin' it at all," Jimmy said, with a squeak.

* * *

It was early nightfall when the tired and hungry threesome arrived at the edge of Apache Springs. Lanterns lit up the saloon, but nearly everyone else had closed up shop and gone home. Only the houses at the edge of town showed lights in the windows. Cotton suspected the hotel's dining room would be closed, so he suggested they try to get some sleep. They'd have to wait until morning to eat. Once the dining room was open, shortly after dawn, they'd all three be famished, but there was little that could be done about that now. Cotton dug into his saddlebags and pulled out some beef jerky. He handed a piece to each of the other men, which they each took eagerly, then he headed for the jail to see if Jack was still there.

He pushed open the door, half-expecting to find Jack leaning back in his chair, feet on the desk, reading the latest penny-dreadful pamphlet put out by writers who really had no idea what the frontier was like. He'd known a few of the men whose exploits had been chronicled by the likes of Ned Buntline, and not one of them even remotely resembled the offbeat characters portrayed. Cotton was surprised not only that Jack wasn't there, but also that no lantern had been lit. He had to stand there for a minute to let his eyes adjust to the dark before he could find a lantern, scratch a sulfur, and touch it to the wick. Soon, the small office was bathed in a warm glow. He checked the desk to see if his deputy had left a message as to where he could be found if needed. Nothing.

Realizing that Jack had no way of knowing when Cotton would be back, the sherrif couldn't really blame him for not being there. After all, he was a deputy, not a slave. He was probably sound asleep, snuggled in Melody's arms. Sleep was exactly what Cotton needed as well.

He blew out the lamp, closed the door behind him, and headed for his own house and the soft mattress that awaited him. As he got closer to the little house at the end of the street, he noticed a light in the window. And Emily's buck-board out front. Something whispered that he should be ready for trouble, so he stepped onto the porch as quietly as he could, leaned over, and peered through the window. He could see nothing. He stepped to the door and gently turned the knob. As the door opened with a squeak, he pushed it farther and slipped inside. His hand rested on the handle of his Colt.

In an instant his hand tightened on the grips, stopping short of a draw, when he suddenly realized that he was looking into the red, tear-filled eyes of Emily Wagner.

"My god, Emily! I could have shot you. What's happened? You look as if you've been crying." He stepped forward to take her into his arms.

"He shot Henry. He meant to kill me, but Henry jumped in front of me at the last second and he was the one to go down. Oh, Cotton, it was so awful."

"Where is Henry?"

"Lying in your bed. He's resting for now. Doc Winters says he'll live, but the ride out to the ranch might kill him. I, uh, didn't think you'd mind if he stayed here for a couple days."

"Of course I don't mind. But how'd you get him down here?"

"One of my new cowhands helped Jack get him here and settled."

"Who shot Henry?"

"I don't know what his name was. He didn't take the time to introduce himself," Emily said through gritted teeth.

"What the hell! What'd this fella look like?"

With eyes still teary, Emily tried to give a description. Jack stepped in the door just as she was struggling to put a face to the evil that had shot Henry. Cotton watched as Emily choked back her emotions with nearly every word.

"H-he was tall, wore a red bandana . . . and, uh . . . I . . . I'm sorry, Cotton, the thought of him makes me . . . sick . . ."

"I think I can describe the hombre, Sheriff," Jack broke

in, coming back after feeding Emily's horses and getting them settled for the night. "The bastard came to the saloon askin' questions about where he could find you."

"And you told him?"

"Hell, no! You should know me better'n that. I could tell he was up to no good, so I said you came and went as you pleased and had no call to give me your itinerary."

"Then how in the hell did he know to show up at the Wagner ranch?" Cotton balled his fists as his expression showed a sudden revelation. "Wait, don't tell me. Melody and her big mouth got this man shot. Am I right?"

Jack looked away with shame in his eyes. "I'm afraid so. She did it behind my back."

"Figures. When are you goin' to dump that whore, Jack? She's no good—not for you, not for me, and certainly not for the town."

Jack could find no words in response. His gaze dropped to the badly worn carpet at the entrance, and he chewed his lip.

"Well, tell me what you can about him, Jack."

"Uh, well, he was a fairly good-sized hombre, with a nose like a buzzard. He wore a Remington .44, a flat-brimmed hat, and, like she said, a large red scarf draped around his neck. From what I could see under his duster, he was also totin' what appeared to be a .38 in a shoulder holster. Mentioned someone named Sanborn."

Cotton stiffened at hearing the description. His eyes filled with recognition.

"Did he by any chance have a limp, Jack?"

"Wh-why, now that you mention it, he did. How'd you know that?"

"He got that limp from one of my bullets. That's James Lee Hogg, and he's one mean son of a bitch. A killer. He calls himself a bounty hunter."

"Why would a bounty hunter be looking for you?" Emily asked with a surprised look.

Cotton took her by the shoulders and pulled her close.

"It's a long story, my love, a very long story."

He'd known for some time that sooner or later he'd have to tell her about his killing of "Lucky Bill" Sanborn for raping and killing his sister. He'd hoped that wouldn't come anytime soon, but circumstances had, once again, brought the matter to his doorstep. Holding Emily tightly, as her tears stained his shirt, he thought back to the Sanborn killing, Thorn McCann's real reason for coming to Apache Springs in the first place, and to his one and only encounter with James Lee Hogg. He found no comfort in any of them.

Chapter 14

———◆———

Cotton took off his hat, wiped his forehead with his sleeve, then replaced the hat, tipping the brim down. He'd left Emily and Jack staring after him as he eased out onto the porch to be alone, to get away from having to launch into an explanation of his checkered past to the love of his life. He had no idea whether her finding out that he'd murdered a man several years back would have any effect on their relationship, but he wasn't eager to find out. The pain of such a consequence might kill him.

His own conscience didn't bother him over the "Lucky Bill" incident because the kid had deliberately attacked Cotton's younger sister, raped her, and left her for dead. He'd also knifed her husband, who bled to death trying to save his wife. Cotton had taken his revenge and shot the young man. Afterward, he turned in his badge and walked away. Killing a monster was something he could live with, although Judge Sanborn, the kid's father, had been unable to let it go, and he sent Thorn McCann out to bring his son's killer to justice. The old judge had put a price on

Cotton's head, even though doing so was illegal. The judge was merely a justice of the peace, without the authority to conduct a murder trial or direct a verdict of hanging.

Cotton's first encounter with James Lee Hogg had been equally justified, although Hogg obviously hadn't thought so. It happened on a ranch just outside Fort Worth several years back. At the time, Cotton was once again a deputy sheriff. He had gone to the ranch to talk over the owner's complaint about some missing cattle. When he got to the place, he found the rancher's ten-year-old daughter crying her eyes out, cradling a wounded dog. The dog was bleeding from a bullet wound.

He remembered asking the girl what had happened. Her story was unsettling to him. She'd described how this man had ridden up to the ranch house asking whether there might be a reward for the rustlers who'd stolen her father's cattle. The little girl didn't know, but said she would go inside and ask. She had, to that point, been carrying a small dog in her arms. When she turned to go inside to find her father, she put the dog down, skipped up on the porch, and disappeared through the door. She heard the dog barking but thought nothing of it until she heard a gunshot. When she ran back outside, her dog was lying on the ground, bleeding from a bullet wound. The man told her she best keep "that mangy mutt" away from him or the next time he'd kill it. He then rode off before the child's father could respond.

The distraught youngster told Deputy Cotton Burke in detail what had happened and described the man with a flat-brimmed hat and the horse he was riding, a dun mare. Cotton remembered seeing someone fitting the description in town. When he got back to town, he spotted the man outside the saloon, sitting in a rocker with a glass of beer in his hand. Cotton would never forget the conversation that took place that afternoon. He had walked up onto the porch and stood in front of the man, casting a long shadow across him. He stared through narrowed eyes at the evil seated before him.

"Somethin' I can do for you, Deputy?" the man asked, sipping from his glass as he glanced up.

"Uh-huh. You just ride in?"

"Been here a couple hours, I reckon. Why?"

"I just came from a ranch where a little girl's dog was shot by a man fittin' your description. You know anythin' about that?"

"I look like a dog-shooter to you?"

"Matter of fact, I'd have to say yes."

"Words like those could get a man in a heap of trouble. Maybe you ought to rethink 'em."

"Don't think I will. I figure you'd best be unbucklin' that gun belt and come with me over to the jail," Cotton said. "We'll wait on a little girl and her father to ride in and identify you as the low-life, cowardly bastard who would gun down a helpless mutt."

"For what reason would I do a damned foolish thing like that?"

"To keep me from pluggin' you where you sit."

"I don't allow no one to talk to me that way, Deputy, so maybe you'd best be on your way and leave a peace-lovin' man to his rest."

Two men who'd stepped out on the porch watched the confrontation. They started back inside, but stopped at the sheriff's next words. They both looked surprised. Neither spoke.

"All right, whoever in the hell you are, I reckon gettin' a judge to string you up for shootin' a dog would be damned nigh impossible."

"That's the way I see it, too. Reckon you might as well be on your way," Hogg said with a big toothy grin on his face. He settled back in his chair and began to rock. He turned away from Cotton, so he didn't see the deputy draw his .45 Colt, take careful aim, and pull the trigger.

The bullet blew through Hogg's boot, taking with it his big toe. Hogg fell out of his rocker, screaming and writhing on the porch as Cotton strolled away as if nothing had happened.

"Reckon the matter's settled now. You and the dog are even." It was Cotton's turn to break into a wry smile.

* * *

After a few minutes, Emily followed Cotton outside. Jack trailed behind.

"I figure to get some sleep, Cotton, if you don't need me," Jack said.

"Yeah, that's fine. We'll talk in the mornin'."

Jack strolled down the middle of the street, heading straight for Melody's Golden Palace of Pleasure.

"Wh-why was that man looking for you, Cotton?" Emily's voice caught as she wiped at a tear. "He *was* looking to kill you, wasn't he?"

"I 'spect."

"Why?"

"Sometimes, when he least expects it, a man's past can catch up to him. Reckon mine has."

"I don't understand. Please tell me."

"Emily, I've told you before that not everything I've done in my life has amounted to something to be proud of. What happened between James Lee Hogg and me doesn't mean nuthin', although I imagine it does to him. But the *real* reason he's here might not be something you want to hear."

"Cotton, there is nothing you could tell me that would make me turn away from you. Please, I have to know what this is all about, especially since it appears to involve me somehow. Please. You owe me that much. And Henry, too."

Cotton flinched at her words. She was right, he did owe her an explanation after she was nearly shot as a result of *his* perceived misdeeds. But could he actually steel himself to the task? It was a question he'd wrestled with for some time. There still seemed no answer in sight.

Chapter 15

Thorn McCann was groggy and disoriented when he awoke. He tried to sit up, blinking his eyes to clear them, to figure out where he was. And why. The stabbing pain in his shoulder knocked him back onto the pillow quickly, with a vague remembrance of Indians and an attack and . . . and Cotton Burke. He groaned and licked his chapped lips. Delilah heard him and came to his side. She sat down on a spindle-back chair next to the bed.

"That you, Delilah? Where am I? What happened?" He tried once more to sit up, but another surge of pain changed his mind.

"We're at the relay station. The Hardins' place. Mrs. Hardin patched you up. Just lie still so you don't undo the good work she did sewing those bullet holes up so no more of your blood leaks out." Her words were barely above a whisper as she leaned in close.

"Holes? Was I hit more'n once?"

"One bullet, clean through."

"I sorta remember being on the stagecoach, and the

attack of them blasted Apaches, and us trying to climb a hill to get you out of there before they saw us, and . . . and that's all that comes to mind. Well, I *do* have some recollection of Cotton Burke, but that could have just been a bad dream."

"Not a bad dream, Thorn. If he hadn't come along when he did, we'd all be dead by now. Those Apaches weren't all that keen on letting us live."

"Saved by Cotton Burke. Damn! That's humiliatin'."

"Owing a man your life isn't nearly as bad as being under a pile of rocks for eternity."

"Yeah, I s'pose you got a point, Delilah," he sighed. "How long I been laid up?"

"Three days now. You got real feverish for a couple days. Looks like its finally broke, thank goodness. Mrs. Hardin said if you lived through the fever, you'd survive."

"Where's Cotton?"

"He took the kid with the shotgun and that passenger, Denby, and went on to Apache Springs. Said he'd be back with a buckboard to haul you out of here. I don't think he figured you'd be able to sit a horse for a week or more, bad as you were wounded. I look for him anytime now."

"The driver, what happened to him?"

"Killed."

Just then Mrs. Hardin came into the room. Thorn could hear some commotion outside but couldn't make out what it was about. Delilah smiled and said, "It looks like your patient might pull through after all, Mrs Hardin."

"Looks like. You up to a little soup, mister?" she said.

"I hadn't given it much thought, but I could use a little somethin', yes ma'am. What's all that hollerin' outside?"

"A couple of Apaches came demandin' whiskey. Jeremiah don't hold with givin' whiskey to Indians. They know that. He tells them every time they come, but they don't give up trying."

Mrs. Hardin turned and left the room. She reappeared only a couple minutes later with a bowl—from which a thin cloud of steam curled—and a spoon. She held out a cloth napkin that had stitching around the sides to stop it from fraying. It had *mostly* worked. She handed the bowl to Delilah.

"Here, child, he'll surely need some help."

Delilah took the bowl from her, spooned out a bit of stew, and thrust it toward Thorn. He sheepishly leaned forward and slurped it, his face growing pink from being fed by a woman. The memory rushed back of being spoon-fed as a young boy after he'd come down with a fever his mother said could have killed him. While his mother was long gone, that same feeling of dependence on another came upon him like a sudden shower. He'd not felt anything akin to this need for any other woman, and yet here he was gazing into Delilah's eyes and experiencing a strange fullness in his heart. That was just before the roar of a shotgun blasted him out of his reverie.

"They've killed him! Those bastards have shot my Jeremiah!" Mrs. Hardin's screams could have likely been heard for a mile.

Delilah raced to the door and opened it just enough to see two Indians standing over Jeremiah's bloody form. He was lying facedown in the dirt. One Indian had a rifle. The other had obviously wrestled Jeremiah Hardin's twelve-gauge away from his aged hands and turned it on him. The old man had had no chance to save himself. Mrs. Hardin was running to her husband when one of the Indians pulled a long knife from his high boot top. Just as he was about to slash it across her throat, another shot rang out.

The Indian's legs went out from under him as he was tossed over backward. His companion looked shocked as a sudden realization came over him: there had been someone other than the old woman inside. The two Apaches hadn't counted on any deadly resistance. He raised his rifle to combat whatever threat showed itself, but was just as quickly dispatched by another deadly shot from inside the building. Mrs. Hardin looked up through tear-filled eyes to see Thorn

McCann leaning on the door frame, a still-smoking revolver hanging limply from his hand. He dropped the gun as he slid to the floor with a groan.

Delilah grabbed him by the arm before he hit his head on a heavy bench. She eased him down. His breathing was labored and coming in short, desperate gasps. Delilah pulled and pulled, trying to lift him up to get him back to bed, but her efforts were fruitless. He was too big a man for such a slight lady to ever hope to even drag across the floor. He closed his eyes and quickly lost consciousness.

Mrs. Hardin stumbled through the door, sobbing and dabbing at her eyes with her apron. Torn over what she should do, Delilah turned her attention to the distraught woman, helping her to a chair nearby. Delilah could feel the tears welling up as she wiped the hair out of her eyes, leaned against the wall, and slid to a sitting position on the floor. She had never known such fear and desperation in her life. She found herself conjuring up images of many more Apaches swooping down on the relay station in retaliation for their two dead comrades outside. Her heart was in her throat and she could feel it pounding in her chest. She glanced over at Thorn's revolver lying near the door. She began to question if she could even lift it, let alone hit anything with it. Her little .41-caliber Remington derringer was easy. It was small, light, and it took no more effort than pulling back the hammer and squeezing the trigger.

Thorn groaned and tried to move.

"Lie still, Thorn, or you'll open those wounds."

He mumbled something unintelligible. She leaned down to try to understand, and heard only the weakest attempt at a whisper—no words came out.

Chapter 16

———◆———

Sitting at the breakfast table, Emily sipped from a cup of tea, which she daintily held in both hands, while glaring across the table at Cotton. He had as yet not been forthcoming about his suspicions regarding the presence of James Lee Hogg in Apache Springs, and any possible explanation of why she might have been a target, even though he knew he owed it to her to come clean. Cotton merely fidgeted in his chair, taking an occasional bite of a plate of eggs. His eyes wandered around, taking in the floor, ceiling, and various pieces of furniture, as Emily remained quiet and patient, blowing on her cup between swallows. Her stoicism told him she would willingly die where she sat waiting until he was forthcoming.

"Haven't you ever done anything in your life that made you ashamed of spilling the beans?" Cotton finally said without looking her in the eye.

"I have. When I was seven, I pushed my little brother off a fence. He broke his arm. At first, I claimed he fell because he was teasing me and not paying attention to what he was doing. I allowed he shouldn't have been climbing the fence in the first place. After a couple of days, my guilt took over and I confessed, expecting the worst. It never came. No recrimination, no anger, no punishment. My mother just hugged me. My brother wasn't even all that mad, although he was pretty uncomfortable until the arm healed."

"I'm not talking about things you did as a child. I'm talking about serious, life-altering things. Life-and-death things."

"How many people have you had to kill, Cotton? Ten, twenty, more?"

"What difference does it make? Probably more than I'd like to remember. And I'm not particularly proud of any of 'em."

"Well, I know that not one was done for anything other than a righteous reason. You're a legally elected lawman, not a murderer. Of that I am certain."

Cotton stiffened at her mention of murder. That was exactly what he considered himself to be. A murderer. *And yet, I'd do it again in payment for the life of my sister.* He wiped his mouth with a napkin, then scooted his chair back and walked to the window. He parted the curtain and stared out on the street. Jack was just entering the jail.

"I get the feeling you know why that man tried to shoot me. Am I right, Cotton?"

"I don't rightly know. I have an idea, a mere suspicion, that's all. I'll know more when I can see him face-to-face."

"So what's your idea?"

"It's got nothing to do with you. It's me he's after. Of that I am certain."

"Something that happened recently?"

"Nope."

"So, he's someone from your past."

"Yep."

"But why me?"

"He knows you're important to me. That's why."

"Then this is about revenge?"

"Uh-huh."

"Why does he want you dead?"

"Payback, money—both, likely."

"Are you saying he's a hired killer?"

"That's my guess."

"People don't hire killers for no good reason, do they?"

"Nope."

"Is that reason what you can't seem to bring yourself to tell me?"

"Likely."

Emily knew she had only succeeded in chasing the goat around the barn and still hadn't caught it. She sighed and took another sip of tea. She sat silently as he continued his gazing out the window. If she was hoping he would relent, he was just as rigid in his intention not to tell her the whole story. After several minutes, he returned to the table, picked up his own cup, gulped the rest of his coffee, which had cooled sufficiently to allow such a daring act, and started for the door.

"I'm going to the livery to rent a buckboard to go fetch Thorn McCann and Delilah Jones. I'll be back in a few days."

"Wait! If you don't mind my staying with Henry until he's able to travel, why don't you take my buckboard? No sense in it sitting here for no purpose. If I need to go out to the ranch, I can ride your mare. You won't be needing her, I presume."

"All right. That is a good plan. I'll tie Mr. Hardin's horses to the back. They'll be needin' them as soon as the stage line gets its schedule back to normal."

Emily stood and walked up to Cotton. She put her hands on his chest and looked up. He leaned over and kissed her, then opened the door and walked out. He went around back to hook Emily's two horses up to the buckboard. That finished, he tossed his saddlebags and a blanket in the back, climbed into the seat, slapped the reins on the horses' rumps, and the conveyance rumbled into the street. Emily watched from the porch as he stopped briefly at the jail, hollering to Jack through the open door. After asking Jack to make sure nothing happened to Emily while he was gone, he waved and started off again.

As soon as Cotton was about to pass the stage line office, he pulled up and called out to the young shotgun guard, Jimmy Culp.

"Hey, Jimmy, you in there?"

Jimmy appeared from the side of the building. He walked up to the sheriff with a questioning look.

"What can I do for you, Sheriff?"

"I'm on my way to the livery to pick up the Hardins' horses. I need to get them back out to the relay station and pick up the two passengers we left out there. I don't know if Thorn will be any help in case of trouble, but if you've gotten some rest and a belly full, you and your shotgun would ease my mind a bit. How about comin' along?"

"Might as well. Until the company gets a crew out to where the stagecoach is lyin' all busted up, we're out of business on that route anyway. Nothin' to do but service the coaches from the two other lines that come through here. And none of them need a guard. Wait till I get my Greener and some supplies." The kid took off at a dead run back around the building from where he'd appeared. He returned in minutes with two boxes of shells, the short-barreled shotgun, and a gunnysack with who knew what stuffed inside. He climbed up next to Cotton with a possum-eating grin.

Jack wandered down to Cotton's house, where Emily stood staring after her buckboard and the dusty trail it left. She had crossed her arms, looking wistfully after her departed love.

"Emily, Cotton asked me to keep an eye on you while he's gone. Reckon that's a good idea since you already had one close call from that hombre James Lee Hogg. Anything I can do for you?"

"Thanks, Jack, but right now the only thing I want is

some straight talk from your boss. But it doesn't appear I'll get that anytime soon."

"I don't understand. Far as I know, he confides in you more'n anyone I know. Sure as hell more'n me."

"He's got something in his past that's eating him up, but he can't bring himself to share that with me. Must be terribly painful for him."

"I don't figure I know exactly what you're talkin' about, but if I was to venture a guess, I'd have to say it *is* something painful. Damned painful. Probably be best if you let 'er lie until he's ready. But that's just my humble opinion."

"I appreciate you opinions, Jack. But if we're ever goin' to make a home for the two of us, there has to be absolute openness about our pasts. I draw the line at secrets."

She spun around and stomped back inside. The door slammed closed behind her, leaving Jack to talk to a slab of pine with a handle and a lock.

"Yes, ma'am," he muttered as he began the trek back to the jail.

Chapter 17

———◆———

A distraught Delilah Jones met Cotton and Jimmy at the Hardins' front door. Her face was tired, devoid of its usual radiance, and dark circles ringed her pretty eyes. As soon as Cotton stepped inside, it became obvious that something terrible had happened during his absence. The smell of death lingered in the air like a musty blanket. He figured Thorn hadn't made it through, even after the heroic efforts of Mrs. Hardin. But when Thorn eased gingerly through the curtains dividing the front room from the sleeping quarters, it became obvious that something far worse had occurred.

"Hey, Cotton. Glad you could get back to us," Thorn said with a voice as weak as a child. He grabbed hold of a chair just within reach and dropped into it with a groan. Pain was obviously a constant companion, and his left arm appeared useless as it lay across his lap like a piece of cordwood.

"You look better than when I left, old pard, but still not the confident pistolero I once knew."

"He-he gets more of his strength back each day, Sheriff, but I'm even more worried about Mrs. Hardin," Delilah said.

"What happened, Delilah? Where is Mrs. Hardin?"

"She took to her bed and I can hardly rouse her to get her to eat a bite. Says she just wants to be left alone. A couple Indians shot and killed Jeremiah when he refused them whiskey. If it hadn't been for Thorn, we'd probably all be dead. He got both of them."

Cotton chewed on his lip as he mulled a way out of this new dilemma. For certain he couldn't leave Mrs. Hardin to fend for herself in the middle of the desert. But he was unsure whether he could come up with sufficient incentive to convince her to come back to Apache Springs with him. He'd known women who'd decided to lie down and die after losing their husbands. He hoped that wasn't what he was dealing with here. He began to pace the length of the long, narrow room. Down and back, down and back. Delilah's lovely lips were pinched. Jimmy Culp was getting fidgety, as if he were uncomfortable with all that had been happening. He opened the door as quietly as possible and slipped outside. Seeing this, Cotton called out for him to look around for signs of anything amiss.

Jimmy began his exploration of the Hardin place at the stable. He figured that since there had been such horror visited on Mr. and Mrs. Hardin over the past three days, he'd best make sure any horses that might be in the stalls had food and water. He wandered across a barren yard, opened a swinging gate that drooped from its own weight and rusted hinges, and stopped at a water tank that looked to have the beginnings of some scum on top. *There haven't been any horses drinking out of this for a while*, he thought. As he approached the barn, he saw that the wide swinging doors were closed and latched with a linchpin. He undid the latch and pulled. It took most of his strength to get the massive door over the dust and dirt blown in front of it by recent winds and a dust storm. As one door creaked open, Jimmy was met with the terrible stench of death. He jumped back, not certain whether he could keep down what little food he'd had that morning.

"Sheriff, you best come look. You ain't gonna like what you see," Jimmy yelled at the top of his lungs.

The urgency in his voice brought Cotton rushing out the door. He hurried to the barn, where Jimmy leaned on a railing, looking wan. The boy turned slightly and pointed to the open barn door, clearly unwilling to accompany the sheriff inside. Cotton stopped short, catching a first whiff of the death emanating from inside like a wandering plague. He quickly pulled his kerchief from around his neck, went back to the watering trough, and dipped the kerchief in the water. He wrung it out and, holding it over his nose and mouth, entered the barn. There, stretched out in front of him were three bodies; two were Indians, and the third was Jeremiah Hardin. Four horses stood in the farthest stall toward the back, obviously skittish about the smell they had been forced to endure.

Cotton came out with a scowl on his face.

"What is it, Sheriff? What's dead in there?"

"Mr. Hardin and the two Indians that killed him."

"How'd they get in there?"

"Someone must have dragged the bodies in there, and there's little doubt who."

Jimmy kept looking back over his shoulder as if he expected a ghost to arise and follow him into the house. He quickened his step to keep up with the sheriff.

"Delilah, how did the three bodies make their way into the barn? I don't see Thorn being much help, and from your description of Mrs. Hardin's state of mind, she probably wasn't up to the task, either. That leaves you."

"You're right, Sheriff. I couldn't leave them lying out there in the blistering sun. Besides, at night there're wild animals roaming around. Hungry, wild animals. So I dragged them one at a time to the barn and closed the door. Didn't have any idea when you'd be back, so—"

"Never mind. I understand. You did the right thing, although you maybe should have put the horses in the corral."

"I-I'm sorry, that never occurred to me. Are they all right?"

"Horses don't like bein' around the smell of death, but other than that, I figure they'll survive." He turned to Jimmy. "Jimmy, see if you can find a couple shovels so we can put the deceased in the ground, quick and proper-like."

Jimmy went back outside with a hint of reluctance. He clearly didn't care for the aroma of the first signs of rotting flesh any more than the horses did. But he went, neverthe-less. Cotton turned back to Delilah, who had gone over to stand next to Thorn's chair. She put her hand lightly on his shoulder and gave him a weak smile.

"I brought a buckboard to take you and Thorn into Apache Springs. Didn't figure he'd be up to climbin' aboard a saddle just yet. But I didn't figure on Mrs. Hardin, either. We sure as shootin' can't leave her here alone."

"You're right, but I don't see talking her into leaving here as being easy. She's a feisty lady, and this has been her home for a good long time. She'll fight the notion of aban-doning her dearly departed."

"Yeah, I figured as much. Think you could sweet-talk her into seein' the facts as they are? This isn't the place for a woman all by herself. The stage line will be back to run-nin' a full schedule soon enough, and it'll require someone who can take care of several teams, feedin', waterin', and makin' food for the passengers while they wait for an exchange of horses. She'd be expected to do that, too."

Delilah looked to Thorn. He shook his head. "Cotton's right. Mrs. Hardin can't be left alone to manage the place."

"But what if she refuses?"

Thorn looked away. "I don't know. I feel powerful bad for the lady. She saved my life, the way I figure it. But I don't allow as how we could force her to do something against her will."

Delilah stared at the curtained doorway to the bedroom.

"I will try my best to get her to see things your way, Sheriff. But I can't guarantee she will."

"I found us two shovels, Sheriff. Where do you figure on plantin' them?" Jimmy shouted, clomping onto the front porch.

"Jimmy, I hope someday you'll gain enough smarts to know better'n to shout such stuff where a grievin' widow can hear you," Cotton said, as he eased outside to keep Mrs. Hardin from overhearing any more.

"Uh, yessir, sorry. I wasn't thinkin'."

Jimmy followed Cotton to the barn to start the most disagreeable task the young man had ever undertaken. The look on his face revealed reluctance to even approach the barn, but he dared not show it in front of the sheriff.

Chapter 18

Several times each day since Cotton left, Emily went to the bedroom to see if Henry was resting comfortably. He hadn't moved one inch from the spot she and Jack had put him in. He kept staring at the ceiling when she asked if he would like some water. It was as if he were in a trance. She wasn't certain if he even heard her. She decided she'd bring a cup from the well anyway. If he didn't feel up to it, she'd try again later.

She had drawn aside the curtain at the bedroom door, her attention somewhere else, when she looked up to see a grinning monster standing in the middle of the front room. It was the man who'd tried to gun her down. It was the one Cotton had called James Lee Hogg. Her hand flew to her mouth to stifle a scream. His expression indicated he liked seeing the fear on her face.

"Wha-what do you want here! Get the hell out! Now! You murderin' piece of trash!"

"Now, now, little lady, callin' folks names don't make for much of a budding friendship," Hogg said.

"Friendship? Why, you pig, who'd have you for a friend?"

"Hmmm. I see your point. I reckon I'm really not all that likable. Oh well—"

"I'll ask one more time before I yell for the sheriff. What do you want here?"

"Well, you see it's like this. Since we're both standin' here jawin', it looks like I've failed in that part of my mission that said you'd be better off dead."

"Why? What did I ever do to you?"

"Oh, little lady, this ain't about me, or you for that matter. It's about that murderin' sheriff you seem to have taken a likin' to. He and I got business."

"You don't know what you're talking about. Cotton Burke never murdered anyone."

"Not the way I heard it. You mean he hasn't taken you into his confidence about his shady past? Ha! That figures. Those kinds of secrets *should* be kept locked away, I reckon. Now, if I was to have found favor with a right smart-lookin' woman like yourself, well, I'd be tempted to keep her as far away from my dark past as I could, too."

"No woman worth her salt would *ever* take up with an animal like you."

"That's not kind. You should watch what you say to me. I take offense awful easy."

Emily took a step sideways, giving consideration to what her chances might be if she tried bolting for the front door. That's when she noticed him following her every movement with his narrowed, hate-filled eyes. She saw him break into a wry smile. She wanted to retch.

"Not a chance. You couldn't get within three feet of that door before I'd plug you." He sniggered.

She could see he was probably right. And it was obvious he wouldn't have any qualms about taking another shot at her, whether he attracted any attention or not.

"Now, let's get down to some palaverin' about whether you live or die. Where is your precious sheriff? When will he be back? I know damned well he can't stay away from you very long. Can't say I could, either."

"You don't know anything about him, or me either for that matter."

"I know more'n you can conjure. For instance, I get a right keen remembrance of the last time the sheriff and I met with every step I take."

"What are you talking about?"

"I got this limp. Don't tell me you haven't noticed. I got it from that bastard sheriff of yours. He shot my big toe off over a damned dog. What do you have to say about that? A damned dog!"

"I'd say you likely deserved that and more. He should have aimed higher."

"Lady, you seem to be full of unfriendly talk today. And that ain't makin' me take kindly to any idea of lettin' you live when I leave this stinkin' town with the sheriff's head in a gunnysack."

Emily's eyes grew wide when she heard his description of what he had planned for Cotton. She was facing pure evil, and there seemed to be absolutely nothing she could do or say to prevent whatever Hogg had in mind. She felt near to fainting as she placed a hand on the arm of a nearby chair to keep from collapsing.

"Go ahead, sit yourself. I know women don't take well to men's realities sometimes."

"Y-you can't really be serious about shooting a man down just because you lost a toe," Emily said. "Y-you're sick."

"Yep, could be, but there's sicker ones out there than me. Why, I do believe I know one that's near to a ravin' maniac."

"What! What're you saying? You'd do a thing like this for money—"

"Oh, yeah. You don't figure I'd come all the way from Texas over the loss of a toe suffered at some son of a bitch's hands, do you? Nah, there's two thousand dollars reward money comin' to me when I kill him. Wouldn't doubt there'd be more if I gun down someone close to him, too. You, for instance." James Lee seemed to be enjoying the psychological pain he was inflicting on Emily. "Yep, that's the kind of money can easy make a man forget losin' a toe."

"Who would pay a man like you all that money? And for what?"

"Why, Judge Sanborn, that's who. He's the one that put up the reward money. Hasn't the sheriff told you about 'Lucky Bill' Sanborn? Particularly how he bit the dust?"

"I have absolutely no idea what you're talking about. I've never heard of anyone named Sanborn."

"I reckon you two aren't as close as I figured. That's somethin' I'd sure as hell tell my woman. If I had a woman, that is," James Lee said. "Course, if you was to get a bit friendlier with me, maybe I'd soften my thinkin' toward killin' you, too."

"I'd rather get friendly with a pig in slop than let a bounty hunting piece of scum like you touch me."

"I've heard them same words told to me before, believe it or not. Can't rightly figure why, though."

"Go on with your lies about who it was that Cotton Burke was supposed to have murdered. I can't wait to hear them."

"Ain't no lie, lady. He killed that poor boy sure as I'm standin' here. Didn't even give him a chance to defend himself. Poor lad." James Lee faked a sniffle as he wiped away a phantom tear. "Leastways, that's what his poor grievin' papa says."

"Then his *poor grieving papa* spews forth an untruth as well."

"Now, I figure the judge would not take kindly to your accusin' him of a falsehood, ma'am, he—"

Emily turned away. She could no longer stand the sight of him. She buried her face in her hands and began to sob.

When Jack left the jail for a trip to the saloon, where he was certain a shot of brandy was awaiting him, he looked down the street and noticed a horse tied up in front of Cotton's house. He didn't recall ever seeing it before and wondered who it belonged to. If Cotton had returned, he would have stopped by the jail to let his deputy know. Cotton was a man of habit, if he was anything. Jack felt an urge to investigate.

He went back inside to pull a shotgun off the rack, load it, and snap the barrel back in place. He carried the gun casually hanging by his side so as not to alarm any of the citizenry that might anticipate trouble brewing. He kept to the buildings and plank sidewalks as far down the street as he could so as not to draw undue attention to himself.

When he got near the small, clapboard-sided house, he stepped gingerly up on the porch from the side so he could peek through the window before knocking on the door. The window was open to allow any cooling breeze that might happen to drift by to refresh stale air inside. A curtain hung at the window, barely wafting from the slight current. Squinting, he could see Emily sitting on one of the few seating choices afforded the place by a stingy town council, and she appeared to be crying. He could make out the figure of a man with his hand on the butt of his holstered revolver, as well. The red bandana and flat-brimmed hat gave no doubt that James Lee Hogg had returned. Jack was instantly fearful for Emily's safety.

With limited choices as to his best chance to catch the man off guard, he decided to try the doorknob. With as much stealth as he could muster, he had started to touch the knob when he discovered that it stood slightly ajar. Hogg had obviously not wanted to make a noise when he entered by letting the door close behind him. Jack wasted no time. He kicked the door as hard as he could, thrusting the shotgun out in front of him. James Lee spun around to face two barrels of potential death staring him in the face.

James Lee's expression turned from one of pleasure at the pain he was inflicting on Emily to an angry growl. Giving it no more than an instant's thought, he eased his hand away from his revolver.

"Good choice, Mr. Hogg. You couldn't have even got that smoke wagon cocked before I blew you to hell. Now just unbuckle your gun belt and let it drop. You and me are going to get you situated in the town's best accommodations for a rattler like you."

James Lee complied, as Emily wiped her eyes and took a deep breath.

"I'll be back soon's I lock this varmint up, Emily." She could only give a tearful nod.

Chapter 19

———◆———

Cotton patted the mound of dirt over the final grave. He wiped sweat from his forehead on the sleeve of his shirt. Jimmy blew out the breath he'd been trying to hold as long as possible as he removed his hat and sank to the ground.

"I hope to never have to do that again, Sheriff. Buryin' folks must take a strong constitution," Jimmy said, "and I ain't got one."

Cotton said nothing as he leaned his shovel against the barn and walked slowly to the house. He knew he would be faced with a struggle to get Mrs. Hardin to leave the place she'd called home for years. The couple had no children, only each other. And while they had sniped back and forth on occasion, it was clear they had been very close and very dependent on each other.

As he came around the corner of the house, Cotton saw Delilah on the porch, holding herself up by clinging to one of the posts, crying her eyes out. Thorn was sitting on the step at an angle that suggested he could barely hold himself erect.

"What is it, Delilah?" Cotton asked. "What's happened?"

"It's Mrs. Hardin. Sh-she's passed away."

"What? You sayin' she died, too?"

"Yes. Looks like her poor old heart just gave out. She was taking Jeremiah's death harder than anyone I'd ever seen before. But, I didn't think . . ."

Cotton turned to Jimmy, who had yet to catch up to him. "Son, gather up those shovels. Looks like we're not quite finished here." Jimmy did an about-face and shuffled off, with a dejected look and a slump in his shoulders.

"When bad news comes, it seems to gather momentum like a rock rollin' down a steep hill," Cotton said, shaking his head.

"I'll get things together so we can start back, Sheriff," Delilah said. "All right?"

"Yep. If Thorn can travel."

"I'll gather up some food and some blankets," she said.

"Might as well. It's clear we can't stay here with Thorn needin' a real doc to care for him. And I can't leave Jimmy here alone to watch the place. One man out here with the chance of Indians comin' back at any time would be a death sentence for him."

Delilah said nothing as Cotton walked out into the barren yard and paced, kicking the occasional clod of dirt and raising dust with every footfall. After a few minutes, he turned back to them.

"Thorn, you figure you can handle the trip back to Apache Springs in the back of that buckboard?"

"One way or t'other, I'm goin' *with* you. No matter what."

Delilah dabbed at her eyes with a handkerchief. "We'll be ready, Sheriff. Just say when."

When Jimmy was on his way back, toting the two shovels, Cotton met him halfway.

"Jimmy, we have to carry the old lady out and bury her. Sorry to put you through this much death, but it has to be done. Also, when we're through, gather up the Hardins' horses and we'll tie them on back and take 'em into town with us. If we leave 'em here, the Indians will just steal 'em and eat 'em."

Cotton put Jimmy in charge of the extra horses. The boy carried his shotgun across the saddle. Cotton drove the buckboard, with Delilah sitting next to him on the seat. Since there wouldn't be anyone left to use it, Cotton had loaded a featherbed into the back to allow Thorn a more gentle ride.

"Delilah, there are some things I've been wanting to ask you. I hope you don't mind my gettin' a tad personal."

"I was wondering when you'd want to learn more about me and Havens. That *is* what you're wanting to know about, isn't it?"

"Well, yes, in a manner of speakin', I reckon it is. Although, I'm not lookin' for any private details about your relationship; there's other things that have me puzzled."

"Like what?"

"Like: I know we've talked about this before, but I still can't figure how you failed to notice Havens was passin' around counterfeit money like candy. Especially since you were handling it every day. And what about that young teller Havens hired? Didn't he ever act the least bit suspicious?"

"If he thought it was phony, he never said a word. It looked like the genuine article to me. I'd never even seen a counterfeit dollar before. I sure wouldn't have spent it if I'd known. Anyway, I was almost arrested for passing some of it myself. Remember?"

"Yeah. Between you and Thorn spending it, you had a passel of folks near up in arms down in Silver City. Of course, when they thought it was good currency, they were happy to take it." He gave her a raised eyebrow.

"And I feel real bad about how it all turned out, too. Why, we neither one would have wanted those nice folks to come to no harm from something we did. You believe that, don't you?"

"For now, I reckon I'll have to."

"So, what else is bothering you?"

"You have any idea where he could have gotten that money?"

"I met up with Havens in a dirty little Texas town. Like I told you before, the man I had been with was strung up by vigilantes for taking, uh, some liberties with a couple of their cattle. So I was in bad shape financially. That's when Havens came along, asked if I'd be interested in helping him with a plan he had, and I fell into his trap. As far as the money, I know he had it at that time. He always kept real close watch on those two valises of his."

"Any idea how long he'd been in town before you hooked up with him?"

"No, but he must have been there awhile. He knew people because he spent a lot of time with a man he kept calling 'cousin something or other.'"

"Any idea what this 'cousin' did for a livin'?"

"From what Bart said, I figured he was a printer."

"What was the name of that town?"

"It was a dismal little town outside Fort Stockton called St. Gaul."

Cotton thought that over for a minute before changing the subject.

"Since you claimed that it was you, and not Thorn, that shot Havens, I wonder if you'd mind lettin' me take a look at the piece you plugged him with."

"No, I don't mind." She opened her handbag, which was gathered at the top with a thin velvet cord. She pulled out the Remington .41-caliber derringer and handed it to the sheriff.

"This is the same gun you shot Havens with?"

"Uh, yeah, that's it. Why do you ask?"

"Curious, that's all."

"Am I in trouble for what I did?"

"No. At least not from me. He deserved killin', and I don't rightly care who did it. Knowin' what kind of a man he was, your claim of self-defense squares up, too."

* * *

They rode on in silence for the next hour, before stopping to rest in the shade of some trees not far off the road. Cotton got down to check on Thorn. Delilah did the same, rushing around to the wounded man's side like a mother hen. Cotton pulled the stopper out of one of the canteens and held it to Thorn's lips. He sipped, then gulped some of the water. Jimmy had tied his horse to a low-hanging limb on one of the trees, under which there was grass enough to feed on. He pulled his canteen from the saddle horn and drank.

Cotton looked over the landscape for any signs of trouble and, seeing none, told the others it was time to get on their way. He didn't like the way Thorn looked. He was pale and seemed weaker than he had when they started out. Cotton hoped his condition wasn't getting worse.

As the buckboard rattled on down the road, Cotton was constantly reminded of all the things about the conveyance that he'd never paid attention to before. Things like wheels needing grease on a regular basis. The squeaks and squeals of tortured wood on metal were getting on his nerves. The sound of rusty springs that had no give when the wheels dropped into one of the many ruts wasn't making the trip any easier, either. His concerns over whether Thorn McCann would survive the rough treatment he had to be experiencing kept nagging at him, too. Then, a sight to bring him out of his misery: as they crested a rise, Apache Springs came into view. What a sight it was, too. Dusty, dirty, and noisy—all the things to give a sheriff a feeling of home.

Chapter 20

———◆———

Jack was taking no chances with James Lee Hogg. He kept his distance behind the killer as they marched down the center of the street toward the jail. When they reached the front door, Jack shoved the barrel of the shotgun into Hogg's back and growled, "Open the damned thing, James Lee, or I'll open it with a blast from this scattergun. Using your body as a batterin' ram, of course." Jack snickered.

"All right, all right! Don't need to go gettin' pushy, you miserable law dog." James Lee pushed open the door, and Jack shoved him inside.

Keeping his distance once they were inside, Jack motioned with the shotgun for James Lee to walk into the first cell. He followed up by slamming the cell door shut and locking it with a key from the ring he'd pulled from a knob on the rifle rack.

James Lee dropped onto the hard bunk. He scowled at Jack, who now busied himself with unloading the shotgun and placing it back in its place on the rack. He went over to the desk and sat, leaning back against the wall with his

fingers interlaced behind his head and looking quite pleased
with himself. He began to whistle, thinking a brandy would
taste real fine about now. James Lee broke his reverie.

"Hey! Law dog! When's some food comin' my way? Ya
can't let a prisoner starve, you know." James Lee's tone was
nasty as well as demanding. "It's against the law."

"I can if he's a pig who'll likely hang anyway."

James Lee leapt to his feet, grabbing the bars of his cell
and shaking them.

"Ain't nobody gonna hang James Lee Hogg, no sir.
Soon as Judge Sanborn finds out what you've done, why,
he'll be on the first stage here. Then you hicks will find out
what's what. I'll be outta here in ten seconds flat. Count on
it. Matter of fact, he's on his way right now."

"Uh-huh."

"And you ain't gonna like it when he gets here."

"I'm shakin' in my boots."

"Yeah, go ahead and scoff at my words. But when I'm
free of this dung heap of a town, you'll be the first one I
gun down. You hear me, you—"

"I *hear* you! You've had your say, now shut the hell up!"

Jack got up and walked outside. He looked across the
street to see Melody push through the batwing doors to her
bawdy house and saloon. She crossed the street with a teasing look on her face, swinging her hips even more than
usual. Jack had always been a sucker for her come-ons, and
now was no exception. Even living with her had not damp-
ened his enjoyment of her sexual provocations. She walked
straight up to him, planted a kiss on his mouth, and took
his arm.

"C'mon, honey, I'm getting real lonely."

That's when he remembered James Lee Hogg inside.

"Uh, I-I can't leave the jail right this minute, uh,
because—"

"Because what? Jack, you know damned well there's
nothing happening in Apache Springs that demands your
immediate attention. Now, let's go to our room and—"

"No, really, Melody, I can't go right this minute."

"Why? You got some boogeyman locked up inside?"

"Uh-huh."

Melody looked at him like he'd lost his mind.

"You got another woman inside, Jack? Is that it? If you do, I swear I'll blow off your—"

Jack took her by both arms, spun her around, and looked her straight in the eye.

"Don't be stupid, Melody. I . . ."

She broke free from his grip, took one agile step around him, and rushed inside. She stopped abruptly as she took an inventory of her surroundings. Her eyes grew wide with fear at the sight of James Lee Hogg, grinning ear to ear, holding on to the cell bars and staring at her as if she were something good to eat.

"Well, hello, missy. Remember me? My, don't you look fine? Did you bring my dinner? I'm near to starvin'."

Melody put her hand to her mouth, spun around, and stormed out of the room.

"What's that pig in jail for?"

"He tried to kill Emily Wagner. You remember tellin' him where he could find Cotton, don't you? Well, that stupid comment of yours got one of her cowboys shot. Better hope when Cotton gets back he don't take it outta your hide."

She stomped across the porch and kept right on moving, making a beeline for Melody's Golden Palace of Pleasure. She didn't look back. Jack merely sighed.

As promised, Jack returned to check on Emily. When he went inside, she was sitting on the love seat, her hands in her lap, looking worried and perplexed. She looked up when he entered.

"He's behind bars, Miss Emily. He can't hurt you now."

"He already has, with his words. All those awful things he said about Cotton. They can't be true, they just can't."

"I'd wait until Cotton gets back before you make any judgments about him," Jack said. "James Lee Hogg is a killer and a liar. Don't you go puttin' stock in whatever filth he's been spewin'."

"I'm sure Cotton appreciates your faith in him, Jack. All of this is a little overwhelming right now, that's all," Emily said.

"When Cotton gets back, things will get straightened out. Right now, however, I'd better get back to the jail and check on that animal I got caged up," Jack said, with a snicker. "That's where I'll be in case you need anything."

"Thank you," Emily said. As he left, she closed the door and locked it.

The shadows of evening had descended when Jack decided to stop by the hotel and grab a bite to eat. He could also see if the restaurant had any slop they were going to toss to the pigs anyway, and have them put some on a plate for James Lee Hogg. He was grinning from ear to ear at the thought of pigs and slop and James Lee Hogg all together. It was almost prophetic. He had taken one step up onto the hotel porch, when out of the near darkness stepped a figure. Jack suddenly felt a sharp pain explode at the back of his head, then his whole world turned to midnight.

Blinking furiously to try to make something come into focus, anything at all, he was barely aware of the people gathered around him. Shadows, garbled talk, or at least he assumed it was talk. Questions emerged from his confusion. *Where am I? Who are these people? Why does my head hurt so damned bad? I don't remember drinking, or did I really hang one on? Am I just so drunk I don't remember falling down? If Cotton finds out, I'm through as a deputy.* All of these rolled over in his befuddled mind.

"Deputy, the doc is on his way. Just lie still," said a voice he thought he knew, but couldn't place. Then other voices joined in. Something was said about drinking too much, but then he heard "No, he's not drunk. He's been hit over the head. Can't you tell? Just look at all that blood."

Blood?

Jack tried to say something, to question those around him, get some answers to whatever dilemma he now found himself in. *That talk about blood, what the hell is that all about?* Then . . .

"Move out of the way. I can't tell what kind of injuries this man has if you don't give me room. Now, stand aside!"

Ahh. That voice I recognize. That's Doc Winters. Wonder if he's been drinking. Hmm.

Jack felt hands taking hold of his shoulders then lifting him. He heard the doc ask for help to get the patient to his office. Then there were muffled voices seeming to agree to the request. He felt himself lifted and being carried. *Who's the patient they seem so interested in?*

After a few minutes of being jostled about, he figured he was being placed on a bed. *No, a table. Too hard for a bed.* Someone said, "Go get Melody. If Jack's going to die, she'll probably want to know."

Die? I'm not going to die! Am I? What the hell? He heard a furious shuffling of boots and the doc's voice shooing people out of the room. Then, a few seconds later—

"Jack, I'm going to lift your head just enough for you to take a drink of this."

He tried to ask what it was, but the words wouldn't come. He felt the doc put a steady hand behind his neck then gently raise him up. He still didn't know what he'd been asked to drink, but he knew it wasn't brandy. In fact it was about the foulest-tasting stuff he'd ever drunk. His head was then carefully placed back onto a pillow.

At least he assumed it was a pillow. That was just before his world began swirling around again and then turned black.

Chapter 21

After three and a half days of driving the rough-riding buckboard, Cotton pulled up in front of the doctor's office. He helped Delilah down, then asked Jimmy to help him get Thorn inside. Delilah was fidgeting as she tried to grab Thorn's hand while the two men carried him onto the porch.

"You better knock, Delilah, in case the doc is asleep."

Just as she raised her hand to knock, the door flew open.

"I thought I told you people . . . Oh, it's you, Sheriff. Sorry. Who is this? How many folks am I expected to handle in one night?"

"It's Thorn McCann, Doc. He's been shot. A lady patched him up as best she could, but he ain't lookin' too good."

"Okay. Bring him inside. Uh, put him on the floor over there. Roll up this blanket for under his head. I'll look after him shortly."

"Wouldn't it be better if we took him into your back office?" Cotton said with an angry look in his eyes.

"It *would* be better, but there isn't room. Got another patient in there and he needs my help more'n this one."

"Who is it?"

"It's your deputy, that's who. Got busted up pretty good. Someone musta taken a rifle butt to his head. I was just about to stitch him up when you come stomping up on the porch."

"Who did it?"

"Don't know, and he isn't up to talking about it yet."

"Can I go in and see him?"

"Had to give him some laudanum. He's not going to even know you're in the room."

"I'll leave Delilah Jones here to help you with Thorn. I better see what I can find out about Jack's attacker. Where'd it take place?"

"Front of the hotel, near's I can figure. Leastways, that's where I found him bleeding all over the place."

Cotton bolted from the doctor's office and headed straight for the hotel. There were several people standing around outside. As he approached them, one spoke up.

"Jack gonna be okay, Sheriff?"

"I don't know yet. Any of you see what happened?"

"Joe, here, came upon him lyin' on the porch bleedin' somethin' fierce. That's all we know. Didn't see no one hangin' around. Got no idea who done it."

Cotton looked perplexed about the whole matter. He glanced up and down the street, seeing nothing unusual. Then it occurred to him he'd better check on Emily. Even if she was all right and knew nothing about Jack, she'd be anxious to take Henry Coyote back to her ranch as soon as possible. He walked back to the doctor's office, took the reins of the horses, and led them back to his place. As he tied them to the rail outside, he saw the curtains part and Emily peering out. He waved, but the curtain was drawn shut in an instant. The door flew open and Emily ran to him, crying.

"Thank god you're back!"

"What is it? Is Henry not doin' well? Are *you* all right?"

"Henry is coming along fine. I'm not doing so well,

however. Come inside. There's something important that needs discussing, and the street isn't the place for it."

He followed her inside and closed the door. He started to sit but stopped when he saw her put her hands on her hips and glare at him like he was a condemned man. His insides turned to jelly. He started to speak but was cut off.

"You got lots of explaining to do, Cotton Burke, and my patience has run out! Did you or did you not shoot down a young man in Texas for no reason? I'm tired of you not coming clean with me."

Cotton took a deep breath and hung his head. The time had come and he didn't like it one bit. If he could have crawled under the door and escaped, he would have.

"Emily, you have to understand, I—"

"Just *tell* me, no backtracking!" Her eyes had narrowed to slits, and her lips were pursed so tightly she looked as if she'd just eaten a dozen persimmons. He held up his hands in surrender.

"Sit down and I'll tell you," he said. She didn't move. "Please."

She complied with his request, reluctantly. Her fists were balled as she laid them on her lap. At that moment, Cotton was certain he'd rather be facing a mountain lion with only his bare hands for defense.

"I did shoot a man, but not for no reason. He was the son of a no-good justice of the peace, and a spoiled rotten son at that. Whatever he wanted, he got. If it hurt someone, Daddy bailed him out. I was the deputy in the town, and I'll admit I hated the skunk. Then one day, I went to visit my younger sister. She was newly married, and she and her husband had settled into a small house at the edge of town. She was beautiful, and I was so proud of her. When I walked in the door, I found her husband on the floor in a puddle of blood. He'd been stabbed to death. When I heard a moan comin' from the bedroom, I rushed in to find Juliet on the bed, clothes ripped off her body. She'd been raped and beaten. She died soon thereafter. Before she passed away, though, she told me who'd done it. I tracked him to his favorite haunt, a saloon, and heard him bragging about his conquest. I was so furious, I pulled my Colt and shot him in the head."

"H-he murdered your sister?"

"Yes. And my brother-in-law."

"And they called what *you* did murder?"

"Yes."

"This is what you couldn't tell me for fear of . . . of . . . what?"

"I didn't want you to think badly of me. I-I'm sorry. I reckon I *should* have told you."

"I reckon you should have, too. Cotton, don't you understand the concept of trust?"

"I—"

"So that's what that Hogg fellow was blathering about."

"Hogg?"

"Yes. He came here and threatened to shoot me if I didn't tell him where to find you. Thank goodness Jack came bursting through that door and hauled him off to jail."

"You're sayin' James Lee Hogg is in my jail?"

"Yes! Jack took him there at the end of a shotgun."

"I'll bet money that he ain't." Cotton jumped to his feet and rushed out the door.

"Cotton! Where are you going?"

He didn't answer her. He ran straight for the jail, with his Colt cocked and ready. When he got there, he burst through the door. He was met with exactly what he had expected. His shoulders slumped when he saw the empty jail cell.

Son of a bitch!

He grabbed a short-barreled shotgun from the rack, loaded it, and beat a path back to Emily. When he opened the door, she was standing at the window, watching him through the curtain.

"Why did you—"

"James Lee Hogg is gone. He must have a confederate in town that whacked Jack over the head to cover the escape."

"Jack's hurt?"

"Badly, I'm afraid. But not as bad as James Lee Hogg will be when I find him."

Emily put her hand over her mouth and shuddered. Cotton could see the fear that had overtaken her. He held out the shotgun.

"Here, take this. It's loaded and ready. When I leave to go check on Jack, you lock the door and don't let anyone in but me. Understand? If James Lee Hogg should come back, don't ask questions, don't even talk, just blow the bastard to hell and gone."

"Y-yes, of course, but what if—"

"Please, Emily, please do as I say. I know you're worried, but *your* safety is the most important thing in my life right now. I'll be back soon."

He turned and all but flew out the door and down the street toward the doctor's office.

Chapter 22

He'll be groggy from the laudanum. You'll get little out of him, I'm afraid," Doc Winters said. "I got him all stitched up right and proper. Going to have one helluva headache for a spell. He'll be his old self in a day or so. He's damned lucky, though."

"Lucky?"

"A blow that hard *could* have caved in his skull. I couldn't have *patched* that up."

"I appreciate what you've done, Doc. What about Thorn McCann?"

"Whoever sewed him up did a right good job. But he'd lost a lot of blood. If that lady in there with him can get him to eat regular so he can build up his strength, he'll be fit as a fiddle in a few days."

"I'll be back later to check on Jack," Cotton said, as he turned the door handle to leave. He hesitated, saying, "Thanks, Doc. Don't know what we'd have done without you." He left in the same hurry that had brought him. Only, instead of going to the jail, or to see Emily, he headed for the clapboard-sided building that housed the undertaker's establishment.

John Burdsall had been Apache Springs' one and only undertaker since the town grew out of the rocky soil in order to serve the needs of the many cattle ranchers and a few small mines. The gangly, long-faced man had few friends, although he always maintained an air of dignity about him, never smiling or joining in any levity that some saw as acceptable but he did not. He never found humor in death. Folks seemed to shy away from him, nevertheless. Cotton knocked on his door.

"Greetings, Sheriff. In what way may I be of service?"

"Sorry to be droppin' in so late, but something's been puzzlin' me for a spell. If I remember correctly, you keep bullets taken from the bodies of men who have been shot. Do you still keep such things?"

"I do, indeed, sir. Would you care to view my collection?"

"I'm interested in one particular bullet. The one taken from the body of Bart Havens."

"Ahh, yes. I have it right here." Cotton followed John to a back room. The man reached for a small jar at the end of a shelf lined with others just like it. He handed it to Cotton. The sheriff held it up to what little light dared enter the room of the dead. Dark drapes hung at the only window, and what illumination could be discerned came from the door left open at the entrance.

"What is your guess as to the caliber of this piece of lead?" Cotton handed the jar back.

"In my experience, while it *is* rather mangled by its encounter with bone, the size and weight suggest a smaller caliber, perhaps a thirty-eight or at most a forty-one."

"No chance it could be a forty-five?"

"Too small. Considerably too small."

"Thanks, John. Your knowledge of such things is a great help."

"What's this all about?"

"I'm tyin' up a loose end. Need to see if I've been told the truth by a couple people."

"Who'd that be?"

"Thorn McCann's lady friend, Delilah Jones, claimed she shot Havens in self-defense. If that's true, she'd have done it with that little derringer she carries."

"I weighed the bullet, and it looks to be a forty- or forty-one-caliber."

"Sounds like she was tellin' the truth."

"You gonna arrest her?"

"Hell, no. Too many folks saw the damage Havens had done to her. He beat her up fairly regular. Her sayin' it was self-defense makes sense. Reckon it's time to let the whole thing drop," Cotton said, as he left the undertaker's establishment. "Sorry to bother you, but this thing has been gnawing at me and I just had to get it cleared up."

This time, Cotton's steps *did* take him to his own house and the awaiting Emily. Before tapping on the door to let her know he was back, he looked around warily. He had a strange feeling he was being watched. It would be just like Hogg to be hiding in an alleyway or in a second-story window, taking a bead on his back with a rifle.

As soon as she had heard about Jack, Melody rushed to the doctor's office to get all the details. She was, of course, her usual snippy self when told Jack was still asleep from the laudanum and wouldn't be able to converse with her. She demanded she be allowed to be by his side anyway. Doc Winters acquiesced by throwing up his hands in frustration and stepping aside as she all but pushed him out of her way. When the doctor attempted to usher her into a plush high-backed chair to wait for Jack to wake up, she became belligerent at seeing he had been laid out on the floor with only a rolled blanket to protect his bandaged head from the hard wood. Another man was lying on the table. It was Thorn McCann. Doc Winters had laid Jack on the floor with plenty of padding under him to keep him comfortable while he attended to Thorn. The situation wasn't satisfactory to Melody, who was used to getting what she wanted, when she wanted it. Her expectations preceded all others.

"Why don't you have him on that table of yours? Why is he relegated to the drafts and discomfort of the floor?"

"I have another wounded patient on the table right now. There simply is no other room. I already attended to him and he's going to be fine. Just needs some rest now."

Melody stood up and stormed out, yelling back that she would return in a few minutes with several men to carry Jack to the comfort of her own quarters. All the doctor could do was shrug and give a giant sigh.

True to her word, Melody did return promptly, knocking at the door mere minutes later with four burly men, each of whom appeared able to lift three times his own weight, to spirit Jack off. They lifted him easily enough, although without much regard for his injuries, and stumbled out of the room, onto the porch, then into the street. All the while, Melody Wakefield made it known that she was clearly in charge, barking out directions and orders like a battlefield general. They carried him through the batwings, across the barroom, up the staircase, and straight into Melody's bedroom. When they had placed him on the wide featherbed, she shooed them off with a thanks and a promise of a free drink as soon as they returned to the bar downstairs.

"Just tell Arlo to set them up for you, gents. Thank you," were her last words before shutting the door immediately at their exit.

"Bossy bitch, ain't she?" said one of the four.

"Yeah, but if I had a woman that looked that good, hell, I'd let her yell at me all day long," said another.

"Crap! If you had *any* woman, you'd let her tell you where to go," said the first, and he let out a belly laugh. "Set 'em up, Arlo, on the house for a change."

*   *   *

"Is everything all right?" Emily asked as Cotton took off his Stetson and dropped onto the love seat.

"Well, Jack's going to be fine as soon as that nasty gash in his head heals up, and Thorn McCann will likely live if Delilah Jones can shove enough food down his gullet, or so the doc says."

"I'm thankful they're both going to be all right. What'll you do now?"

"Same as always, keep the rabble from taking the town apart board by board," Cotton said with a silly grin.

"But you're all alone—the town's only protection. What if that awful James Lee Hogg comes back?"

"Oh, he'll be back, of that I'm damned sure. It's a couple of other things that are bothering me more than that, though." Cotton again grew very serious.

"Like what?"

"Like who hit Jack in the first place?"

"And why did he do it?" Emily added.

"Seems likely he did it to keep Jack away while he freed Hogg. Have you noticed anybody hangin' around town with Hogg or lookin' like someone who might be of the same low-down character?"

"Most everyone fits that description. This town isn't known for its society types, you know. Would you like some coffee?"

"I would, indeed. I'll be right back after I put away the horses and get them fed."

"When did you last eat something?"

"Can't rightly say. But now that you've brought it up, it's somethin' I should probably attend to."

"You go ahead and take care of the horses, and I'll worry about your empty stomach." Emily seemed to have gotten over her snit and gave him a "glad you're back" smile.

Chapter 23

———◆◆———

Damned good thing you come along when you did. Probably saved my bacon," James Lee Hogg said, tossing a small piece of deadwood on the campfire. "That damned sheriff will be none too pleased about my threatenin' his woman. He'll be lookin' hard to find me. That ought to make the judge happy," he added.

The man looking across the flickering flames at James Lee was Lazarus Bellwood, a scrawny piece of bone and weathered flesh, an aging mountain man who could always be seen carrying a Sharps carbine in a deerskin scabbard, with Indian beadwork and fringe down the side. He was a man with a unique skill as a sharpshooter and a deadly streak a mile long. A man who left a trail of blood from here to yonder.

"Sure appreciate your help. By the way, just who are you?"

"Name's Lazarus Bellwood."

"How come I ain't never seen you before? How'd you happen to break me out?"

"Keepin' outta sight and layin' low is part of my job."

"Job for who?"

"The man who hired you."

"So, Judge Sanborn sent you?"

"That he did."

"I'm obliged to you. *Whatever* your connection is to the crazy old judge. He told me there'd be someone to watch my back."

Lazarus remained silent, eyeing James Lee like he would a target that needed a hole punched through it.

"You look like you got somethin' more to say, Mr. Bellwood. Spit it out," James Lee said.

"I come out here to bring you a message; it's from Sanborn. A fella came to the hotel this mornin' with a telegram," Lazarus said, motioning for Hogg to add another log to the fire.

"Well, what does that paper say?"

"Says he's a-comin'. Soon."

"When?"

"Like I said, real soon. Says he's gotta wrap up a, uh, minor detail about his, er, new appointment to the bench. That's all."

"Boy, is that damned Sheriff Burke gonna be surprised when he finds out a circuit judge is on the way, and he's lookin' to settle a score."

Lazarus chuckled.

"Don't know whether you knew this or not, Hogg, but Sanborn's gonna have an *extra* surprise in his black satchel. Our elusive sheriff's soon gonna be faced with a deputy U.S. marshal to contend with, too," Lazarus said.

"Yeah? Who's that?" Hogg asked.

"You!"

They both roared at that revelation.

"How's he gonna do that?" Hogg said, suddenly puzzled.

"Didn't say how. But he plans to pin a badge on you, one way or another."

"Even that dumb sheriff wouldn't try to arrest a deputy marshal," Hogg said with a grin that stretched almost from ear to ear.

"Reckon you're right about that," Lazarus responded, without much conviction.

"Sanborn's a clever old fart, ain't he? Wouldn't surprise me none if he turned this town into dust before he's through," Hogg said.

"How's that?"

"First, he plans to make life miserable for any of them that's sided with Cotton Burke in any way . . . ever! Then he'll get even for the killin' of his son, Billy. Didn't he tell you? That's what he brought me here for."

"Of *course* he told me; I'm here to make sure it happens accordin' to his plan." Lazarus squinched up his face and narrowed one eye. "And his plan is to give Burke a death sentence."

"That old devil's got ways of makin' a person look guilty when he ain't done one thing wrong."

"Just you remember that," Lazarus said.

"He, uh, didn't go into detail about you and what you'd be doin' whilst I'm causin' the sheriff pain," Hogg said.

"Once he gives me the go-ahead, I'm to tack up some notices all over town tellin' of the court's opening. It'll give a few particulars about the cases he intends to make judgments concerning."

"Uh, but there ain't no cases pending, are there?"

"No, at least no real ones. The first thing he'll do is mention some cases he's made up, and then he'll dismiss them all. That's to make him look like he's the forgivin' type," Lazarus snickered.

"But he ain't?"

"Hell, no!"

"And then . . . ?"

"He's gonna announce to the mayor that the sheriff is a wanted man, and he'll order you to put Burke in jail for murder, and then announce a trial date. Probably let the fool sit and worry about his fate for a day or two."

"What makes him think Burke will jus' hand over his gun to me?"

"Well, the judge don't think for one minute that he will.

The aim is to get the sheriff so angry and flustered by all your dastardly doings, he'll be eager to pull on you."

"Then I'm gonna shoot 'im?"

"You can bet on him gettin' shot down. And I guarantee you'll be in the middle of it all. Remember, that bastard sheriff's the one that shot off your big toe."

They were both engulfed in laughter. Hogg was holding his stomach and quaking uproariously when he lost his balance and nearly fell into the fire. When things settled down, Lazarus once again got serious. Hogg leaned forward to catch every word, lest he miss something and find himself in trouble with the new judge.

"Sounds like you're givin' the orders until Sanborn gets here. That right?" Hogg asked.

"You can bet on it."

"So, what do I do next?" Hogg raised one questioning eyebrow.

"First thing is, you got to lay low. Don't draw no attention to yourself. It'd likely be a good idea for you to stay out here. Looks like it's a darned fine place to hide one's self. I'll be makin' myself scarce, too, in case anyone happened to see me club that deputy. When things are ready, then you can come back into town. Not before I let you know, though. Understand?"

"Not sure I like that arrangement, Bellwood. Sanborn told me somebody'd be comin' along to help, but he never said who. Anyway, a feller can get real lonely, not to mention damned hungry, sittin' out here all by hisself."

"You'll get used to it. After all, you stand to collect a tidy sum for bein' patient and followin' orders. *My* orders."

"Uh-huh. Sanborn hasn't actually told me jus' how much that *tidy sum* is goin' to be. How about a hint?"

Lazarus put his hand to his mouth, stroked his chin, and looked off into the distance. "Well, let's see, how much money have you made in, say, the past ten years?"

"Workin' or stealin'?"

"All told."

Hogg scratched his head, frowning as if deep in thought.

"Hmmm, countin' the ol' miner I clubbed for his poke, the stage I hit where the only thing I came away with was some grumpy woman's broach, the general store I broke into and took all the cash in the till, and, of course, the hides I took from a trapper in Colorado, I'd reckon about two hundred seventy-five dollars."

"That's *all*?"

"I *did* work for a ranch in Arizona for about three months, but that didn't work out so well. I figured to get thirty dollars a month, but the foreman and me got into it over a card game and I had to shoot him. So I didn't get paid for none of that time."

"The feller die?"

"You ever see what a Remington forty-four can do to a man at close range?"

Lazarus nodded his head.

"Well, if you can follow orders, and I mean *every* order I pass on from the judge, he's promised to pay you two thousand dollars."

Hogg gave Bellwood a wry grin.

"You already knew how much the poke was, didn't you?" Lazarus said.

"Just makin' sure I wasn't getting' cut out of any of my rightful 'reward.'"

Lazarus gave Hogg a scowl that suggested he didn't like being played. He stood up to leave. "Now, you just make yourself comfortable here and I'll be back in the morning with supplies—food, ammunition, and some blankets." Lazarus wasted no time making himself scarce. He had a lot to do in preparation for the arrival of Judge Sanborn. Of course, part of his problem would be to stay clear of both the sheriff and his deputy. Sanborn had made it clear that Lazarus was to remain as anonymous as possible. He didn't think he'd raised any eyebrows since his arrival, but even one tiny slip of the tongue could be disastrous.

Until Sanborn got to Apache Springs with the tin badge he'd promised to secure for Hogg, even if it was one that carried no real authority, Lazarus would have to rely on

Hogg to follow orders and stay out of trouble. As he rode back to the outskirts of town, his thoughts turned to what the judge would think when he found out his *almost* deputy marshal had foolishly allowed himself to get hauled off to jail in the first place. He knew there would be a price to pay for the man's clumsiness, even if it did come from a phony judge.

He grinned widely at the thought. He even began to hum to himself.

Chapter 24

———◆———

Cotton felt his stomach start to growl the very moment he walked in the door. The smell of biscuits and beans cooking on his little stove in the back reminded him that it had been a spell since he tasted Emily's good cooking. At the sound of the door closing behind him, Emily appeared from the small kitchen at the back of the house with a cup of steaming coffee in her hand. She thrust it toward him with a smile.

"Thanks," he said.

"There's food coming," she responded.

At just that moment, they both whirled around at the sound of a familiar voice, an unexpected voice.

"Smell coffee," Henry Coyote said as he pushed open the curtain that divided the front room from the bedroom.

Emily's eyes were as big as saucers. She began to sputter. "H-Henry! Wh-what are you doing out of bed? Get back in there!" She tried shooing him back.

"No need. Have coffee now."

"Right here, my friend," Cotton said, handing his untouched cup to the Indian. Henry took it gratefully and eagerly. After each sip, Henry let out a gentle sigh.

"Are you certain you're well enough to be up?" Cotton asked.

"Feel better. Ready to work."

"Work? Henry, you've been *shot*. You nearly died saving me. I-I can't even think of letting you go back to work yet," stammered Emily.

"I have to admit, Henry, you look pretty darned good for a wounded man," Cotton said. Emily shot him a serious frown.

"No more wounded. Healed," Henry managed between sips of coffee.

"B-but, the doctor said you would need to rest up for a week . . . or more . . . t-to get your strength back," Emily said. She settled onto the love seat, shaking her head, apparently unable come to grips with Henry's miraculous recovery. She seemed dazed by all the events of the past few days—Henry, Cotton, *and* James Lee Hogg.

"Have all strength I need."

Cotton wasn't certain he was up to getting between Emily and Henry at the moment, so he decided the best course of action was to change the subject.

"Excuse me, Emily, but I think I smell something burning."

"Oh, my . . . oh, damn!" She burst from the room muttering something about needing four hands and a kitchen big enough to turn round in. Cotton and Henry each gave a shrug.

Emily couldn't take her eyes off Henry while he ate. He wolfed down his beans and biscuits like he'd never been wounded, merely away on a long trip without food or water . . . or coffee.

"Henry, I-I don't understand how you can possibly have healed up s-so quickly."

"Spirit father visit while I lie on bed. He touch me where bullet go in. Take away pain."

"Spirit father?" Obviously puzzled by his explanation, Emily leaned on her elbows as she studied the Apache's weathered face.

"Spirit father protect all Apache," Henry said nonchalantly.

Cotton sat silently, marveling at Henry's resolute belief in the healing powers of something he couldn't see or touch. While Cotton had been raised in a religious home as a child, he had drifted away from churches and organized religion, although he knew that he'd come close to losing his own life too many times not to believe that someone or something had been looking over him. As Emily and Henry delved into Henry's beliefs, Cotton tried silently to find some reason for his failure to continue his youthful education in a spiritual world. His conclusion was a rude awakening, a self-evaluation of his own shortcomings as a man with little more than a Colt .45 for protection. While he also saw small hope for humanity in general among the despots and criminals he dealt with on an almost daily basis, he had to admit he'd often yearned for evidence of the kind of peace his mother had gone through life with. She said she'd found it in that little black book she kept on the table next to her bed.

"Cotton!" Emily's sharp command yanked him from his reverie.

"Uh, yes. What is it?"

"Would you like more coffee?"

"Oh, yes, that would be good."

As she went out to the kitchen to retrieve the coffeepot, Cotton watched the old Indian's face for signs of whatever it was he'd obviously missed. He saw nothing. He was left to his own devices, once again.

"Where were you, exactly, while Henry and I were exploring my ignorance of his spirit father?" Emily said as she returned and sat down.

"I'm sorry. I reckon I was doing the same thing with

my own failings to follow a path my mother would have approved," Cotton answered. "Kinda lost in my own thinkin'."

"Well, whether you think so or not, I'll bet she'd have been proud of you."

Just after midnight, a figure moved stealthily in the shadows behind the general store. A dog barked from somewhere inside a house across the alley. The man moved tentatively, then deliberately, toward the one window at the back of the store. A moonless night made his mission more difficult, but it also kept others from seeing him and calling out a warning. In his left hand he carried two burlap bags. When, by feeling his way along the back wall, he reached the window, he placed one of the bags against the glass, picked up a rock, and struck the pane one swift blow. The glass shattered; the shards all fell inside. Standing as still as a cigar store Indian, Lazarus Bellwood waited for several minutes to see if the noise had awakened anyone. Since he heard nothing to indicate an alarm had been sent out, he proceeded. Feeling confident he'd accomplished his first goal, that of securing a way into the store to purloin the supplies Hogg would need, Lazarus reached through the now glassless frame and undid the lock at the top. He pushed the window open and crawled inside.

Since he'd never been inside Russell's General Store and Sundries before, he had to take it slow. There was no light, and stumbling into a stack of brooms or canned goods would most certainly bring about an unwelcome response from the owner, along with the inevitable shotgun. *Easy, easy.* He stopped short when his foot hit something that felt suspiciously like a pile of clothing, or perhaps blankets. He reached out to pull a piece off the top. Feeling it, he could tell it was a wool blanket. *Perfect.* He gathered up another for good measure. Then he moved toward where he figured a counter might stand. He kicked something metal that clinked and rattled to the floor. *Damn!* It was a bucket. When he bent down to retrieve it, his hand felt others just like it, only they were in a stack. *If I'd knocked that over, I'd be a dead man now.*

He'd been fumbling around for nearly thirty minutes when he thought he heard a voice outside. Keeping as low as possible to aid him in feeling his way back to the window, he carried a sack full of items he'd secured from the shelves. Of course he had no notion of whether he had cans of peaches, tomatoes, or rat poison. He'd just have to take his chances. Even lighting a match was too much of a gamble for this midnight stalker. He found the window just in time and stuffed the burlap bag with his booty through and eased it to the ground. He was nearly through himself when he heard a loud voice.

"Hey! You there! What're you doin' in the general store?"

Lazarus scrambled to his feet and took off at a dead run down the alley. He'd left his horse tied up behind the hotel, but the voice seemed to be coming from somewhere in between. He'd have to make a quick detour around the gunsmith's shop, cross the street, and slip down an alley between the sheriff's house and a corral. No time to worry about being seen by the sheriff now, he figured. He was on a dead run with no intention of being waylaid by anything or anyone. He raced through the night.

Perspiration was pouring down his face when he reached his horse, swung aboard, and galloped down the alley, into the main street, and headed out of town in a cloud of dust. He heard the crack of a revolver as he turned the corner before the town limits sign. Something sang by his ear. It could have just been an insect buzzing around, but he had the uncomfortable feeling it was made of lead.

I hope to hell Hogg appreciates what I've gone through just to feed his belly, Lazarus thought.

Thompson-Nicola Regional District Library System

Chapter 25

A white-haired old man with a wrinkled, deeply lined face sat uncomfortably in a curved-back captain's chair waiting for an army officer to return, stressing his impatience by repeatedly tapping his cane on the floor. His bony butt was causing him discomfort because he'd been in that same position for almost three hours. He kept scooting around in the chair like an old hen on her nest. In front of the man was a wide, well-worn walnut desk. The nameplate indicated the desk was the official workplace of a Captain John Berwick. The captain's post was obvious in its placement as the gatekeeper in charge of all visitors hoping to gain an audience with the governor of New Mexico Territory. Berwick and Berwick alone oversaw who did and did not get an audience with the territory's most powerful man, Governor Lew Wallace.

Berwick was no mousy clerk, but a powerfully built example of the army's finest officers. A man with a voice that clearly demanded attention. And respect. And obedience. The captain had already informed the visitor that the governor was making no new appointments to the judiciary. That should have been sufficient, but not for the crusty old Arthur Sanborn. Fidgeting in his seat in vain to find a comfortable spot, the old man had insisted that if the governor would only see him for a few minutes, he was certain an exception might be made. His efforts, his insistence, his excuses, his references were all made to no avail. Eight times he'd sent the captain back into the depths of the cavernous room. And eight times he'd returned with the same answer. The captain came out of a wide set of double doors behind his desk, frowned at the old man, then strode to the desk.

"I'm sorry, Mr. Sanborn, but, as I've already told you many times, the governor has no interest in seeing you, let alone bestowing a judgeship on you. I'll not bother him again. So, if you'll allow me the courtesy of escorting you out, I'd be happy to suggest several fine hotels or rooming establishments. It *is* rather late in the day and not the best time to be setting out on a journey."

The old man pushed himself out of his hard chair, rubbed his backside, frowned, and nodded his acceptance of his fate. Arthur Sanborn's options had been exhausted. He must continue his quest to destroy Sheriff Cotton Burke without the cover of legitimacy. He didn't see it as the end of the world. He'd lied his way into positions of power and influence many times before, and he could do it again. It might take a little more time than he'd have liked, but since a dead sheriff was his goal, he'd wait for hell to freeze over to see that goal accomplished. He muttered under his breath as he walked from the Territorial Government Building in the capital, Santa Fe.

I'll get him for you, son, don't you fret. I swear it on your grave.

Sanborn slowly strolled down the street, peeking into windows, surveying the merchandise. There was nothing he had in mind to buy, but perusing anything and everything was simply his way of clearing his mind. He needed a new plan. As he was walking by a bookstore and bindery, an idea came to him. *If I arrive in Apache Springs with a bound set of legal opinions, the mayor should take me at my word that I'm a judge. Why would any man travel around with volumes of books on the law unless he was well versed in their content? Only a fool would do otherwise. And Arthur Sanborn is no fool.*

He chuckled at his evaluation of himself. When he entered the store, a bell tinkled above the door. In the back of the room filled with stacks of books, empty book covers, and presses, upon hearing the announcement of a customer, a man rose up from behind a pile of newly bound volumes.

"Good day, sir, what might you be interested in? *Tales of the Knights of the Round Table*, perchance? Or something documenting the exploits of the settlers in Jamestown and their encounters with savages?"

"Neither, I'm afraid. My interests lie with the law. I'd like to see whatever volumes you might have of cases, legal opinions, and trials—anything postwar."

"Ahh, a learned man, eh? Well, sir, I don't believe I have anything concerning actual cases, but let us see if there isn't something here to accommodate your taste for the law. Follow me to the rear and I'll show you what I have."

Before they even reached the stack the book purveyor had in mind, Sanborn spotted several leather-bound books that struck him as appropriate for his subterfuge. The covers had been embossed with a gold leaf title that read *Laws of Nature*. The word "Laws" was centered and quite a bit larger than the rest of the title. He felt certain he could scrape "of Nature" off with a sharp penknife. No one would know the difference. Besides, spending his valuable time reading anything in a bunch of dusty old books was the very last thing he intended to do.

"I'll take those two there," Sanborn said with authority. *I only need for people to think I'm a real judge for one very important pronouncement*, he thought. *Then I'm gone.*

The bookseller gave him a curious smirk, then realized that his best bet was to acknowledge the man's keen eye, take his money, and get back to his task of cataloging the store's contents. He shrugged, picked up the two books, and asked if his customer would like them wrapped in brown paper.

Sanborn nodded and proceeded to fish a wad of bills out of his vest pocket. He asked the man what the price was, agreed to it, and handed over the precise amount. He left the establishment with a crooked grin on his craggy face.

Sanborn continued along the boardwalk, ever cognizant of his quest to find any article that might help him convey an air of legitimacy as a judge. When he came to a clothing store, he noticed a stylish black Chesterfield coat. He went inside to inquire as to the price. The clerk told him it just so happened he'd come at a very opportune time, as the coat in question had been placed on sale that very morning. It had come in with a minor flaw in the broadcloth, and he had been forced to reduce the asking price. Sanborn eagerly shelled out the proper amount and left the store quite pleased with his purchases thus far. He was wearing the coat as he passed a cigar store.

A couple of cigars sticking out of the breast pocket of this fine coat should impress anyone who sees me, he thought, turning in to the store. He was beaming as he continued on. Approaching the jail and the office of the town marshal, he eased up a bit. The sudden reluctance he felt to confront a lawman, even by accident, unnerved him. He started to cross the street to avoid any possible contact, then thought better of it. He continued on in a manner that suggested he was a visitor to the community and one merely curious about its many offerings. As he came to the door to the jail, he noticed it was open. He stopped to peruse the meager furnishings. His gaze fell to something quite unusual: a young deputy had laid his head on his desk and was sound asleep. In fact, he was snoring loudly.

Sanborn's fertile brain began to conjure a less than legal idea, staring not so much at the man but at several objects conveniently lying on the desk not five inches from the lawman's hand, gleaming from a ray of sunlight that had invaded the darkened room. *How can I be having such a lucky day?* he thought. On the desk lay not one but several deputy marshal's badges, there for the taking, begging to be lifted by nimble fingers for a surreptitious purpose. The deputy had obviously been assigned to clean them of any tarnish.

Looking about for signs of anyone watching, and seeing no one, Sanborn tiptoed into the office and went straight to the desk. He bent slightly to make sure the man was truly asleep, and observing no evidence to the contrary, he nimbly lifted one badge from the table and eased out the door. As he hurried away from the proximity of the jail, he pulled the badge from his coat pocket and polished it on his lapel.

"Here is my ticket to a successful venture," he muttered almost—but not quite—loud enough to be heard. He fairly danced down the street, tapping his cane as he went toward the hotel where he intended to secure a room for the night.

Sanborn rose early the next morning in order to be ready when the stagecoach was scheduled to start off. As he sat on the bench in front of the stagecoach office, he glanced up to notice a sign posted above his head that said the line had experienced some Indian trouble and schedules might be changed at the last minute. With a sigh, he got up and went over to discuss any possible delays with the agent on duty.

"Unless I hear otherwise, the stage will leave in one hour. Rest assured we intend to take precautions so we don't get hit like we did a couple of weeks back. Can't abide any dead passengers, you know."

"Precautions?" Sanborn asked, with a surprised look. "What precautions?"

"There'll be a small detachment of soldiers accompanying the coach to Socorro, Apache Springs, Silver City, and all the way to Lordsburg."

"I'm getting off at Socorro," Sanborn said.

"Makes no difference. You still need protection. No tellin' where those savages might strike."

"I-I wasn't aware of any recent Indian trouble. You say there was someone killed?"

"Don't you read the papers?"

"I must have missed it."

"Yeah, well, them Apaches killed a driver and wounded a passenger not too long ago. Then, last week they hit another coach down near Las Cruces. Can't take any chances anymore. Don't worry, the army will take good care of you."

"What do Indians want with a stagecoach?" Sanborn asked.

"Guns, ammunition, money, and food," the agent said.

"Food? What food?"

"The horses. They always take the horses. They eat them."

Chapter 26

I'm going down to Doc Winters's office. Need to look in on Thorn McCann," Cotton said, taking a last gulp of coffee then wiping his mouth on his shirtsleeve. Emily rolled her eyes. "When I get back, if you'd like, I'll ride with you to get Henry back to the ranch and settled in. Regardless of how well he thinks he is, he was shot and that's something to take damned seriously."

"That's a good idea. I'll tell him we're going home."

"Where did he go? I haven't seen him since we ate."

"Said he was going out back to, uh, become one with the sun, or something like that. I didn't know what he meant, but I wasn't going to question him," Emily said, carrying cups and plates back to the kitchen.

"I'll look in on him before seein' the doc."

When he stepped out the back door, Henry Coyote was sitting cross-legged on the ground, head tilted to the sun with his eyes closed. He was chanting softly.

Cotton was loath to interrupt, but he'd seen ceremonies

similar to this before: Indian death chants. It sent a shiver up his spine.

"Henry, are you feeling, uh, well enough to return to the ranch?"

Henry continued his chanting without interruption. For several minutes Cotton silently watched the Mescalero rock slowly from side to side, half-singing, half-muttering in his native Apache tongue. Finally, he stopped, got up, and brushed the dirt from his legs and knee-high moccasins. His face was dark and lined. His eyes had a vacant stare.

"You got a worry, old friend?" Cotton asked.

Henry nodded.

"I must admit, you had several folks round here concerned about you. But from what I see, you're doin' just fine. We're hopin' to take you home in a bit."

"Worry not about me."

"Oh, there's someone else on your mind?"

Henry again nodded.

"I think Emily is doin' jus' fine, too, thanks to you."

"Not Miss Emily."

"Well, who then?"

"See vision of evil coming to friend."

"What friend would that be?"

"Sheriff Cotton."

"Me? Well, uh, what did the vision tell you?"

"Evil come to kill you. You must leave."

"I'm aware of a fella gunnin' for me. I can handle him."

"This evil will hide in dark, not face sheriff."

"I can't just pick up and leave on account of a vision, Henry. Besides, men have come for me plenty of times before. I'm still standin'; they're not. Don't worry yourself about me. I'll be all right."

"I stay here until danger has passed. Not go to ranch."

"You're welcome to stay here, old friend, but Emily has need of you, too."

"She okay. You not okay." He pushed past Cotton and walked onto the porch.

Cotton followed the old Indian. Inside, Emily was packing various items in a cloth bag, what little there was to pack. She'd had to buy a few necessities since she'd been in town, but for the most part, she had been able to scrounge up enough to keep a body together from Cotton's stores.

She looked up as he stood in the doorway. Henry had slipped past her and seemed to be very intent on finding something. Emily gave him a questioning glance then looked back to Cotton.

"Is everything okay, Cotton?"

"Ask Henry. I'm not the one with the ability to see spirits."

"See spirits? Oh, you mean the one that appeared to Henry and made him well. Yes, well, I'm quite certain there's a perfectly rational explanation for such doings."

Henry continued to search the rooms—behind furniture, in corners, and even on the front porch. Finally, out of curiosity, Emily spoke up.

"Henry, what *are* you looking for?" She stood with her hands on her hips, like a mother quizzing an errant child.

"Need rifle."

"Oh, Henry, I took it down to the jail and had Jack clean it real good. I'll bring it back to you after I see Doc Winters," Cotton said.

That seemed to satisfy the Indian, but then a questioning frown came over him.

"Why you go see doctor?"

"While I was away—before you were wounded—I came across a wrecked stagecoach. The driver had been killed. I found several people hunkered down in a ravine trying to fend off some Chiricahuas, probably Victorio's followers. One of the men was badly wounded. I brought him to the doctor's to get him patched up. Thought I ought see how he's comin' along."

"You not have need of doctor?"

"Nope."

"That good news."

"So, are you sayin' the vision you had about me might not be what you figured it to be?"

"Vision not change. Good you are able to defend self . . . with help from Apache."

Emily looked stricken by the news of some vision having to do with Cotton that she had as yet not been privy to.

"Wh-what's Henry talking about?"

"Seems he saw some danger comin' to town that I'm unaware of, and the way he tells it, the threat was to me."

"Is that right, Henry? You saw Cotton in danger?"

"Maybe see death." Henry looked solemn.

"B-but . . . from who? How?" Emily stammered, her face turning pasty white.

"Evil spirit. *Devil!*"

Emily's hand flew to her mouth. Her eyes were wide, terrified. Tears began to form, threatening to overflow her pretty eyes. Cotton pulled her close as Henry turned around and went outside.

"Don't worry, Emily, I'm not in any danger. You'll see. Maybe Henry saw it wrong."

"He *knows* things you and I don't, Cotton. You've seen it before. You know what I'm saying is true. Henry has some sort of mystical powers."

Now Cotton began to get a worried look. He *did* know that what she'd said carried with it more than a modicum of truth. Something in the back of his mind made him stop. It was coming back, slowly, and without clarity, but he, too, had experienced Henry's inexplicable ability to see things others couldn't. He'd always brushed it off as nothing more than a cultural difference between white men and Indians. But after seeing him recover from a serious wound in a near-miraculous manner, he now realized that Henry Coyote, a Mescalero Apache who'd been raised in a culture of spirituality and uncanny insights—little of which Cotton understood—should not be ignored. The Indian's vision might very well be much more than fantasy.

Cotton swallowed hard.

Chapter 27

———•◆◦—————

It was morning when Lazarus Bellwood tossed the burlap bag on the ground at the feet of James Lee Hogg.

"I come close to meetin' my maker just to get you this food and some blankets and ammunition. I hope to hell you appreciate it."

Hogg stopped whittling on a stick and slowly raised his head.

"Oh, I do 'ppreciate it, Mr. Bellwood, I surely do. Yassuh!" His smile was anything but sincere. Lazarus took notice of the man's sarcasm but decided to let it pass. *This one time.*

"Damned near got my head blowed clean off. Some stupid storekeeper with one of them *toy* guns they keep behind the counter, most likely. Those idjits never sleep. Always watchin' over their precious stores, scared to death a body'll run off with their goods. I swear . . ."

Hogg had wasted no time plunging his knife into the lid of a can of peaches and was now prying it off. Before the can was completely open, he held it to his mouth and began slurping the sweet juice.

"Ahh, the nectar of the gods," he said, and he began rummaging through the bag for whatever else Lazarus had thought to bring.

"Well, don't eat it all at one sittin'. I ain't goin' back for no more."

"I didn't ask you to, did I?"

"No, but the way you're attacking that bag, I figure you'll have eaten your way clean to the bottom before noon."

Hogg shook his head with a disgusted frown as he pulled out a box of pepper and threw it away. He fished around and pulled out a strip of jerky and began gnawing on it. He sat down and leaned back against a large log that was burned on one end from a lightning strike many years before.

"You know any more than you did yesterday about the *great man*'s plan?"

"If I was you, I wouldn't never let him hear you talking sassy-like about him. The man's got the fires of hell in him, and he don't forgive easy-like."

Lazarus pulled his saddle from his horse and tossed it on the ground. He turned the horse loose to forage for whatever grass might be found at the edge of a nearly dried-up spit of a creek. He plopped down beside Hogg and pulled out a cigar. He lit it and blew out a small cloud of smoke, making certain the aroma wouldn't be missed.

"I don't suppose you thought to bring me one of them?" Hogg said with a narrow-eyed frown.

"Nope. This is my reward for takin' all the risk." Lazarus couldn't keep a chuckle from spilling out.

"So, how long are we supposed to sit out here like a couple of wampus cats?" Hogg asked.

"When I got back to town, it was still daylight. So I went to the hotel to get a little sleep. A telegram was waitin' for me at the desk. Sanborn said he'd changed his mind and for us to go on over to Socorro and he'll meet us there. Wanted you and him to get to Apache Springs on the Butterfield stage, *together*. Said I was to ride in on my horse and not make it known that we know each other. Don't know why. Reckon he's got his reasons. I'm not all that damned eager to meet either the sheriff or his deputy, anyway. I figure Burke is goin' to take it real hard that Sanborn's got hisself a judge appointment."

"The old man's got sand, I'd say," Hogg said.

"You're sure right about that."

"Hope he's got it all figured out to the minute."

"Things could get hot real quick, if what I've heard about this sheriff is right," Lazarus said.

"What've you heard?"

"Probably best if I keep quiet. Don't want to scare you to death," Lazarus cackled.

"You don't need to worry about me. I can take care of myself."

"He shot off your big toe, didn't he? And he done it without any warnin'?"

"I'm not about to be caught off guard this time. Besides, I'm a better shot now."

"I hear he is, too."

Lazarus looked off into trees with a strange expression on his face. James Lee noticed and spoke up.

"What? You sittin' on a burr or somethin'?"

"Just thinkin' about that telegram I got. What if the operator decided to spill the beans to the sheriff? He'd know everything we got planned for him and be waitin'."

"We better hope he don't," Hogg said.

After two days of riding, James Lee Hogg and Lazarus Bellwood arrived at the edge of Socorro, a centuries-old village on the eastern edge of the Magdalena Mountains on the Rio Grande. The conglomeration of adobe huts and dusty streets was kept safe by a contingent of buffalo soldiers stationed at Fort Craig. James Lee intended to stay clear of soldiers, of any type, as he was still wanted in Texas for shooting two of them in a saloon. His popularity with the army revolved around their desire to see him dangling from the end of a rope.

"Ain't much, is it?" Lazarus observed, looking around with a scowl.

"Nope. Didn't figure it to be. I figure Sanborn picked it for the best place to meet up because we wouldn't attract much attention. Uh, I forgot to ask, you ain't wanted in these parts, are you?"

"Nope, I ain't wanted around here, anyway. I'm too slick for any lawman to corral," Lazarus answered.

"Uh-huh."

"Lets see how bad they cut their whiskey in that saloon over there."

"Probably a lot of tequila and not much whiskey in a place like this. I *do* know what they got a lot of, however."

"Yeah. What's that?"

"Mexicans. Lots and lots of Mexicans."

"Maybe that's why they call it *New Mexico*," Lazarus said, raising one eyebrow.

"Don't need no smart-asses ridin' beside me, you know."

They pulled up in front of the saloon and dismounted. Each tied his mount to the railing and climbed the steps to the front of the narrow adobe building with many small, round chinks taken out of its walls.

"Looks like this place has seen its share of battle damage," Lazarus said, trying to count the many indentations.

"Yeah, that damned war got all the way down here, too."

Inside the dark, gloomy room, the smell of whiskey, beer, and burned beans was overwhelming. James Lee stepped up to the bar. A small-framed Mexican turned to look at him, then returned to what he had been doing, which appeared to have been nothing. James Lee knocked on the bar top.

"Hey! How about a couple of whiskeys over here?"

Apparently unfazed by the gruff American's impatience, the man made no response. This infuriated the gunman, and he drew his revolver and fired a shot into a stack of glasses just to the left of the nonchalant bartender. Just as he was about to send another bullet directly at a mirror behind the bar, James Lee heard a voice behind him. He whirled around to see two dark-skinned men in sombreros, wearing conchos on their vests and holding rifles pointed his way. Both also wore badges.

"I beg your pardon, señor, but what is it that makes you think shooting up our saloon is permissible?"

"Just tryin' to get a little service out of that wet . . . er . . . fella behind the bar. I take it servin' customers ain't part of the business." James Lee's face was red with rage. Lazarus nudged him in hopes of calming him down. Two men with guns pointed at them didn't seem to be the best odds to him.

"The man you want will be back in a few minutes. He went out back to relieve himself. The one you are shouting at only mops the floor and cleans out the spittoons."

"Oh. Well, how the hell was I supposed to know that?"

"You probably weren't, but I believe an apology is due him anyway."

James Lee was getting antsy about the guns being pointed at him. His instincts told him to leave well enough alone, but his anger told him to try for it. He could tell Lazarus was not going to be any help, since by the time he got the Sharps up, cocked, and aimed, it would all be over. He slumped at the obviousness of the only decision he could make and stay alive long enough to meet the stagecoach.

"Sorry. I'll, uh, pay for them glasses."

The man with the badge gave him a toothy grin as he lowered his rifle.

"That would be appreciated."

Chapter 28

———✦———

Cotton kicked at a clod of dirt lying in the road on his way to Doc Winters's office, exploding it into a thousand pieces. His mind was still miles away when he reached the door and knocked. He was surprised when Delilah opened it. He removed his hat and gave her a questioning smile.

"Good day, Sheriff," she said. "I'll bet you've come to look in on Thorn. I'm happy to report that he's coming along nicely, thanks to the doctor. And you, of course. Won't you come in?"

"I'm glad to hear Thorn's on the mend. He up to talkin' some?"

"Reckon he'll talk to you." She waved him into the reception area and pointed to the back room, just beyond a curtained doorway.

He walked up to the makeshift bed the doctor had constructed. Thorn was trying to lean on one arm, but was obviously struggling to keep his balance.

"Howdy, Sheriff. Glad *you* come through that little dustup with those Indians all in one piece."

"Yeah, but the Hardins weren't so lucky. Any idea where those two drunken renegades came from?"

"Nah. Pretty raggedy pair. Probably been kicked out of the tribe or somethin'."

"Well, we need to talk over some recent happenin's. You ever heard of a loudmouth goes by the name of James Lee Hogg?"

"I ran into him a couple times, if he's the same Hogg as I'm thinkin' on."

"Got a nasty limp."

"Yeah, that's him. Heard some lawman shot his big toe off. Had to laugh the first time I heard it. Who you suppose'd do such a thing?"

"Me. Now, let's get down to business. Hogg's in town, or he was. Came and went under troublesome circumstances. Someone busted him out of jail by cracking my deputy over the head. And I have reason to believe—if Hogg's words are worth a tinker's damn—that Arthur Sanborn is lookin' to finally make me pay for Billy."

"What for? He can't be thinkin' to take you down himself. Why, that scrawny old fart likely couldn't even *lift* a revolver bigger'n a thirty-two."

"Since you know him, what's your thinkin' on the matter?"

"Could be that Hogg was hired to finish what I didn't. Sanborn's a strange one, and I doubt he'd give up the hunt just because of my failure to bring you back to Texas."

"I figured as much. So you're sayin' he's hired Hogg for . . . what? Thinkin' he'll try for a shoot-out?"

"Be a damned fool if he did," Thorn said.

"Something else, then? Jack said Hogg was spoutin' off about Judge Sanborn arrivin' in Apache Springs soon. You know anythin' about that?"

"News to me. But anything that old coot might come up with wouldn't surprise me."

"If he is on his way, you reckon he would *personally*

push me and Hogg into a smoke wagon meetin'? Just so he could watch it come down?"

"Wouldn't be the first time. At least that's the way I heard it."

"Oh? What was it you heard?" Cotton asked.

"They say that before you took justice into your own hands and blew that no-good straight to hell, Lucky Bill Sanborn left a trail of destruction everywhere he went. A real hellion, so they say."

"And Sanborn was the one to clean up all the messes?"

"Yep. And he seemed to get the job done by makin' certain his son was the last one standin'."

"How'd he go about that?" Cotton asked with a squint.

"He'd first make sure the whole town knew that there was a disagreement between Lucky Bill and some other feller. He'd start rumors that Bill was being taunted and had no choice but to defend himself. The other feller always ended up facedown in the dirt."

"Bill wasn't that fast. How would Sanborn know his son would win?"

"Never figured on takin' any chances."

"You mean—"

"That's right. Hired his own personal sharpshooter," Thorn said.

"Know who that was?"

"No one ever saw him. Shot came out of nowhere. Wasn't James Lee Hogg, though. James Lee hadn't made the judge's acquaintance that early on in Lucky Bill's career of destruction. I do know that whoever he was, he was one helluva shot. Rifleman, likely."

Cotton rubbed his chin. He'd never regretted shooting Lucky Bill Sanborn, but he was getting concerned now about what effect his having done so might have on Emily, his friends, and the town of Apache Springs. If the rumor was true, and the old man *was* on the road to retribution, things could get pretty hot for everyone. Considering James Lee Hogg's willingness to shoot at Emily, it was obviously time to make some serious plans to ensure her safety.

* * *

"How is Thorn doing, Cotton?" Emily asked.

"He'll be good as new in a couple more days. Doc said that Mrs. Hardin saved his life. I feel bad I wasn't still there when those Indians came. Two damned fine people are now dead because of it."

"There was no way you could have known. Quit blaming yourself. If those renegades hadn't come by when they did, they'd probably have been there two days later, or four days, or who knows when. If they were bent on getting liquored up, that's all that was on their minds."

"Maybe. But right now, I've got another worry."

"And what would that be?"

"You."

"Me?"

"Yes. Don't forget, James Lee Hogg took a shot at *you*. He more'n likely did it because old man Sanborn had paid him to kill anyone who was unlucky enough to be close to me. That's the kind of thing Sanborn would do."

"How can anyone be that evil?"

"Like father, like son. Lucky Bill Sanborn was the most unscrupulous boy I've ever known. Satan himself. And his father made him that way."

"And you figure he's coming here for his revenge, since he failed before?"

"That's right. While I'm his main target, if he can make anyone I love suffer, it makes his revenge even sweeter. That's the kind of man he is."

"What do you propose to do?"

"I'm still cogitatin' on it."

"Don't cogitate too long. We don't know when he'll be here. Could be tomorrow."

Chapter 29

———◆•◆———

In Socorro, James Lee leaned on a post while Lazarus sat on the boardwalk, hat pulled down, snoring away. The stage was due any minute, and James Lee wanted to be sure to be there when Arthur Sanborn arrived. He jumped at the sound of a whip commanding the six-horse team to do the driver's bidding. A block down, the stagecoach rounded a corner and came to a shuddering, skidding stop. The driver jumped down and hastened to the door to open it for his passengers. James Lee nudged Lazarus as soon as he saw a frail old man step gingerly off the step of the coach.

"That's him. That's the old geezer that's goin' to make me some real money," Hogg said.

"I know."

"Oh, that's right. You already met the old highbinder."

"More than just met him."

"You've known him for a long time?"

"Done considerable business with him, *several* times."

"Doin' what?"

"What I do best," Lazarus said, patting his Sharps rifle.

James Lee stared at him for a minute trying to decide whether what he'd just heard was true or more of Lazarus's bull. He was getting more than a little ruffled by the man's continual evasiveness at almost every question he'd asked. But the promise of a lot of money seemed to calm his temperamental tendencies.

James Lee grabbed Lazarus by the sleeve and pulled him up. They started walking fast down the street to meet Sanborn. Halfway down, when it was obvious the old man had recognized them, he turned abruptly and quickly entered the nearest saloon. James Lee followed Sanborn inside. Lazarus remained outside to watch for . . . hell, he didn't know what, but it seemed a good idea at the time, especially since Sanborn had always been touchy about them being seen together. Without a word, Lazarus held back and seated himself on a bench near the front doors.

I know Sanborn don't want to be seen with us, but I'm supposed to be riding in on the stage with him. Just don't make sense, thought Hogg.

As soon as his eyes grew accustomed to the dark and smoky room, James Lee spotted Sanborn leaning on the bar. He walked over cautiously, not knowing what to expect.

"Mr. Hogg, I see your companion remained outside."

"Uh, yessir, but I don't completely understand why."

"You will understand, and soon, Mr. Hogg. I have instructed Mr. Bellwood that he is to ride into Apache Springs alone and not acknowledge either of us for the time we're there."

"Yessir. But—"

"No buts, Mr. Hogg."

"Uh, yessir."

"Good. Lazarus Bellwood and I are not to be seen together, either here or at our destination. I expect you to do my bidding to the strictest terms. I'll not expect to spell it all out, again and again. I need you to use your brains at all times. Clear?"

"Absolutely, Judge. Oh, before we leave, I almost forgot

to mention a fact of which I figure you'll be wantin' to know."

"And just what is that, Mr. Hogg?"

"When I was in town, I happened to overhear some fellers in the saloon talkin' about a man that had been wounded in some squabble with Indians."

"Why should I care about that?"

"Well, sir, the man's name is Thorn McCann."

"McCann?"

"Yep. Ain't that the man you sent after the sheriff before me?"

"It was. This doesn't bode well for our plan. If that damned McCann sees me, he'll likely figure out what my plans are and how I intend to pull off the seemingly impossible."

"That's what I figured. Did I do right in tellin' you?"

"You certainly did, Mr. Hogg, you certainly did." Sanborn frowned and began rubbing his stubbly chin. "It may cause me to make a minor change in plans."

"Why's that?"

"If McCann is still in Apache Springs, then it means he's probably thrown in with that damned sheriff. That may be why he didn't return. We'll have to deal with him, too."

"Ahh, yes, I see what you mean. What do you figure to do?"

"Go ahead and send Lazarus into town ahead of us. You and me, we'll stay another night here in Socorro to make sure he's got a good head start."

"What'll I tell him?"

"Give him a description of McCann and tell him to keep an eye on him."

"What's he supposed to be on the lookout for?"

"I want to know if he's chummy with Burke. If so, he'll have to be dealt with harshly, if you get my meaning."

"Oh, yessir, I think I do at that."

"You haven't told me what you observed when *you* went to Apache Springs."

James Lee Hogg suddenly grew glum, fidgeting around like a nervous rabbit in a trap. He started to hem and haw, but it was now clear that Sanborn had caught on that things had gone astray. Hogg cleared his throat.

"Well, you see, when I got there, I found out that the sheriff had a lady friend. And since you told me to eliminate anyone close to Burke, just like what he'd done to you, well I figured to shoot her. As it happened, an old Indian jumped in front of her just as I let loose with my thirty-eight. He's the one that caught the bullet."

"You kill him?"

"No."

"And the woman?"

"She's, uh, doin'—"

"Never mind. I got it figured out."

"But since I failed the first time, I just naturally figured you'd want me to get the job done, so, I went after her in the sheriff's house in town."

"Good. Good. You got her that time, I presume."

"Uh, n-no, things didn't go well that time, either."

"What! You had two chances to shoot down a woman and you messed it up both times?"

Sanborn sighed and threw up his hands. "What the hell happened?"

"That damned deputy sheriff come in just as I was about to pull the trigger. He arrested me and hauled me down to the jail. Lazarus had to club him later that night so he could get into the jail without bein' seen. He set me free."

"Do you have any idea how important it is to me to see that sheriff dead? I can't abide any more bungling. Do you understand?"

"Yessir. Won't happen again."

"Damned right it won't. Because if it does, and I'm cheated once more out of the justice I seek, you'll be the one lying in the street."

"I-I understand, sir, er, Judge."

"You damned well better."

Hogg stared at him with a worried look.

"Is there something else I should know, Mr. Hogg?"

"I was just thinkin' about what the sheriff might do when I arrive back in town. Won't the sheriff be lookin' to put me back in jail?"

Sanborn fished around in the pocket of his coat and pulled out a shiny piece of tin. "I think we can get around that problem if you pin this on. Just let me do the talking."

Hogg stared at the badge for a moment before breaking into a wide grin. "Yessir, that should do the trick."

"All right, now you go tell Lazarus to get himself back on his horse and scoot. After all your slipups, *you* can bed down at the livery. I'm going to get a room at the hotel. We'll meet at the stage depot early in the morning."

Sanborn had a scowl on his face as he spun around and headed off to the hotel. James Lee knew that what he'd had to tell the old man didn't sit well, but he figured it was better coming from him than someone else. Sweat was dripping from his brow as he went to tell Lazarus of Sanborn's orders. And to show off his new badge, too.

Chapter 30

———⊱◆⊰———

Early in the morning, two days later, Lazarus Bellwood rode into Apache Springs, being careful not to attract undue attention, twenty-four hours ahead of the Butterfield stage from Socorro. He arrived to a town awakening. James Lee had briefed him of the old judge's plans, and he'd been pondering just what he could do to help things along. After all, James Lee had fouled things up, twice, so Lazarus figured he'd take a shot at an idea that had come to him in the middle of the night while he rocked back and forth in his saddle just trying to stay awake. His idea was not to make the sheriff angrier, but to put a scare into him, make him fear for his very life. He wanted the sheriff to be looking into every dark corner every time he stepped outside. His plan involved something less drastic than shooting a woman. *James Lee Hogg is a fool. I'll not make the same dumb mistakes. Before I'm through, Cotton Burke will be shooting at shadows.*

Since he hadn't eaten for a whole day, the first thing he did was to order breakfast at a small diner near the livery.

From a seat near the one and only window, he could see the comings and goings of half the town's inhabitants. For instance, he saw Emily emerge from the sheriff's house, the location of which he'd learned from the hotel desk clerk. He watched her climb onto the seat of her buckboard and drive away, heading straight out of town. *Must be the sheriff's lady*, Lazarus thought. *Perfect. I'll just follow and see where she goes.* He hurried to gobble up his eggs and beans, shoved a biscuit into his mouth, and dropped some coins on the table before rushing out the door.

Lazarus pulled the reins loose from the hitching rail and climbed into the saddle. It was a calm day, and he could still see the trail of dust left by Emily's wagon. He'd stay a decent distance behind so he wasn't spotted. Considering the heat, he was just as happy his roan mare wasn't exhibiting any need to increase her gait anyway. He leaned over and patted the horse on the neck. Lazarus stayed well out of sight as Emily Wagner drove her two-horse team toward her ranch. Lazarus steered his roan into a copse of cottonwoods at the bottom of a lane when the ranch house came into view and it was obvious that's where the comely lady was headed. He sat with his hands stacked on the pommel, well back in the shadows as he watched her climb down and go inside. He took off his floppy hat and scratched his head. His loosely formed plan could use some more thought, but time was of the essence. He wanted to put his idea in play before the Judge and James Lee Hogg arrived back in town the next day.

The last time he'd been in Apache Springs, no one had caught even a glimpse of his shadowy movements as he stalked the town's deputy sheriff to the hotel, then clubbed him into unconsciousness with the butt of his Sharps rifle, in order to free Hogg from jail. That had been his plan, too, carefully considered and executed. No evidence left behind, no one the wiser as to his clandestine presence. He was not only one of the best rifle shots west of the Mississippi River, but also a cold and calculating killer. And, notably, one without any record of his despicable deeds to follow him

around as so many gunmen's did. Buoyed by a sudden flash
of confidence, Lazarus clucked his tongue. The roan stepped
forward, out of the shadowy overhang of the leafy canopy,
her hooves clicking a rhythm on the rocky path to the ranch
house.

Emily spotted the lone rider as he came up the path to
the porch. She called out to one of the cowboys, Teddy Olander, to come quickly and be armed. She stepped through the
door, the scattergun from over the fireplace gripped firmly
in her hands. *This time*, she thought, *I'll not hesitate to pull
the trigger if it looks like this fellow is as unsavory as he
appears.*

Lazarus reined the horse in front of the porch steps and
leaned on the pommel, making certain to keep his hands
well away from his rifle, so as not to signal a threat. He
carried no sidearm.

"Howdy, ma'am. I was passin' by and wondered if you
could spare a traveler a spot of water. Mighty hot out here,
today," Lazarus said, tipping his dusty hat.

Emily pointed to a well off to the side of the house.
"Well's over there. You're welcome to a drink for yourself
and your horse, and then move on." She kept the shotgun
pointed in his direction.

"Obliged, ma'am," Lazarus said as he dismounted and
led the horse to the well. Beside the round stone well there
stood a wooden trough filled with water and a slight scum
of green algae around the edge. Lazarus swished the algae
aside so the horse could drink. He then pulled up the bucket
from the well and dipped a long-handled tin cup into it. He
drank deeply. He hadn't really realized just how thirsty he
had been until that cool water touched his lips. "Mighty
kind of you."

"Something else I can do for you?" Emily asked, taking
notice of Lazarus's lack of enthusiasm for leaving. Lazarus
looked over at Teddy standing by the porch, his rifle in his
hand, hat pulled low, and looking more than a bit uneasy
with the man's presence.

"Uh, oh, no, ma'am." He hesitated. "Well, maybe one

thing. In addition to needin' a drink, I also dropped by to show you a little bit of what I do best. Never know when you might need a man with my expertise. If that'd be all right."

"Your expertise?"

"Yep. I'm a champion rifle shot. Won all sorts of prizes from here to Kansas City and beyond. Hell, that's how I got my horse and my saddle. Of course, my pride and joy is the Sharps rifle that's restin' in the saddle scabbard. Won that in Fort Worth. Turkey shoot."

"I don't reckon I'll be needing any demonstrations today. Thank you, anyway." Emily had taken a few steps backward to let him know she was through talking, when Lazarus made his final plea.

"Only take a moment of your time. Besides, I figure you'll be wantin' to pass on what you've seen to the sheriff."

"Just what do you mean?" Her eyes narrowed at the man's barely concealed message.

"As I rode in, I set an unopened can of peaches on the gatepost at the end of your lane. I propose to take one shot. You'll surely get the point of my little demonstration." Without waiting for a response from her, Lazarus slipped the Sharps from the scabbard and brought it cleanly to his cheek. He flipped up the adjustable Creedmore sight mounted on the tang, made one slight change, cocked the rifle, and slowly squeezed the trigger. The gun bucked as it roared to life in a smoky cloud. Almost a hundred yards away, the can of peaches exploded in a spray of juice, peach parts, and tin shrapnel, spreading the contents for twenty feet. He was all grins as he replaced the rifle in its scabbard.

"All right, I'll grant you that you've just made a formidable shot. But I fail to see your objective in doing so." Emily's trigger finger was twitching.

"Just thought you'd want to let that lawman friend of yours know that not every bullet comes from ten feet away. He should keep his eyes peeled. A careful sheriff is a live sheriff," Lazarus said, as he gave her a wry grin, swung into his saddle, and spurred the roan to a run toward the gate.

Emily was frowning as she turned to Teddy. He appeared as puzzled as she was.

"What the devil did we just witness?" she said.

"Damned if I know, er, pardon my language, ma'am."

"One thing's for sure, you better ride to town and tell Sheriff Cotton about our visitor," Emily said, "Oh, and if you see Henry, fill him in, too."

"Yes, ma'am," Teddy said, as he trotted off to the corral to saddle a horse.

Cotton looked pleased as Delilah and Thorn McCann came strolling into the jail, arm in arm and all smiles. The sheriff leaned back in his chair, interlacing his fingers behind his head.

"Good to see you up and around, McCann."

"Thanks to you, I'm still able to walk about with this beautiful lady."

Delilah blushed and tried to avoid direct eye contact with Cotton.

"If you hadn't come along when you did, I fear we'd all be coyote bait," Thorn said.

"Luck of the draw, McCann, luck of the draw."

"Well, I like your kind of luck. But I am somewhat confused by what the hell you were doing out there in the first place."

"Didn't you send a telegram to me askin' me to come save your worthless hide from a rope necktie?"

"Reckon I did, at that."

"Then, when I got there, you were gone. Escaped with the help of some unknown individual, likely that same beautiful lady clingin' to your arm. Am I guessin' right?"

"Depends. She gonna face charges if she *did* happen to come for a visit at just the right time?"

"Nope. Marshal in Silver City said he's just as happy to have you gone. Wasn't all that certain how he was goin' to prove you knew it was counterfeit money you were spreadin' all around, and he didn't favor a vigilante hangin'."

"Yeah, well, I think I can explain. As I now see it, all that money Bart Havens was flashin' around turned out to be phony. I didn't know until I got wind that some folks in Silver City were questioning whether it was good or not. When I mentioned it to Delilah, she was as surprised as I was. Hell, I never saw no fake bills before, well, other than Confederate, that is."

"That's when you two decided to break out of their jail?"

"That's right. See, it was all just an innocent mistake," Thorn said with a shrug.

"I will say the Apache Springs banks' depositors were right pleased that you brought *their* money back safe and sound. Nobody hereabouts got stung too bad. However, by what you've just told me, you've pretty much convicted yourself by admitting you knew it was fake when you broke out of the Silver City jail instead of hangin' around and tryin' to make things right to a judge. Did I miss anything?"

"It's like you said, some of them folks was bein' a bit unreasonable about things. Seemed the best option to skedaddle."

Cotton just grunted.

Chapter 31

Teddy Olander spurred his horse to a dead run. Dust swirled behind him as he left the dusty road to cut across country and save time in his rush to get the message out to Sheriff Burke that there had been some strange doin's at the Wagner ranch. Teddy had been raised not far from Apache Springs, and he knew the country like the back of his hand. He was a good horseman and an eager worker, both virtues in Emily Wagner's sight. When he splashed across the last of the many small creeks that wandered down from the hills and nearby mountains, pulling up just at the edge of town, he smiled to himself. He pulled out his pocket watch and grinned big. One half hour better than the time it would have taken had he stayed on the trail.

Teddy reined in at the hitching rail in front of the jail, jumped to the ground, and rushed inside. Fortunately, the sheriff was at his desk and Henry Coyote was lying on a bunk in one of the cells. Teddy's eyes grew wide at the sight.

"Sheriff, h-how's come Henry's in jail? He didn't do nothin', did he? Why, I've never knowed . . ."

"Calm down, Teddy. Henry is taking his leisure in there because he wants to, not because of anything he's done."

Teddy took off his hat and wiped the sweat from his brow. "Whew. That's a relief. Miz Wagner wouldn't like it none if Henry was in some sort of trouble."

"Well, he's not, so you can stop frettin'. Now, what're you doin' in town?"

"Miz Wagner has had an unsettlin' experience out at the ranch. Wanted me to hurry in and tell you about it."

Cotton stared at the boy, not saying a word. He waited a full minute. Then he waited some more. He sighed.

"Teddy, I swear I could die of old age before you spit out what it was that brought you here. Get on with it."

"Oh, yeah, sorry. Well, there was this feller come ridin' in pretty as you please, got down off his horse—without no invitation mind you—and asked Miz Wagner for some water for him and his mount."

"Yeah?"

"Miz Wagner, bein' the generous soul she is, said he could have all he wanted at the well. The man led his horse around to the well and proceeded to let the horse drink from the trough. He ladled himself a cup or two, spillin' half of it down his shirt and . . ."

"Teddy! How about we get to the good part? The unsettlin' part you mentioned."

"Uh, sorry to be so long-winded, but I just don't want to leave nothin' important out."

"I understand. Go on. But be kinda quick about it, if you could."

"Yessir. Well, this feller said he wanted to show her somethin' she would find interestin'. She didn't act like she wanted to be bothered, but he proceeded to pull a Sharps rifle from his saddle scabbard, cocked it, and aimed down the sights. Said he'd placed a can of peaches on the fence post at the gate as he rode in. He pulled that trigger and let fly. And whooee! That can of peaches exploded like it had dynamite in it. I checked the can when he left. Hit the darned thing dead center."

"He did this from where?"

"Just about fifteen feet from the well, towards the house."

"What was his point? Why'd he think she'd be interested? Was he lookin' for a job?"

"Nope to all of that. Said he thought she'd want to tell you that you should keep an eye peeled 'cause you never know where the next bullet might be comin' from. Said you'd understand."

"He mention his name?"

"Don't rightly recall that he did. But he was a rangy feller carryin' a Sharps that looked like he mighta slept with it. Shiny frame, polished stock, and one of them Creedmore rear sights that mounts back of the hammer on the stock."

Cotton fell silent. He rubbed his chin for a moment before speaking.

"You hear any of that, Henry?"

"Hear all."

"The description suggest anyone you know?"

"Not know of such a man."

"Teddy, I appreciate what you've told me. We'll keep a lookout for such a man. Now, you better skedaddle back to the ranch. Tell Miz Emily I'll be on the alert, and she can stop worryin'."

"Yessir. Uh, you don't suppose it would hurt to stop for just a tiny sip of whiskey, would it?"

Cotton almost laughed out loud but kept his composure.

"No, Teddy, I don't think it would hurt a thing."

After Teddy scampered off, Henry rose and came into the office. "You want me to keep watch for man with fancy rifle?"

"Yes, I do. He doesn't seem like a man to take lightly. And if you run across Jack, tell him, too."

Henry picked up his Spencer rifle and slipped out the door as silently as a wolf tracking its prey.

Jack sat on the edge of Melody's bed, sloshing brandy around in a glass. He stared at it so intently that Melody was sufficiently incensed to inquire what could possibly be so important as to take his mind off her charms. She raised herself up on one elbow, reached over, and stabbed him playfully in the ribs with a long-nailed finger.

"Jack! Look at me! Don't you like what you see? Am I getting old and haggard?"

"Huh?" Jack suddenly realized he was being addressed. He came out of his fog trying to reconstruct whatever it was that Melody had been muttering. "I . . ."

"Don't toy with me, Jack. Do you think I'm pretty or not?"

"Not pretty, Melody, beautiful. And you always will be . . . to me."

"Well said, sweetie, but I'm *concerned* about you."

"Why?"

"You've been distant, lately, off in another place." She sat up suddenly. "You're not thinking of another woman, are you?"

"Of course not. My head still hurts a mite, that's all."

"If I find out you're lying to me, I'll shoot your . . ."

"Melody! Stop it! There's no other woman, and I've had enough of your jealous tantrums. I'm concerned about Cotton, that's all."

"Cotton! Always Cotton! Damn! Sometimes I think you'd rather be with him than me." She swung her legs off the bed, got up, and slipped into a pink robe with feathers all down the front. She stood in front of the full-length mirror she'd had sent from Chicago, twisting and turning, checking to make sure Jack wasn't lying about her losing her looks.

"Now, Melody, don't go gettin' all huffy on me. Cotton's my boss and whatever happens to him affects me, too. Don't you see that?"

"Uh-huh. But whatever happens to that rattler don't mean a hill of beans to me. When we're together, I expect your *full* attention. You got that?" Melody stormed out without waiting for an answer, slamming the door behind her.

Jack muttered one under his breath anyway.

"One of these days, my dear, you're goin' to push me too far."

In a foul mood when he left the saloon, Memphis Jack had no more than stepped out the swinging doors than he came face-to-face with Henry Coyote. He stopped and started to say howdy, but Henry cut him off.

"Have message from sheriff. Come sit, we talk."

"Where is he? Has something happened?"

"He concerned about Miz Emily. He get bad news."

"Bad news? What—"

"I talk. You listen."

Chapter 32

The next morning, Cotton was cleaning his coffee cup in a bucket of water when someone burst into the jail. He finished wiping the cup dry, then poured some fresh coffee. He didn't bother to look around. He could tell by the way the door slammed it was Memphis Jack.

"Cotton, got some news, and it ain't good."

"Yeah? Well, I already got some of my own."

"Henry already told me all about the sharpshooter," Jack said. "But that ain't all."

"There's more bad news?" Cotton said, with a questioning squint.

"The stage from Socorro just got in. Couple of fellers got off that're bound to spell trouble."

"How do you know that?"

"One was a scrawny old, balding man, bent over and lookin' disheveled. Had a glint in his eye that sent a chill up my spine, I'll tell you."

"A chill, and that spells trouble?" Cotton raised one eyebrow.

"Indeed it does."

"And the other one?"

"James Lee Hogg."

"What! Are you certain?"

"Sure as water runs downhill, I'm that dead-on certain. Don't forget, I'm the one who put him in jail for rousting Emily. My eyesight ain't givin' out on me," Jack said.

"Where'd they go?"

"Straight for the mayor's office. I 'spect that's where they are right this moment."

"Tell me more about the old man. What'd he look like? How old? Fat, tall, short? Were his clothes store-bought or handmade? How'd he walk?"

"Hold on, Cotton, one question at a time."

"Sorry."

"For starters, he was, like I said, kinda bent over. He used a cane with a silver handle. He had white hair, or what was left of it. And he was frail, I'd say, bony and frail. But that look on his face, I'll tell you—"

"I know, chilling. What color was his suit? Or was he wearing a duster?"

"How'd you know about the duster?"

"Just a guess. Pretty dusty ridin' the stage, and some men don't want to get their clothes trail dirty. Especially if they think they're real important."

"Yeah, well he *did* have on a duster."

Cotton set his cup on the desk and walked to the door. He gazed at the town hall, where the mayor had his office. He leaned back against the doorframe and watched. Didn't say anything, just watched. Jack frowned as he squeezed by Cotton and went outside to sit on the bench. They both remained there keeping a vigil on the door to the town hall. After about twenty minutes, the mayor and two other men emerged, one old and stooped, the other the man who'd escaped jail after someone had cracked Jack's skull with the butt of a rifle. The identity of that someone remained a mystery.

"I say we go down there and arrest Hogg for breaking

out of jail," Jack said. He spoke through gritted teeth. He looked up to see Cotton chewing his lip. "What do you think, Sheriff?"

"I think you're right about that trouble you spoke about."

"If I am right, it looks like it's comin' sooner rather than later. They're headed this way."

Mayor Orwell Plume led the way, with the old man following a step or two behind. The third man, James Lee Hogg, broke off and headed for the saloon. Jack kept his eyes on Hogg, then got up.

"Think I'll wander over to Melody's place and keep watch over things," Jack said, not waiting for permission. Cotton just grunted his permission as his deputy stepped off the boardwalk.

When the mayor got close enough for him to hear, Cotton spoke up.

"Looks like you got company, Orwell."

"Indeed, Sheriff. I'd like you to meet the new circuit judge for the district. He tells me that Territorial Governor Lew Wallace himself has appointed him to set up his court right here. It sounds like it'll be a good thing for the town. Should bring in lots of folks from all around to see the court in action. It also means not havin' to travel all the way down to Silver City for trials. Well, anyway, this here is Judge Arthur Sanborn, recently from—"

"Texas!" Cotton said, barely able to control his anger.

"How'd you know that, Cotton?"

"We've met."

"Ah, well, I wanted you to be the first to know that Judge Sanborn will be starting his trials very soon. He hasn't set a date yet for the first one." Plume turned to Sanborn, who looked as if he had bitten down on something very sour. His gaunt, wrinkled face was ashen gray. "Uh, exactly what *will* be your first case, Judge?"

"It'll be one that's bound to shake the community up quite nicely, Mayor. I'll give you the particulars in a day or two." Sanborn slowly turned and shuffled away, headed for the hotel.

"Oh, one thing, Judge, who was that man with you?" Cotton's voice was unmistakably bitter.

"Oh, that's Deputy U.S. Marshal James Lee Hogg. I believe you've already met. A judge needs someone to enforce his rulings, you know." Sanborn was chuckling as he stepped away and went on down the street alone.

"Is there something I should know, Sheriff, about the judge and all?" Plume asked. "You seem, er, upset."

"I figure you'll find out soon enough, Mayor. Soon enough." Cotton spun on his heel and went inside. He slammed the door behind him just in case the mayor took a notion to follow him.

Shaken by the experience of seeing his enemy face-to-face, Cotton sat morosely at his desk. He'd drawn his Colt and was cocking and uncocking it over and over. He was faced with a dilemma and he knew it. *How could that crooked, evil old man have gotten an appointment to the bench? Is it even legitimate or just another of that wily old fool's tricks?* He was boiling inside when he heard a light knock at the door. At first he ignored it, but after the second *tap, tap, tap,* he hollered, "Come in! The damned thing ain't locked!"

Emily cautiously eased the door open and peered around the corner. When he saw her, he was ashamed that he'd let his anger spill over. He was, after all, the sheriff, and it was imperative for him to maintain a sense of civility toward the citizenry at all times. Over the past few minutes, civility had been the furthest thing from his mind.

"*Emily!* Uh, I'm sorry for shouting. You, er, caught me at a bad time, I reckon. Come in, please. Didn't know you were in town. I got your message from Teddy."

"Good. But after he left, I got to thinking about all that's happened with Hogg and now that man with the rifle. I'm concerned. So I came on in myself."

Having drifted into the room with an air of worried expectation, Emily Wagner stood in front of Cotton with a questioning look, head cocked.

"I wish there was something I could say to ease your fears, but . . ."

"I expected that's what you'd say, and I don't blame you one bit. I don't know what's going on, but I did see some old man and that awful James Lee Hogg coming out of the mayor's office. Hogg wasn't in chains, so I figured he wasn't under arrest. Why is that?"

"It's a long story and one that's proving tough to swallow."

"That's what you said when I asked you about your past."

"Uh-huh. I remember. And this time I expect it's goin' to get me in as much trouble."

"It will if you can't see the advantage in being honest with me and not keeping all your secrets inside."

"That old man is the father of the young hellion I shot, the one who raped and beat my sister, Juliet, to death. He's somehow found a way to follow me here and make my life pure hell."

"Hell?"

"That's what the devil cooks up, isn't it?"

"How can he cause you any trouble here? Didn't that all occur in Texas?"

"He has somehow conned our governor into making him a circuit judge for this district and has given him Apache Springs as his court location. Looks like he somehow got Hogg made a marshal, too. At least that's his claim."

"What're you going to do about it? You can't just let him chase you out!"

"He's not interested in chasing me anywhere. He wants to see me gunned down in the street."

"Is there any possibility that the man who stopped by my ranch and entertained Teddy and me with his shooting ability could play into things?"

"Emily, I think it's far more than a possibility."

Distress clouded Emily's face. She was visibly shaken by Cotton's words. Cotton took her by the shoulders and pulled her close. She buried her face in his shoulder. He could feel her shaking. Comforting a fear-stricken woman wasn't something that came naturally to him. But it was important that he try.

"It's goin' to work out, Emily. I'm sure of it."

She pulled back enough to look him in the eye. "How can you know that?"

"I feel it."

Emily sighed and pushed out of his arms.

"I-I'm going back to the ranch. I can use this opportunity to pick up some supplies I forgot to have Teddy get. That sharpshooter that dropped by has me frazzled. Why don't you come out and stay the night? I'd feel much safer if you would."

"All right. I'll be out as soon as I finish up some things here."

She started out the door, then stopped suddenly and put her hand to her mouth. "My god! That's him. He's here." Her eyes were wide with panic as Cotton rushed to her side.

"Where?"

"There. Just going into the hotel. That's the man who came to the ranch."

Chapter 33

———◆◆◆———

Jack, I want you to go to the hotel and see what you can find out about a man who checked in a little bit ago. He's a scraggly old feller who looks like he'd spent too much time in the mountains and carryin' a Sharps in a fancy scabbard. He's wearin' a floppy-brimmed hat."

"What's he done?"

"Scared the hell out of Emily for starters. He's the one that gave her a shootin' demonstration."

"Did he threaten her?"

"Not directly, but I think his aim was for her to warn *me* of somethin'."

"Warn you of . . . what?"

"Not sure. Just do it."

Jack pulled his Remington and half-cocked it, spun the cylinder to assure it was loaded and ready, slipped it back into his holster, and walked out the door. When he got to the hotel, he looked around to see if there was anyone fitting Cotton's description in the lobby. He walked over to the dining room and glanced about, then wandered over to the check-in desk. The old man who owned the hotel was on duty. He looked up as Jack approached.

"What can I do for you, Deputy?"

"You know how the sheriff and me kinda like to keep an eye out for any troublemakers that might be passin' through. You check anyone in recently that might look the least bit suspicious?"

"Jack, you know if a man has the means to pay for his room, I don't ask questions. In fact, I try not to look 'em in the eye if I can help it. You got a particular someone in mind?"

"Could be a grizzled old man carryin' a Sharps rifle in a fancy scabbard. I'm told on good authority that a man like that came in a while ago."

"Don't know a thing about him, but a gent with such a rifle did check in." The old man spun the sign-in ledger so Jack could take a peek at the signature.

"Hmmm. Lazarus Bellwood. Never heard of him."

"You ain't plannin' on bracin' the feller right here in the lobby, are you, Jack?"

"Not on your life, pardner. Wouldn't mind, though, if you'd sorta keep an eye on him for me. Just report any suspicious doin's, if you could see to it."

"Sure, Jack, sure. Whatever you say."

With that, Memphis Jack Stump strolled out onto the wide hotel porch. He noticed a couple of the town's drunks sitting in rockers under the portico exchanging stories and sipping from bottles of whiskey. They looked up as Jack came out. Obviously uncomfortable at being caught drinking on the street, they quickly slipped their bottles behind their backs. They grinned sheepishly at the deputy as he looked away with a knowing grin and said, "Gents. Nice weather we're havin', ain't it?"

Both men grunted when he passed by on his way back to report to the sheriff.

"Name's Lazarus Bellwood. You ever heard of him?" Jack sat on the edge of the desk.

"No."

"You want me to keep an eye out for him? See where he goes, who he talks to?"

"Wouldn't be a bad idea. He's up to somethin', and I'd like to be at least one step ahead of him if it turns out to be what I'm thinkin'."

"You're thinkin', uh . . . what?"

"He doesn't haul that rifle of his around like it was made of gold for nothin'."

"He surely doesn't figure on facin' one of us with a rifle."

"He thinks he's damned good with that thing."

"How do you know that?"

"Remember, Emily got a shootin' demonstration from him."

"Oh, yeah."

Cotton looked at the clock on the wall as if he'd suddenly remembered something important, then said, "I'll be back later. Keep watch on the store." He gave Jack a nod and walked out the door as casually as a man with no worries whatsoever. Jack scratched his head and shrugged. He sat at Cotton's desk and began shuffling through a stack of wanted dodgers to see if any of them sounded like this fellow Lazarus Bellwood.

James Lee Hogg was making certain that everyone in the saloon saw that he was wearing a badge. While James Lee had no idea that Sanborn had not secured him an appointment as a deputy U.S. marshal, he *had* progressed far enough in school to recognize a few simple words. He recognized the word "Town" etched right into the top of that shiny badge. In the middle was a star. Across the bottom it said "Marshal." That was good enough for him, although he'd taken steps to scratch any reference to the word "Town" off the silver. In fact what had been written there was so completely obliterated, it couldn't have been deciphered by a university professor. But the word "Marshal" was as clear as a street banner proclaiming an upcoming horse race. And did he ever play up that word.

He stepped boldly up to the bar and stared the bartender right in the face. "Do you remember me?"

"Uh, yessir," came the response.

"Good, real good. You see this here badge I'm wearin'?"

"Uh, yessir."

"I'll expect a helluva lot more respect from you than the last time."

"Yessir, Marshal. What would you favor?"

"Whiskey and lots of it. Bring a bottle and I'll pour my own."

While he waited for the bartender to put a bottle in front of him and secure a clean glass, he glanced around the saloon. There were only a couple of tables occupied. One had four cowboys playing poker while one of Melody's whores in a low-cut dress observed them. She had her hand on one cowboy's shoulder and every few minutes she'd shake him.

She chided him. "Donny, if you don't start playin' better'n that, you'll never get enough money for a poke." The cowboy swallowed hard and gave her a hopeful smile. Cards were dealt. He picked up his hand and his shoulders drooped. He threw his cards on the table, got up, and left. The girl was left standing. She seemed to take it in stride as she turned her attention to the one with the biggest stack sitting in front of him. She reached over and ran her fingers through his hair.

"Ervin, it looks like you're about to earn a treat."

The one called Ervin must not have agreed, for he stood up, scooped all his earnings into his hat, and left right behind the other cowboy. "Maybe another time, Lucy," he called back over his shoulder.

James Lee looked at the girl called Lucy with a licentious grin. *I think I'm goin' to like this town*, he thought. He walked toward her. When she saw him approach, she gave him a coy smile and tilted her head.

"Lookin' for companionship, mister?"

"Yup. You and I can share this bottle and have us a grand old time," James Lee said, taking her by the wrist and pulling her toward the staircase like she was a rag doll.

"Now hold on, mister, we haven't even discussed the price."

"Don't care about the price. Just get your scrawny body a-movin' and let's get to it."

The girl looked around the room. There weren't any others lining up to be with her, so she followed James Lee as he stomped upstairs.

Lucy and James Lee could be heard laughing for nearly an hour before James Lee's voice grew into something angry and vicious. Suddenly, the sounds of pleasure turned to terror.

Lucy's screams could then be heard throughout the saloon. Melody bolted from her room.

"What is it? What's going on in there? Lucy, are you all right?"

Just as she began pounding on the door to Lucy's crib, James Lee Hogg burst out with a nearly empty bottle in one hand and a bloody six-shooter in the other, roaring with a villainous laugh. He stumbled past Melody, brushing her aside so hard she was nearly knocked over the balcony railing. His drunken tirade could be heard above Lucy's pitiful moans for help as he stumbled from the saloon.

When Melody stepped inside the crib, she took one look at Lucy, put her hand to her mouth and started crying. The poor girl was lying facedown on her pillow in a bloom of crimson. Her screams had become little more than a whimper. It looked like James Lee had repeatedly hammered her with his pistol.

"Somebody go get Jack! Hurry!" Melody screamed, "He'll kill the son of a bitch!"

Chapter 34

———✦———

Jack had accompanied Melody to Doc Winters's office. She'd had the bartender and a couple of cowboys who were drinking in the saloon help carry Lucy out of her crib, down the long stairs, and up the street to the whitewashed building that housed the town's only doctor. Jack couldn't tell if Melody's angst was because of Lucy or the gall of James Lee Hogg in disrupting the usually calm demeanor of her establishment. As she paced back and forth, wringing her hands and muttering one oath after another, Jack felt obliged to try calming her down.

"Melody, I'm certain Lucy will be all right. Sit in that chair over there and try to be patient. The doc'll let us know as soon as possible how things are goin'."

"I won't be satisfied until that animal is blown to hell and whatever's left of his unholy body tossed out for the buzzards to dispose of."

"You need to understand, I must talk to Lucy before I can go after Hogg. I have to know what happened. As soon as we know something, I'll get Cotton and we'll take care of Hogg. Don't worry."

"I want *you* to do it, Jack. I don't even want Cotton involved. This hits home for me, and you are my protector. It could have *been* me! Don't you see that? *You* do it!"

Jack bit his lip and turned away. He would have been more than happy to oblige Melody, but if he did it without Cotton's blessing, it could spell the end to his last chance at being a lawman. There were, after all, protocols that must be followed. He'd learned that lesson the hard way once before. He wandered over to the door. The three men who'd helped get Lucy to the doctor had disappeared back into the noisy, smoke-filled saloon, presumably to pick up where they'd left off with whatever game they'd been engrossed in when all the excitement began.

As he was deciding what to do, Jack heard the door to the back room open and Doc Winters stepped out. He was wiping his hands on a cloth and looking very grim. Melody rushed to him.

"How is she, Doc. Will she be all right?" Melody's voice shook as she looked to the doctor for hope. He dropped his gaze.

"It's too soon to tell, Melody. I've done all I can for her right now. All we can do now is wait and see."

Jack reached out to take Melody by the shoulders, but she shrugged him off and hurried out of the office. Jack watched as she left, then turned back to Doc Winters.

"Jack, I have to tell you I've never seen anybody so badly injured. He must have hit her twenty times with the butt of a revolver. Her skull was damned near crushed. Plain and simple, she was *bludgeoned*. I wish I could do more to help her."

"I'm sure you're doing everything you can, Doc. Thanks."

Jack hurried from the doctor's office with mixed emotions. He wanted to see James Lee Hogg gasping for his last breath, but he dared not do it without Cotton knowing why. Melody's words flooded his brain, his inner conflict growing by the second. Before stepping inside the jail, he stopped to glance up and down the street. James Lee Hogg was nowhere to be seen. As he went inside, Jack realized his hand was resting on the butt of his Remington and his thumb had cocked the hammer. Cotton was not in his office. Jack's thoughts of going about the situation in a professional manner were diminishing by the second. A fury was growing inside him almost to the point of exploding. He grabbed a shotgun off the rack, loaded it, and stormed out, heading to who knew where. Even Jack didn't know. He was driven by such a blinding anger, he had to keep moving. He thought about maybe stopping for a quick brandy, just to calm his nerves, but decided against anything that might slow his reflexes. Hogg had to be somewhere nearby and Jack was intent on finding him. His fear of losing his deputy's badge had been pushed back farther and farther in his mind as the image of that poor young girl, beaten to a bloody pulp, kept coming back, again and again. The fact that she was no more than a whore played no part in what drove him. She was a person, a young girl who'd done harm to no one, and now she lay unconscious at the hands of a man so full of evil it made Jack's heart hurt.

He rounded the corner of the jail to cut through the alley and came face-to-face with Cotton. "Whoa, Jack, what's got you so bent?"

"Lucy! Melody's young girl from Kansas."

"What about her?"

"J-James Lee Hogg! That bastard gave her a beating with the butt of his gun. Hogg's goin' to die and damned soon if I got anything to say about it."

"You're sure it was Hogg?"

"Sure as you're standin' here takin' valuable time away from my finding that rattler and cuttin' off his head."

"You're mad, I can see that. Goin' after someone who's a known killer when your head is full of hate is a good way for you to end up on your back. I can't have that."

"Try and stop me!" Jack tried to push Cotton from his path. Cotton wasn't going anywhere. Jack took a swing.

Cotton dodged and landed a left cross on Jack's jaw that sent him ass over elbows into the dirt. He was rubbing his chin as he tried to get to his feet, lost his balance, and fell back. This time he sat, blinking.

"What the hell did you do that for?"

"I'm committed to savin' your life, you dimwit. Didn't you hear anything I just said?"

"Yeah."

"Good. Then brush yourself off and let's go inside and make a plan. I'll gather some men to spread out in town and look for Hogg. You start loadin' some rifles." Cotton strode into the jail. Jack got to his knees, working his jaw to make sure nothing was broken, then got to his feet. He wobbled for a bit before finally getting a firm footing. He followed Cotton inside.

Melody burst into the jail, fuming and sputtering.

"What the hell are you doin' sittin' there as if a precious young woman was *not* beaten no more than ten feet from where we sleep every night? I told you what I wanted!"

"Sit down, Melody. We're workin' on a plan to corral this critter," Jack said.

"I'll *not* sit down!" Melody screamed. "Not while that animal is roaming the streets!"

"We need to put togeth—" was all Jack could get out.

"You two haven't the guts to tackle that son of a bitch, and you know it!"

"Melody, either sit down and shut up or get the hell out of here!" Cotton roared. He slammed his fist down on the desktop. Jack jumped.

Startled by his unexpected response, Melody whirled around, hands on hips, and made a beeline for the door. The last thing she said as she exited was "Never mind! I'll handle that bastard myself!"

Jack started to get up, but Cotton put his hand on his shoulder.

"Let her go, Jack. *We'll* get him; I make you that promise."

*   *   *

James Lee Hogg staggered into the dining room at the hotel. He saw Arthur Sanborn and dropped into a chair at his table. Sanborn gave him a serious frown, taking note of the man's bloody hands and the crimson on the butt of his gun.

"What has happened, James Lee? What have you done?"

"Nothin' much, Judge. Just a little dustup over at the saloon. I can handle it."

"Was someone hurt? You have blood all over you. Go wash up."

James Lee shrugged and stared across the room.

"If you've done something I can't undo, Mr. Hogg, you're on your own. You know that, don't you?"

"Yeah, uh, sure, Judge."

James Lee pushed out of his chair and slumped out of the room by the back way. He left just as the mayor was coming into the dining room.

Chapter 35

———◆◆◆———

When he saw Judge Arthur Sanborn sitting alone at a table in the hotel's dining room, Mayor Plume decided to take advantage of the opportunity to quiz the old man. Since he'd been in town, Judge Sanborn had scheduled no cases, nor had he indicated his preference for a place to hold such trials if he did.

"Judge, may I join you?"

"Why certainly, Mayor. Always happy to share a meal with a man of your caliber."

"Thank you, thank you. You are *too* kind," Plume gushed.

"You look as though you might have something on your mind. You looking to discuss anything in particular?"

Tugging at his collar in embarrassment for being so transparent, Mayor Plume cleared his throat and said, "As a matter of fact, Judge, there is a question I'm bound to bring up. That is to say a certain curiosity as to when you planned on having your first trial."

"I'm gathering information as we speak, sir. And I'll happily announce the first such exhibition of a properly run court's vital role in controlling the outlawry so often found in the Territory."

Plume gave the old gent a curious stare.

"Uh, I assume you mean the rustlers and shootists that roam freely about to do their devilry."

"Indeed, I do. Wherever there are men who take it upon themselves to place their own brand of justice on the populace, there will always be a need for a court to deal with those men in a proper manner."

"And that manner is . . . ?"

"Death, my good man. Death at the end of a rope or a gun."

"Certainly whenever there is a death caused by such a man, a hanging is proper. But there is also a need to deal with petty thieves and vagrants who prey on merchants in less serious crimes, but crimes nevertheless."

"Don't give a hoot about vagrants, sir. Murderers! That's all I'm interested in. And a spectacular hanging will be a good lesson to all who would indiscriminately impose their self-righteous authority upon the innocent." Sanborn's face had turned red in his rant.

Plume could say nothing. He motioned for the waiter to bring him some coffee.

"I believe I understand what you're saying, Judge, but as a man not well versed in the law, I'm really more interested in what having a judge right in our midst might mean to the community. Whenever a court is in session in other towns our size, business usually picks up considerably. The folks would like that."

"Ah, yes, I see where your interest lies."

"So, is there a trial of someone that I haven't heard about coming soon?"

"As a matter of fact, yes there is. Very soon."

"Wouldn't it be wise to set up a courtroom, then? The town doesn't have one, you know."

"Won't need one. We'll hold the trial near where prisoners are normally incarcerated and the sentence carried out. For me, that will be on the street for everyone to see. It will be spectacular."

"Y-you'd hold court in the street?"

"I believe that's what I said, yes."

"But the dust and dirt from horses and wagons passing by would be most disruptive. Not to mention the sounds coming from the saloon, dogs barking, horses whinnying. I fail to see the advantage."

"Fail as you will, sir. The site for my first trial is not only perfectly situated but most apropos."

Sipping from his steaming cup, Mayor Plume displayed confusion and surprise that a judge would not wish his courtroom to be properly appointed with a bench, chairs for a jury, not to mention for the many onlookers who would undoubtedly wish to see the doings. It was obvious from the mayor's words that he was unaccustomed to the ways of the law. At least, Sanborn's interpretation of it. Sanborn abruptly set his empty cup on the table and wiped his mouth. With that, he excused himself.

"Good day to you, sir."

Plume sat stunned at the conversation he'd just had with the town's new judge. He couldn't fathom how any judge worth his salt would actually believe holding court in the middle of the street would work to the court's favor, toward achieving a fair trial for some poor soul. His confusion also encompassed a fair amount of doubt about the sanity of such thinking. It just plain didn't seem judicial to him. If this man wasn't all he'd claimed to be, it was up to Mayor Orwell Plume to get to the bottom of it. If all was on the up-and-up, so be it. But if not, the sheriff should be told and appropriate action taken. Whatever the appropriate action might be Plume had absolutely no idea. Seeking out the sheriff was exactly what he intended to do.

Cotton's concerns about Sanborn being in Apache Springs were growing by the minute. After Jack made tracks for the saloon in an attempt to get Melody under control, the sheriff stood staring out the open door to the jail. He'd not seen Emily since she'd left to go back to the ranch. The latest developments concerned exactly how dangerous things were becoming and how it appeared that James Lee Hogg was completely out of control. So Emily didn't yet know about the prostitute's beating at the hands of one Hogg. Cotton knew he should have learned his lesson after the problems that arose from his keeping secrets from her before, but that had had to do with his own actions, not the potential for several lives to be affected by someone else's actions. And the consequences thereof. He was scratching his head, considering if he should ride out and tell her, or send someone, when he saw Thorn McCann coming toward him. *I'm not certain I'm up to listenin' to McCann, right now*, the sheriff thought.

"Sheriff, got a minute? There's something I feel obliged to discuss with you."

Cotton knew he was trapped. He just shrugged, went back inside, and dropped into the chair at his desk. He waved Thorn to a chair and offered him some coffee, which was declined.

"All right, McCann, what's on your mind?"

"Delilah."

"What about her?"

"For starters, she's the best thing that ever happened to me."

"Nice to hear it, but I fail to see how that affects me. Or why I might find it noteworthy."

"I reckon you won't, but there's a point to all this if you'll hear me out."

"Do I have a choice?"

"You'll be glad you did, assuming you'll give me your undivided attention for ten minutes."

"You got ten minutes."

"I got more than that, I got a proposition."

"Huh?"

"I seem to be a big part of the troubles that have been visited on you. If I hadn't found out from Bart Havens where you were when he hired me to help take you down, Arthur Sanborn would never have known how to find you. That old reprobate would still be lookin'."

"You told Sanborn?"

"In a manner of speaking, yes. Since he'd hired me to find you and bring you back to Texas, he asked if I had any idea where to start lookin'. I told him I'd hired on with a man named Havens to track you and that Havens might know. He told me to stay in touch."

"And you did?"

"Not exactly. When I realized takin' you back to Texas was the wrong thing to do, as well as dangerous as hell, I sent Sanborn a telegram sayin' I was no longer workin' for him. I told him I thought you were a good man and didn't deserve what he had planned for you."

"And he figured out where you were by where the telegram came from. He also figured out we'd met by your judgment of my character. That about the way it happened?"

Thorn hung his head and bit his lip. "Uh-huh."

"Your ten minutes are up. Go back to Delilah. She'll give you more sympathy than you're goin' to get here."

"I'm not lookin' for nothin' except a chance to make things right."

"And how do you figure on doin' that?"

"I got a friend in Santa Fe who owes me a favor. A big favor. He works for the governor."

"Go on."

"I got a hunch there's something smelly about Sanborn bein' made circuit judge. I'd be willin' to ride up there and maybe get a look-see at the appointment he's claimin' to have received. If you think that'd help matters any."

Cotton rubbed his chin pensively. He slowly began nodding his head.

"Matter of fact, I think it might help. And it *could* answer a whole passel of questions. Get some supplies from the general store and charge it to the town. Let me know the moment you find anything out, whether you figure it'll be helpful or not. And the sooner the better. Oh, and take the Butterfield. You still look a tad peaked after your run-in with the Indians."

Chapter 36

The day dawned with a slight overcast. Cool and breezy. Thorn McCann stood under the portico outside the Butterfield office awaiting the departure of the stagecoach that would take him first to Albuquerque and then on to Santa Fe. His shoulder wound was nearly healed but still giving him occasional stabs of pain. The doctor had told him not to worry about those twinges; they were normal. It would take time to completely heal. Those *twinges*, as the doctor called them, came frequently enough to dissuade him from trying to ride his horse all the way to the capital.

The driver and the shotgun guard stepped out of the stage office with a steel box between them. They hefted it up and dropped it into the forward boot. The driver then turned to the awaiting passengers and told them it was time to get aboard. Thorn stepped aside to allow the others, two men and a woman, to board before him.

He tossed his valise up to the driver with a groan, keeping another smaller bag with him. As he settled at a window seat, sitting next to the lady, one of the men across from him kept eyeing him. That made Thorn nervous. He didn't think he'd ever seen the gent before, but when you carry a gun for a living, there are probably lots of people you run across that you don't remember. Not all of them are that eager to forget you. The man kept staring at him. Thorn's uneasiness was growing by the second. Finally, after they'd been on the road for about a half hour, he spoke up.

"Mister, you've been eyein' me ever since we got aboard this buggy. Have we met?"

"Oh, yeah, indeed we've met, *Mr. Thorn McCann, bounty hunter.*"

"You've got a better memory than I do, then. So, who are you and when did our paths cross?"

"You really don't remember?"

"Nope."

"Three years back. Fort Worth. A gambling hall named Big Nellie's."

"Go on."

"You claimed I was cheatin', and you knocked me out of my chair and dragged me over to the sheriff's office. Then you demanded I be put behind bars. I never cheated at the pasteboards in my life. Never had to. I'm the best cardplayer you ever saw."

"I vaguely remember somethin' like that. So, what happened to you?"

"The sheriff couldn't prove I did anything wrong, and none of the other players claimed I had, but they ran me out of town anyway. Just on principle, I reckon. Cost me all my winnin's. Near to five hundred dollars."

"Sorry, mister. No way I can make it up to you now, however."

"You could cross my palm with five hundred greenbacks."

"Not likely. I'm flat broke. Besides, there must have been somethin' about the way you were shufflin' the deck or dealin' that raised my suspicions."

The man turned to look out the window without answering Thorn's veiled conjecture. He made not a sound the rest of the way to Albuquerque, even with two stops for food and a change of horses. The man's sullen silence had infected the other passengers, as well. Only the occasional flirtatious comment from the other man to the lady broke the silence. The lady did manage a smile at McCann on a couple of occasions. He returned it only to have her turn away suddenly, drawing a lacy handkerchief to her dainty mouth. *I wonder if she thinks I did her wrong somewhere in my past, too.*

As the coach lumbered on, hour after hour, he decided to dwell on something pleasant for a change: Delilah. That brought a smile to his lips.

"I just saw Thorn McCann boarding the stage. I suppose that means you aren't plannin' on makin' a fuss about the counterfeitin'," Memphis Jack said to Cotton as he approached the jail.

"Nope. That's a thing of the past. Instead, I decided on makin' a trade."

"A trade? What kind of trade?"

"I let the counterfeit charge go up in smoke if he can dig up a snag in Judge Arthur Sanborn's appointment that'll help me take him down."

"How the hell's he gonna do that?"

"Says he's got a friend on the governor's staff, that's how. If, that is, there is *anything* to find."

Jack raised an eyebrow, suggesting he had some doubts but was willing to let it go. He crossed in front of the sheriff's desk and picked up an empty cup. He lifted the pot and started to pour some. When nothing came out, he opened the lid and peered in. Empty.

"Someone around here drink all the coffee?" he said.

"Uh-huh."

"Why didn't that someone make some more?"

"I don't make coffee."

"Why is that? You too good to do such a menial task?"

"I'm the sheriff, that's why. I don't make up the bunk beds in the cells, either."

"We don't have bunk beds in the cells," Jack replied.

Without looking up from his perusal of a heavy, leather-bound volume that looked very much like a legal book, Cotton said, "That may be the reason."

Jack threw up his hands and poured coffee beans in the pot, along with a half teaspoonful of chicory, and then went out back to the well for water.

About fifteen miles short of reaching Albuquerque, the driver slapped the reins and started shouting to the horses in order to spook them into a run. The guard leaned over and yelled at those in the stage that they were about to be receiving visitors. Thorn muttered something about being damned tired of Indians. He leaned through the side window to see up ahead. There were two riders wearing sugar sacks over their head with holes cut out for eyes.

Bandits! Damned if I haven't had enough excitement for a lifetime!

He opened the door and swung an arm out and up to grab on to the top railing. He had to use his right arm, the one attached to the shoulder that *hadn't* recently had a hole blown clean through it, to get the strength to haul himself up to climb onto the roof. The guard saw his struggle and leaned over to lend a hand. Once topside, Thorn pulled his revolver and asked if there was an extra rifle in the boot. The guard said no. So there they were: a shotgun with two barrels and a smoke wagon with six shots. There was soon going to be a need for some very accurate shooting.

Thorn's estimate of two minutes was shortened to about thirty seconds as another masked rider came out of the brush barely ten feet behind them, just as the coach passed. He had a Colt in his hand and looked ready to blaze away. Thorn decided not to give him a chance. He fired at the rider with a sudden swing of his gun. The rider was obviously not prepared for such a quick response, as he hadn't even cocked the hammer on his revolver. He tumbled backward over the horse's rump. Landing on his head, he was dead before hitting the dirt.

The other riders, seeing what had happened to one of their own, made a dash for the brush. Only one made it. The shotgun guard unloaded both barrels of his twelve-gauge coach gun into the back of the slowest of the bandits. He wouldn't be much help to his partner in crime on any future get-rich-quick schemes—if, that is, he lived.

The coach barreled down the sloping road toward a curve the driver knew to be treacherous. He hauled back on the reins sufficiently to slow the team and get around the curve safely. Behind them, the third bandit was bent over his bloodied partner. He fired a couple of quick shots at the coach as it faded into a dusty haze. One shot sang past Thorn's ear and the other buried itself in a piece of luggage.

When the coach reached the Butterfield station in Albuquerque, the driver was quick to praise the fast action and deadly shooting of Thorn McCann. Thorn, on the other hand, passed his congratulations on to the shotgun guard. The two of them shook hands and Thorn headed inside to cool off. The stage to Santa Fe wouldn't leave until the next morning, and he needed to rest his aching shoulder. The pain he thought he'd left in Apache Springs had returned in Albuquerque.

Maybe a little whiskey and a soft bed will help, he thought, mounting the steps to the hotel. He looked back to see the passenger he'd apparently arranged to have jailed in Texas talking to a rider who had just arrived in town. The horse looked familiar. They appeared to be arguing, one poking his finger in the other's chest repeatedly.

That fellow, Thorn thought, *doesn't seem to make friends real easily.*

Chapter 37

————◆◆◆————

The peaceful, sleepy town of Albuquerque was any-thing *but* calm and restful that night. Thorn could hear shouts of a celebration of some sort, a mariachi band play-ing, people singing, and guns being fired into the air. *Those Mexicans sure do know how to have a good time*, he thought.

It was after midnight before the noises on the street sub-sided and Thorn could get to sleep. A half-empty bottle of tequila likely helped, though. He struggled to roll out of bed when the desk clerk began pounding on his door.

"Señor, it is time to rise. You said to wake you before the stage left. And now it is that time. You must hurry!"

"Okay, okay," Thorn mumbled. His best attempts to wake up were falling short. He fell back on his thin pillow. Twice. Finally, he was able to toss his legs over the side of the bed, reach down for his boots, and try to tug one of them on. He was failing miserably until he realized he had the wrong boot on the wrong foot. He cursed under his breath and started all over again. He sat up fully, stretched, and pain-fully reached a standing position to look into the Chatham

mirror above a pitcher of water and a bowl. He was greeted
with a frown. He splashed water on his face, wiped it off
with a towel, pulled up his suspenders, and left the room.
Stopping halfway down the hall, he turned around and went
back into the room. He sighed as he grabbed his shirt, picked
up his two pieces of luggage, and again tried to negotiate the
hallway. When he finally did manage to locate the bottom of
the stairs without tumbling down them, he saw the shotgun
guard leaning on the stair railing, grinning ear to ear.

"Figured we owed you somethin' for that fine shootin'
on the road, yesterday. Without your help, one of us might
not be here today to tell about it. We've been holdin' the
stage for you."

"Damned nice of you, son, thanks." Thorn followed the
younger man outside into the bright sunlight. Thorn found
it necessary to shield his eyes from the glare by pulling his
hat low over his bloodshot eyes.

As he got into his seat, he noticed that the man who'd
claimed he had been wronged was not on board. The lady,
however, was and she was beaming at his presence. This
time when he smiled at her, she didn't look away. He figured that amounted to a certain degree of progress.

Ten miles out of Albuquerque, on the road to Santa Fe,
Thorn was fully engaged in a cozy conversation with the
young lady. She wasn't beautiful, certainly not at all as
pretty as Delilah, but she was attractive and enjoyable to
talk to. It didn't take him long to find out she was from Ohio
and had trained to be a teacher. She'd heard there was a
shortage of teachers on the frontier, and she was excited to
make a place for herself. She said she had been engaged
once but that her intended turned out to be somewhat of a
rounder and she dumped him. *She's got spunk, I'll give her
that*, Thorn thought.

If the conversation hadn't been going so nicely, Thorn
might have been tempted to look out the window and watch
the scenery. But, of course, he was too busy engaging a

pleasant young thing to be bothered by scenery. As it turned out, that mistake nearly cost him his life. It was the bark of a rifle that brought him out of his reverie. One shot, then two, three. A bullet crashed through the coach, barely missing him. The lady screamed, and Thorn stuck his head out the side window just in time to see the driver tumble from his seat and plummet down a steep ravine that ran alongside the road.

Thorn squeezed out the door and, once again, found himself trying to hang on to anything that would hold his weight as he struggled to climb up top. It took only a second to see that the horses, panicked by the shooting, were racing hell-bent-for-leather toward a narrowing of the road between several huge boulders.

There was little chance of the coach making it through traveling at such speed.

The shotgun guard was doing his best to grab the one rein that was still within reach, while also pushing on the brake handle as hard as he could with his foot. His shotgun had fallen between his legs, into the forward boot. Thorn took over the driver's position and drew his revolver. So far, he hadn't been able to locate the source of the shots. After several attempts, he got hold of the one rein and began yanking on it. With only one, however, he was mostly just pulling the lead horse's head to the left, right toward the ravine. He reached down and retrieved the shotgun and shoved it into the guard's hand. He signaled that they should change places. He'd take over the brake and the guard could seek out the position of the shooter. With a broader pattern of lead pellets, Thorn figured they stood a better chance of hitting something while he wrestled with bringing the coach to a halt.

With every ounce of force he could muster jammed against the brake handle, the coach finally skidded to a dusty halt fifty feet short of the boulders, where, if they'd continued on at the speed they were, the stagecoach would surely have been reduced to kindling. The guard gave a huge sigh as he jumped from the seat and began gathering

up the other three reins. But before he could climb back
aboard, two men stepped from behind the boulders, both
pointing rifles at Thorn and the guard.

"Throw them hands up, gents, or say your prayers," one
of the masked men said. "And drop those weapons on the
ground."

The guard followed the instructions without hesitation.
Thorn wasn't quite as interested in acquiescing. He was
prompted to comply by the other bandit, who fired a shot
into the dirt two feet in front of him.

"The next one won't miss!" the bandit said, and Thorn
tossed his gun in the dirt.

The man's voice sounded familiar. Thorn searched his
memory for what face might fit the gravelly sound coming
from behind the sugar sack. *Sugar sack. That's the same
thing those owlhoots were wearing on the first attempt to
rob us.* That's when he remembered where he'd heard that
distinctive voice: the man on the stage who'd said Thorn had
wronged him. He also remembered seeing the man and
another arguing on the street in Albuquerque just after
they'd arrived there.

"All right, miss, climb down out of that coach and be
quick about it. I want everyone's valuables, and right now!"
The second bandit handed his rifle to the first one, then drew
his revolver, and approached the young lady. She stepped
gingerly from the coach, shaking like a wet puppy.

"I-I d-don't have any v-valuables," she stammered.
Something caught her eye. She was staring at the bandit's
shoes, dark brown brogans with a cream-colored stitching.

"Don't give me that bull, lady; I can see a broach around
your neck that ought to fetch a pretty penny."

"And I know who you are, too, you thieving coward.
Hiding behind a mask can't change those shoes. I remem-
ber them from when you were on the stage from Apache
Springs. You ba—"

"Don't be givin' me any of your backtalk, bitch," the
bandit yelled as he stepped forward, raising his gun to
strike her.

That was Thorn's opportunity to change the course of events. He dove for his revolver, grabbed it up in both hands, and rolled over while the bandit with both rifles fumbled to get rid of one of them so he could shoot somebody. Thorn thumbed back the hammer with his left hand and pulled the trigger with his right, a trick he'd seen Cotton use. He fired three shots, so close together they didn't register more than a single echo off the towering rocks. Both robbers lay writhing in the dirt. The one with the fancy brogans coughed a couple of times, trying to speak as blood bubbled from his mouth. He quickly stopped moving and died after one last gasp.

The other bandit was hit in the upper chest. He struggled to get his breath. He had dropped to his knees, then fell back against a boulder. Thorn figured the bullet had gone through his lung. He bent over the stricken man.

"Too bad you fools didn't learn your lesson the first time. I don't figure you're goin' to make it, friend. Any last words you'd like me to pass on to a mother, father, wife?"

"T-tell 'em I'm sor-sorry." He began spitting up blood. "Name's B-Benjamin Wil . . ."

He died before getting his name out. Thorn stood up and shook his head at the guard.

"I gotta tell you, mister," the guard said. "I'm damned glad you were with us . . . both times. When we get to town, I'm givin' up this job. Makes the fifth time someone's tried to hold us up in just the last month alone. And the driver, nicest fellow you'd ever want to meet, he didn't deserve what he got." The guard took off his hat and held it over his heart.

Thorn glanced around at the carnage. "I s'pose we best load 'em onto the stage and get 'em into Santa Fe. Have to send someone out to fetch the driver's body. We'll never be able to reach him down in that ravine."

The girl stood frozen with fear as she watched the two men pile the deceased outlaws onto the rear boot and strap them on. She blinked through tear-filled eyes. "Th-thanks, mister," she sobbed.

Thorn put his arm around her and walked her back to the open stage door. He helped her inside and then climbed up to take a seat next to the guard.

"I'm prayin' for an uneventful trip the rest of the way," he said. "But I do have to say, the Butterfield Stagecoach Company *sure* does offer a man plenty of excitement for his fare." They both chuckled.

Chapter 38

——◆——

As the day waned and darkness began its descent over the buildings in Apache Springs like pouring maple syrup, Cotton's thoughts drifted to sudden unexpected feelings of remorse. He couldn't explain exactly what had come over him, but when, as the town settled down for the night, he finally had an opportunity to sit in the stillness, accompanied only by his thoughts, a nagging fear crept in as an unwelcome stranger. *What would I have done if Emily had been killed by James Lee Hogg?* He shuddered at the thought. He began to blame himself for all the killing and his involvement in it. *Would this town have been more peaceful if I weren't a part of it? Maybe I should pack my things and move on. Leave Jack in charge. I always figured he'd make a decent sheriff given the time to shake off some shortcomings.* His remembrances of when they'd both been lawmen—before Jack went around the bend in a drunken stupor and accidentally shot a man to death—came back, not as regrets but as fond memories.

And then the trials he'd gone through when Emily was kidnapped, his feelings and his fears of that time, all rushed in like an overwhelming storm. *If I were still in Texas, she would not have had to suffer the indignities Virgil Cruz put her through. It was all because of me and the fact that I love that woman.*

How much death has been directly attributed to me? Havens would never have come here and brought his cutthroats had I not been here. And now my actions have brought Judge Arthur Sanborn to town seeking his own demented revenge—on me and my town. Evil seems to seek me out like a hawk seeks a rabbit.

He was brought out of his misery by the sound of boots on the boardwalk in front of the jail. He unconsciously dropped his hand to his Colt and drew it, placing it on the desk in front of him. Just then, the door opened and Jack stepped in, grinning. His smile changed when he saw the look on Cotton's face and the .45 lying in front of him.

"Hey, ol' buddy, why the firepower?"

"Uh, I reckon you caught me off guard. Lost in my own doom and gloom."

"You figure a boogeyman was coming in to grab you?"

"Somethin' like that. Why aren't you snuggled up next to that wh—er, woman of yours?"

"Not sure. For the time being, at least, I reckon we solved our little difference of opinion. Guess that's what you'd call it, or maybe it's just a temporary truce."

"So, she told you to come sleep in the jail until you come around to her way of thinkin'?"

"You all of a sudden some sort of a mind reader, Cotton?"

"Just an observer of things you seem unable to see, that's all."

"Like . . . ?"

"See what I mean?"

"I don't get what you're tryin' to say. I know you don't like Melody, but she certainly doesn't pull me around on a leash."

"So you say."

"Well, never mind me and my situation, what's eatin' at you that you can't go home and get some sleep, yourself?"

"You ever have terrible regrets that eat at you like the gangrene?"

"Some. I try not to let it get me down, though."

"Yeah, well you haven't had several piles of human waste come here to do you in. Try not lettin' *that* get you down."

"Which one of all them gunslingers you've had to deal with seems to be most distressin'?"

"All of 'em."

"Heavy load."

"Yeah."

"Since I'm havin' to bunk down here for the night, I thought to bring some liquid company. Join me?" Jack pulled an unopened bottle of brandy from a sack. He'd also put in some biscuits and a couple pieces of beef jerky.

Cotton drew in a long breath and let it out slowly. "Don't mind if I do." He reached into a desk drawer and pulled out a couple of small tin cups. "I just knew these would come in handy someday."

Jack smiled knowingly as he poured each cup nearly full to the brim.

"Now, let's talk over what's got you all tangled up in barbwire."

"To start with, I have absolutely no idea how to handle Sanborn. If he's really a judge, I'm sure to meet my maker, and soon. If he's not a judge, I can't just gun him down. He's never been known to carry a gun. And if I let him go, he'll not stop tryin' to figure a way to see me dead, not till the day he drops over himself."

"Hmm. That might be the answer."

"What?"

"If he was to, say, have a heart attack or a fatal case of the ague, well, you'd be free as a bird. Now, ain't that right?"

"Yeah, but you can't just will a man into a failure of his ticker."

"Might have to encourage him a little," Jack said, with a most devious grin.

"And how do you figure to do that?"

"You ever hear of some aged gent keelin' over due to a frightful incident, like almost bein' run down by a runaway team, or nearly losin' his balance and fallin' off a balcony? Or some fallen angel gettin' too frisky?"

"I suppose, but those are accidental, not planned."

"How do you know that?"

"Don't reckon I do, but—"

"But nothin'. Happens all the time. I know, I read about such things in a gazette once. Why, back East, there's been some poor women who got to be rich widders in some very suspicious ways."

"What's all this got to do with me?" Cotton scratched his head.

"Well, what if the old judge met with some bad luck?"

"Like?"

"Like drinkin' somethin' that didn't agree with his delicate stomach."

"What are you suggestin'?"

"Uh, well . . ." Jack raised both hands with a questioning shrug.

"Forget it, Jack. I know you're lookin' out for me, but I can't stoop to murder, no matter how dire my circumstances become. That's how I come to be in this mess in the first place." Cotton leaned back and downed the cup of brandy. "But, I do appreciate your wantin' to help. I'll figure it all out. G'night." The sheriff got up, wobbled a bit from the brandy, and walked out the door and toward his house, looking for some welcome sleep.

Chapter 39

Lazarus Bellwood left the hotel by the front door and went down the street looking in various windows as he went. He appeared to anyone watching to be nothing more than a man out for a leisurely stroll on a cool summer evening. Looking behind him, he turned suddenly into an alleyway between two stores and circled back to the hotel. He reentered the three-story building by the back door, checking and rechecking his back trail, taking care to be seen by no one. He quietly climbed the rear stairs to the floor Judge Sanborn's room was on. He tapped lightly on the judge's door, looking around nervously to make sure one more time that he hadn't been seen. The door opened a crack and one eye peered out.

"Come in, but be quiet about it," Sanborn whispered.

"I done what you said, sir, checked out the perfect place to do our deal."

"Good, very good. Let me hear about your plan."

"Well, sir, just like we done all those times when Lucky Bill'd get hisself tangled up with a shootist, I found me a perch up above the street, and when the other fella goes for his gun, that's when I'll plug the owlhoot with my Sharps. Never miss. Everybody always figured Bill done the killin', and you got him off with a self-defense claim."

"I know how we did it all those times before, Mr. Bell-wood, but this time is different. This sheriff is *very* good with a gun. He also has a curious deputy that'll likely be watchin' his back. This must be foolproof. No hitches, no mistakes. It must appear as though James Lee Hogg outdrew and outshot the sheriff, no questions asked."

"And I got me the perfect spot for just such a gunslinger greetin'"

"Not only must the place you're shooting from be perfect, your timing has to be down to the split second. Do you understand?"

"Yessir."

"Now, as at the other times, you pull the trigger exactly when the sheriff starts for his gun. James Lee couldn't possibly beat Burke, so you'll have to keep an eye on Hogg, as well. He's a real nervous type, and there's a chance he'll actually be dumb enough to try beating Burke."

"What'll I do if he does shoot and actually manages to hit the sheriff? Two bullets in the body is gonna be frowned on when the shooter only fired once."

"I've already thought of that. You ever heard of a dummy bullet?"

"Uh, no. What is it?"

"You pull the lead out of a cartridge and replace it with candle wax. The gun still goes off, but the only thing that comes out is a harmless wad of melted wax. That way, the sheriff only gets hit with one bullet."

"I ain't sure James Lee is gonna like it if he knows he's slingin' a candle at the sheriff. I figure he actually thinks he's gonna win the shoot-out."

"If he practiced for a month of Sundays, he couldn't beat Burke. Believe me, I've seen him. Fact is I was in the saloon the day he shot down my son. Bill tried to outdraw Burke when he saw him come through the door. Bill was pretty quick, but that damned Cotton Burke drew, shot him, and had put the Colt back in his holster before poor Bill hit the floor, gun barely in his grip."

"Should I tell James Lee what our plans are?"

"No. I'll be the one to inform our hapless gunslinger about what must happen, when it will take place, and where. Everything has to happen perfectly, timed to the exact second. If James Lee knows ahead of time what we're planning, he'll mess everything up. I didn't choose him for his brains, his expertise with a gun, or his ability to follow orders. I picked him because he's nothing more than a second-rate gunman with a nasty disposition and a powerful need of the almighty dollar. He's too stupid to be anything else. In fact, I may let you kill him when this is over. That way he can't blab to some lawman."

"I understand, sir. You can count on me to keep my mouth shut."

"Now, where have you chosen as your position to take the fatal shot?"

"Right about where I'm standin'."

"Here? From *my* hotel room?"

"Yessir. The angle is perfect, and I figure when James Lee calls Burke out, the sheriff will walk out in front of the jail. He'll likely start down the street toward James Lee, who'll be standin' right about there," Lazarus said, pointing through the lacy curtains to a spot right below Sanborn's room. "If he walks to that particular spot, it gives me a perfect shot, and I can watch them both without moving my head."

Sanborn's mouth twisted into an evil grin. "That seems almost prophetic."

Henry Coyote had spent the last two days squatting on the front porch of Cotton's house. He leaned his back against the wall with his Spencer rifle lying across his knees. He never took his eyes off the front of the jail, yet he was keenly aware of everyone's movements throughout the whole town.

Nothing got by the old Mescalero's notice. Jack or Cotton stopped by several times each day to ensure that the Apache had fresh coffee, food, and a blanket, in case he continued his refusal to sleep inside at night, when the air could get quite cool. One man whose movements had caught his attention was one of the town's newest arrivals, a man who went nowhere without his rifle, the one in the fancy scabbard. While the man had done nothing in particular to draw attention to himself, Henry Coyote could sense something was amiss. The way he walked, always checking behind him to see if he was being followed, avoiding conversations with folks he passed along the boardwalk, and staying in shadows as much as possible. Cotton had asked him to be especially watchful of the man's movements. He had no intention of letting his friend down.

Thorn was stopped at the gate to the territorial capitol building. He asked specifically to see Captain John Berwick and was told to wait. The guard left and returned several minutes later carrying a piece of paper with very official writing on it.

"Show this to the guard at the main door, sir, and he'll show you in to see the captain."   ·

"Thank you, Private." Thorn followed a brick pathway to the porch of the capitol. Another private was standing stiff as a board just outside the huge oak doors. Another soldier stood on the opposite side. Thorn handed the first soldier the paper and was ushered inside. Across a wide room and sitting at a desk that could easily have hidden a squad of soldiers beneath it was a man about Thorn's age in a snappy uniform with captain's bars on the shoulder. The captain seemed not to notice as Thorn approached.

"I see you finally conned the army into giving you a nice pay raise. When we were just lieutenants, I never figured you for a lifelong professional soldier."

The man looked up at the obvious insult. Then his stolid expression turned all smiles.

"Thorn McCann! Good grief, is it really you? How long have you been out of prison?"

He reached a hand across the desk. Thorn returned the favor, but with a frown.

"Nice talk from a friend, John. I've never been in prison, and you know it. Now, maybe a short stay in a jail a couple of times, but that didn't count." They both laughed.

"What the hell are you doing in Santa Fe?" Captain Berwick asked.

"I'm lookin' for something."

"Something or someone?"

"Depends."

"On what?"

"On whether the 'something' is granted."

"And that something is?"

"A favor. A very *big* favor."

Chapter 40

James Lee Hogg was hiding out. After getting completely sober, he found out he'd beaten one of Melody Wakefield's prostitutes badly during one of his well-known drunken furies. He had no doubt the sheriff would be hot to find him, even if he figured the badge he wore was legitimate. Considering his past with Cotton Burke, he couldn't count on leniency, either. And since the whole thing had occurred at Melody's Golden Palace of Pleasure and Deputy Sheriff Memphis Jack Stump was romantically tangled up with the whore that owned the joint, he was running from more than *one* lawman. He wasn't certain if Judge Sanborn had gotten wind of his blunder, but when he did, James Lee knew there'd be hell to pay. So, for the time being, he figured he'd better lie low in the woods above the town. He sat poking at a small fire with a stick, wishing he'd thought to steal some food before he took flight as if the devil himself was on his tail.

Just in case the judge still expected him to confront Cotton Burke, he figured he'd better sharpen his skills with

the .45. It had been a while since he'd faced another man
with the intention of putting a bullet in him. As a matter of
fact, he'd never actually faced anyone. Every man he'd
killed, all three of them, he'd had to ambush or shoot in the
back and then ride like the wind to avoid capture and hanging. As an accomplished gunslinger, he was nothing more
than a sham, a fraud. His hand dropped to the revolver he'd
carried for at least five years. Truth be told, he'd taken it off
a man who was lying dead drunk in the street one night.
He'd exchanged his old Colt percussion revolver, a .36-cali-
ber Navy model. He got a crooked grin whenever he remembered that night, wondering what that drunk thought when
he found his new Remington had changed into an old gun
with a tendency to misfire half the time.

He drew the Remington and picked out a target, a small
rock the size of a man's fist lying on top of a larger boulder
fifteen feet away. He held the revolver at his side, then suddenly yanked it up and fired. He blinked through the smoke
to see how many pieces he'd blown that rock into. As it
turned out, none. He pulled and fired again. Same result. He
emptied the cylinder, six shots total. He hadn't hit his target
once. And, as close examination revealed, he'd even missed
the larger boulder it sat on. He looked at the Remington like
there was something wrong with it. He stuck it back into the
holster without putting more bullets in it. The disgusted
look on his face told a discouraging story. He was no gunslinger, probably never would be. And he damned well
knew it.

*How the hell am I going to outshoot a man like Cotton
Burke? I'm dead as dead can be if I try facin' him down.
How did I let that old buzzard, Sanborn, talk me into this?
Oh, yeah, two thousand dollars.*

He sat on his saddle, which was straddling a fallen tree
trunk. He stared at the dying embers for a long time. He
needed a plan. Unless he gunned the sheriff down from the
darkness of an alley, he hadn't a prayer of coming out of the
mess he'd gotten himself in. He sat shaking his head, dis-
mayed at his prospects of living more than a few more days.

* * *

"What's eating at you, Cotton? You've been moping around like your best friend ran off with your woman, and we both know that isn't going to happen," Emily said.

"This Sanborn thing has me grasping at straws. How *am* I goin' to beat that old devil?"

"Come into the dining room and eat something. We'll talk about it. You probably haven't eaten anything since you rode out."

Cotton got up and followed her into the same room she used to feed her wranglers. She didn't have a cook, having chosen to save the money by doing all the cooking herself. She was good at it, and she enjoyed doing things around the ranch house. The hands all loved being served by the boss lady, too. She had several sets of china cups, saucers, and plates she'd ordered from a catalog. She said it gave the place a homey air. Cotton sat down, pulled his chair up close, and started to pick up the coffeepot and pour a cup.

"Let me do that, Cotton. You have a tendency to pour it too full."

"You're right. I am kinda clumsy around your fancy china cups."

"You're not clumsy, you're just . . . eager."

Cotton laughed at Emily's attempt to ease the situation with a compliment, or at least a sort-of compliment. Then his expression turned from light to serious. Emily looked at him askance.

"What is it, Cotton?"

"Eager. You said I was eager . . ."

"I didn't mean anything by it. I was just kidding you. You know that."

"Yes, of course. But that word has given me an idea."

"I don't understand."

"James Lee Hogg beat up that girl at Melody's saloon. He's on the run. He has to know both Jack and I are just waiting for him to show his ugly face in town. I figure if I went to Judge Sanborn and let him know all about Hogg's indiscretion and made him understand that Hogg's a dead man if he comes round, he'd be forced to change his plan."

"How do you think he'll take that?"

"The same way most people would, he's goin' to have to hurry up his plans to take me down. He'll also try to get word to Hogg to either stay away or to come sneakin' into town at night to back-shoot me."

"Wouldn't you be better off to face him in the daylight, out in the open?"

"Yes. But if I can make him rush his play, he might make a mistake. And that's to my advantage."

"Just how good is he?"

"I don't know. I don't know of any man he's ever faced down."

"How're you going to get Sanborn to lead you to him?"

"I think I'll just hit him with the truth. His marshal is a woman-beater and is going to jail for it. I'll let the old bastard know it's his duty to set a trial date as soon as I bring him in."

"Won't that make him tell Hogg to stay away?"

"Won't make any difference. He, or someone he sends to tell Hogg of my intentions, will lead us straight to him."

"You're going to be kept busy keeping an eye on Sanborn. Don't you think he'll know if you're dogging him?"

"I won't be."

"Okay, then Jack."

"Nope. Not Jack, either. I have a special weapon."

"What weapon?"

"Henry Coyote."

Emily poured another cup with an acknowledging smile.

Chapter 41

———◆———

Is Judge Sanborn in his room?" Cotton asked at the hotel's front desk.

"No, Sheriff, I believe I just saw him come down and go into the dining room. Shall I fetch him for you?"

"Nope. I'll just join him. He's, uh, waiting for me," Cotton lied.

The sheriff located Sanborn reading a newspaper and sipping coffee at a table across the room, somewhat away from any table where other patrons were eating. *I reckon he likes his privacy*, Cotton thought. *He'll want it even more after he hears what I have to say.*

Cotton walked up to Sanborn's table and sat. "Well, Judge, I hope you're enjoying our little town."

"I *was* enjoying the solitude afforded me here, before your arrival, that is. What is it you have to say? I'm sure you're not here just to share pleasantries."

"You are absolutely right. So I'll just have my say and leave you to your dinner."

"That would be most appreciated. What is it, Sheriff?"

"It's about some trash you brought to town, your deputy marshal, James Lee Hogg. He beat up a whore over at the saloon late yesterday in a drunken fit. He's now a wanted man and on the run. I'm surprised you haven't heard by now. When I catch up to him, I expect you'll want to set a quick date for the trial. I'll inform you as soon as he's in my custody. Unless of course you'd rather not be bothered, in which case I'll handle the matter myself."

The shock on Sanborn's face was the exact reaction Cotton had hoped for. Fear filled his cloudy gray eyes, telling the whole story. The old man acted as if he had suddenly realized he'd picked the wrong man to do his dirty work and he was now in a corner. And it was obvious he didn't like it one bit. He began chewing his lip nervously. His complexion seemed to turn paler as his expression darkened.

"Good day to you, sir," Cotton said with a snide, contempt-filled smile, as he strode from the room, thinking, *If the old man is going to have one of those "accidents" Jack suggested, now would be a perfect time.* Leaving the hotel, Cotton broke into a wide grin, giving a group of ladies on the porch a cheery "Howdy."

Arthur Sanborn saw his best chance to take his revenge on Sheriff Cotton Burke begin to go up in smoke. If the sheriff got a posse together and went on the hunt for James Lee, the chances were they'd find him. There weren't that many places to hide while staying near the town. Sanborn knew that Hogg wouldn't go far from the payout he expected for killing the sheriff. Therefore, Sanborn concluded that his only recourse was to enlist Lazarus Bellwood to find James Lee and smuggle him back to town. The plan wasn't complete as of yet, but if he could keep Hogg under wraps for only two more days, he figured to be ready to set the trap and have James Lee call the sheriff out. Only difference now was he'd have to get rid of James Lee, too. He dabbed at his mouth, pushed his plate away, and left the dining room.

When he got to the desk, he asked if the clerk had seen the man who had checked in carrying a rifle.

"No, sir, I haven't seen him since earlier this morning. Shall I run up to his room and see if he's there?"

"That won't be necessary. I'll do it myself if you can you tell me his room number."

Sanborn took the three sets of stairs slowly and gingerly, holding tightly to the handrail all the way. He had an arthritic knee, and putting weight on it gave him severe pain. He stopped halfway up, pulled a silver flask from his inside coat pocket, unscrewed the cap, and took a long swig. Replacing the cap, he took a deep breath and continued up the stairs, each step bringing a reminder that choosing a first-floor room would have been more advisable. However, after hearing Lazarus's plan for shooting Burke, he was glad for the pain the second floor brought him. It seemed a small price to pay for such sweet revenge. And its perfect vantage point.

Cotton's gleeful revelation about James Lee Hogg almost drove Sanborn to buy a gun and do the job himself. He wouldn't, of course, not because he thought it might place a stain on him as a judge, but because the truth was he was a coward. Always had been. In fact, his son, Bill, had suffered from the same trait. That's why the judge had paid large sums to Lazarus Bellwood to shoot any unfortunate fellow who made the mistake of crossing "Lucky Bill's" path. The scheme had worked several times, and each time with great success. Until, that is, Bill made the fatal mistake of pushing himself on a deputy sheriff's sister and killing her when she rejected him.

Having to climb to the third floor to reach Lazarus's room, Sanborn was nearly out of breath by the time he reached the right number. He tapped lightly with the handle of his cane. He heard some shuffling coming from inside, and he stood back as Lazarus opened the door only slightly. The first thing Sanborn saw was the muzzle of the Sharps rifle, followed by one sleepy eye.

"Oh, it's you, Judge. Sorry. I was taking a siesta. Won't

you come in?" Lazarus stepped aside as Sanborn breezed by him, making his way for a chair. He slumped into it and sighed.

"Would you like a drink of whiskey, sir? You look plumb tuckered out."

"No, thank you. I have my own right here," he said as he again pulled the silver flask from his pocket.

"Is there something wrong, Judge? I sure didn't expect to see you at my door." Lazarus seemed fidgety, more nervous than usual.

"Yes, there is. We have a very large problem on our hands. That jackass James Lee Hogg went and lost his mind while in a drunken rage. He beat up a whore at that bawdy-house saloon. Now he's on the run, and the sheriff's going after him."

Lazarus stood silently, stunned by the news. He looked around almost as if he were looking for a way out of there. He shook his head.

"What do we do now?"

"It is imperative you find him before that damned sheriff does. I'm guessing you know where he'd go to stay out of sight."

"Not for certain, but I have an idea."

"Good. Go get that idiot and sneak him back into town in the middle of the night. Bring him to your room and make him stay here until I'm ready for him to confront Burke. If you have to tie his ass to the bed, so be it."

"I'll do it. I'll leave right after the sun goes down."

"Fine. And one more thing, I figure we'll have to change the plan a tad to get that deputy in a position to take James Lee down as soon as you shoot Burke. That way, there's no one left alive to connect you and me to the killings."

"I understand, Judge. But how do we make sure the deputy is where we want him?"

"I've heard talk that the whore that owns the saloon has him wrapped up tighter than a pig for roasting. I'll have to drop a hint in her presence that there's a gunslinger looking to kill the sheriff. If she wants to make certain her lover is out of harm's way, she should demand he stay off the street at a certain time and day."

"Think she'll do what you suggest?"

"You bet she will."

"Will *he* do *her* bidding?"

"Not if what I've heard about their relationship is true. He'll do just the opposite, which is just what I want." Sanborn chuckled.

Lazarus walked to the window, parted the curtain, and said, "Judge, I think you've got yourself a mighty sound plan."

Chapter 42

———◆◆◆———

"Cotton! Bad news!" Jack was yelling at the top of his lungs as he burst into the sheriff's office. "That bastard Hogg is a dead man!"

"Wh-what the hell are you hollerin' about, Jack?"

"Lucy! She's dead. Hogg's beating ended up killin' her. Doc said she never regained consciousness. The son of a bitch crushed her skull."

Cotton jumped up and went to the gun rack, grabbing a rifle.

"We better gather ourselves up a posse. Round up some fellows who might have an interest in catching Lucy's murderer and bring them over to the jail, pronto. Make sure they can ride and shoot," Cotton said.

Jack turned on his heel and raced across the street to Melody's. What better place to find those who'd had a friendship of sorts with the young lady? Jack wasted no time at all. He came busting out of the saloon with half a dozen cowboys eager to take their revenge on James Lee Hogg.

Cotton stepped out and held up his hand. "Hang on,

fellas. I need to make certain you understand what we're set-tin' out to do."

"Aww, hell, Sheriff, we know you don't want no hangin' on our way back. We can wait for it to be done all legal-like. So feel free to go ahead and deputize the lot of us," said a grizzled cowboy who had likely had his share of friendly relations with the popular Lucy.

"All right, boys, as long as you understand the rules. Hold up your hands."

Six arms shot into the air.

"Okay, that's good enough. You're all deputies. Get your horses and meet here in twenty minutes." Cotton went back inside to retrieve some extra ammunition. Jack followed him through the door just in time to catch the box of cartridges Cotton tossed his way.

"We really goin' to bring him back for trial? Ain't that like leadin' the fox right to the hen house?" Jack said, with a tone of incredulity.

"You mean because the only judge we got is Sanborn? And of course everyone knows Hogg's in Sanborn's employ? And Hogg sure as hell ain't gonna get found guilty?"

"You know damned well that's what I mean," Jack said.

Cotton ignored the question. He continued gathering whatever he figured to need for the mission. When he had tied a wide kerchief around his neck and put on his hat, he led Jack outside to the six anxious cowboys, mounted and ready and lined up in front of the jail.

Cotton and Jack swung into their saddles. Cotton took the lead, but he had gone no more than a hundred feet when Jack pulled alongside him with a quizzical look on his face.

"Far be it from me to question a sheriff as famous as Cotton Burke, but don't you think headin' in the direction Hogg most likely took would be more productive?" Jack had kept his voice down so as not to let the others know there might be a disagreement building in the ranks.

"No, I think we're headed in exactly the right direction. Do you figure differently?"

"Well, you know I do or I wouldn't have brought it up.

Hell, there's nothing for fifty miles goin' this way. Hogg ain't real smart, but he's smarter than to put himself on a run across a desert when he could be hiding safely in them piney forests to the north."

"Uh-huh."

"I take it you think I'm wrong."

"Nope."

"You agree?"

"Pretty much."

"Then why don't we just turn around and pick up that owlhoot's trail in the right direction?"

"Because this is the right direction."

"But you just said . . . Aww, hell, never mind. We'll just follow the wind and see where it takes us. That'll do as much good as what you're doin'."

Jack's dissatisfaction over the way things were progressing was growing by the minute. He knew Melody would make his life miserable if he didn't come back with Lucy's murderer in tow. He also knew Cotton was the one in charge, and he couldn't change that, either.

Jack dropped back with the others, wearing a scowl as dark as the color the sky was turning over the distant mountains. Darkness would be on them in another hour or so. They weren't counting on camping overnight. The theory had been that the chase would be short. Hogg would be easy to find, and that would be that. They'd figured to grab him before he had a chance to get even farther away than he probably already had, and drag him back to Apache Springs; at least that was the way Cotton seemed to have figured it. Jack still hadn't climbed aboard that log wagon, though. That's when he made his move.

Jack reined his horse around and began heading back the way they'd come. He was a couple hundred feet behind the group when one of the other cowboys called out.

"Hey, Sheriff, where's Jack goin'?"

Cotton turned around and started after Jack like he was

a misbehaving child. He told the others to continue on and keep a sharp lookout for anything indicating they were on Hogg's trail. As he caught up to Jack, pulling alongside him, he reached over and took one of his deputy's reins.

"Hold up there, pardner, we haven't played this hand out just yet. I'll be needin' you when things start to get hot."

"The only things hot around here are me and the weather. Goin' that direction won't ever find James Lee Hogg, and you damned well know it."

"I do?"

"Yeah, you do. Why, only an idiot would try to evade a posse with nothing but scrub brush for cover. I could track someone across this sandy ground in the dark after havin' finished off a half bottle of brandy."

"Uh-huh."

"So why are you leadin' us nowhere? Don't you want to catch that no-good filth and see him get what's comin' to him?"

"More'n you know, Jack, more'n you know. Don't forget, he tried to kill Emily, too. You don't figure I plan to let him get away with that, do you?"

Jack rubbed his chin. "Naw, I reckon not. So why're we headed west?"

"Think, Jack, *think*! You already know the answer to that."

"What the hell are you talkin' about?"

"You said it yourself. If we bring James Lee Hogg back to town, he'll have to be locked up for trial. With that no-good Judge Sanborn callin' the shots, Hogg will undoubtedly be found not guilty and set free. I can't risk that. Besides, I know this wasn't what Sanborn had planned for me. I have to play it out."

"What if Hogg suddenly shows up in town and calls you out?"

"I'm countin' on it."

"Then what in tarnation are we doin' followin' a nonexistent trail to catch a killer who ain't gonna be at the end of it?"

"Come on, pardner. Use that thing sittin' on top of your shoulders. James Lee needs time and probably the cover of darkness to sneak back. That's just what we're givin' him . . . time."

"So this was a wild-goose chase all along?"

"Yup."

"Hmm, best you keep a distance from these fellas when they find out they been duped."

"You're goin' to take care of that."

"Me? How? And why me?"

"Simple. You tell Melody we were unsuccessful at finding Hogg, but that we'll be trying again tomorrow. Tell her she needs to keep these boys interested in keepin' up the search after some sleep. Tell her she can play an important part in seeking retribution for Lucy by plying these gents with lots of whiskey.

Jack grinned. He nodded and wheeled his horse around. "You're a devious man, Cotton Burke, a very devious man. But I like the plan."

Chapter 43

———◆———

Knowing his time was limited to set things in place for his plan to work, Arthur Sanborn made a beeline for Melody's Golden Palace of Pleasure. His footsteps along the boardwalk were accentuated by the distinct tapping of his cane with every other step. When he came to a woman's millinery shop displaying a long cotton dress with blue cornflowers, he stopped to gaze in the window, using the glass to see if he was being watched. He didn't think it was particularly strange to see a man peeking inside a woman's shop, but a couple of ladies passing by apparently did, as they clucked their tongues at him. He gave them a steely-eyed glare and moved on, tapping his cane ever more urgently. He started across the dusty street, stopping suddenly as a heavily loaded wagon from the lumber mill nearly clipped him.

"Hey, old man, why don't you look where the hell you're goin'?" shouted the driver. He whipped the mules with the reins to keep them moving.

Shaken by the near miss, Sanborn hollered back and

shook the cane at the man. He didn't really see why he should be careful about crossing a street. After all, he was a judge, and judges have the power over the life and death of any who would break the law. And, of course, that was his mission: taking the life of one Sheriff Cotton Burke in retribution for the loss of his only son. The fact that Lucky Bill Sanborn deserved to die didn't deter Arthur Sanborn from his own deadly intent. He wasn't even mildly interested in hearing about the whys and wherefores of Bill's demise; he was only interested in the judgment he fully intended to mete out. He stepped up onto the boardwalk in front of Melody's saloon a bit nervously, this being his first visit to such a disreputable establishment.

Stepping inside, he looked around the smoky, dimly lit room with tables full of men gambling or just chatting. Several men were leaning on the long bar, sipping glasses of whiskey, and two or three girls wandered the room wearing barely more than undergarments, at least that was Sanborn's impression. As his eyes adjusted to the poor lighting, he thought he spotted the proprietor, Melody Wakefield, standing at the top of a curving staircase, like a queen glaring down on her subjects. He went over to the bartender, ordered a brandy, and began the process of coming up with a way to approach a whore and engage her in a conversation that would lead to another piece of his plan being put firmly in place.

A disagreement over a poker game at one of the tables almost erupted in gunfire, but Melody swooped down and broke it up with a stern warning to a couple of cowboys before things got out of hand. Her method of dealing with disagreements gave Sanborn an idea. When she walked over to the bar, he approached her.

"Ma'am, I wonder if I could take a moment of your time."

"Sorry, mister, I'm not available, but there are two other girls here that I'm sure would find you charming. We don't get many men, uh, *your age* looking for a poke." She gave him a smile then started to turn her back on him.

"Uh, no, ma'am, I feel you've misunderstood. I'm not

seeking to become a customer; I'm merely wishing to talk to you for a minute. Won't take long. Could be important."

Melody gave him a quick appraisal, then shrugged. "I reckon that wouldn't hurt. Let's sit over here and you can buy me a brandy." She led him to a table near the stairs where she could see everything that went on around the whole floor. She motioned for Arlo, the bartender, to bring her a bottle of brandy and a couple of glasses.

Sanborn pulled her chair out and pushed it back in as she sat. He then took a seat himself.

"First of all, I have to commend you for the masterful manner in which you handled those two ruffians. Quite a lesson for your other patrons to see your authority over them in action."

"That's kind of you, but I have a feeling you didn't just want to talk to me about this little incident."

"You are most perceptive, ma'am. I am Judge Arthur Sanborn, the new circuit judge for the county. As a judge, I'm sure you can imagine the information I find myself privy to."

"A judge, huh?"

"At your service."

"This, uh, information, does it come at a price? And why would it interest me?"

"Why, dear lady, there could be no charge for coming to the aid of a beautiful woman. I do this to prevent any unnecessary bloodshed."

"Bloodshed? What do you mean? Whose blood could be shed?"

"I believe you are quite attached to a certain Memphis Jack Stump. Am I correct or have I been misinformed?"

"Jack and me, well, we're, uh, close, yes. But what does Jack have to do with this?"

"My dear lady, he's the one we're talking about."

"Jack? Are you saying he's in danger?"

"Imminent, I'm afraid."

"I don't understand. How?"

"Is he not closely associated with your sheriff, Cotton Burke?"

"That scalawag? Yes, yes, I suppose you could say that. But I can tell you he's not *my* sheriff. What does that have to do with what you're intent on telling me? He wouldn't hurt Jack."

"No, not him personally, but his association with your friend could, indeed, bring great harm."

"How?"

"I'm privy to information that suggests there is a gang of desperadoes on their way here at this very minute. Their intention is to engage your sheriff in a gun battle with the end result being his death."

"That means little to me. If I could get away with it, I'd probably shoot him myself."

"Ahh, yes, I believe I recall hearing about the two of you having a bit of a squabble some time back. But, that notwithstanding, this gang would have reason to include in their shooting spree anyone who might be siding with the sheriff. As a way of guaranteeing a successful escape, of course."

"So, if Jack were on the street alongside Cotton, he, too, would be a target?"

"That is correct. Now, me being a judge, of course I'd have to demand a trial for any such lawbreaking, but, with the sheriff dead, and possibly his deputy, who would be left to arrest them? We need to ensure the safety of your Memphis Jack. Do you understand?"

"I most certainly do. I thank you for your concern. You can rest assured I'll do all I can to keep my precious Jack safe." Melody got up from the table, shot Sanborn a smile, and turned to scurry upstairs to her room to mull over her approach to this new dilemma.

Chapter 44

"James Lee, James Lee Hogg, you in there?" shouted Lazarus Bellwood.

There was a rustling of leaves as James Lee burst from a thicket of brush like a bull moose. "Keep it down, you damned fool," he said. "You want someone to hear you and come roarin' in here guns a-blazin' and do us both in?"

"Course not. But the judge sent me to find you and bring you back. I been lookin' high and low for your worthless hide for nigh on to four hours in this stinkin' woods. Maybe you ain't noticed, but there's somethin' dead in here."

"Yeah, well, you found me. So what's the judge want me back for?"

"His plan, you idjit. Did you forget?"

"He cain't still be figurin' on me ridin' back into town to confront that damned sheriff. I'll get shot down the moment I'm seen on the streets. Hell, that gal probably poked every man in the county at some time or another. They'll all be gunnin' for me. How's she doin'?"

"She died from the beatin' you gave her."

"Damn! I hadn't counted on that. I didn't mean to kill her."

"Sanborn knows that. He was pretty pissed off at first, but he's got a new plan that'll work sure as bees make honey."

James Lee wrinkled his mouth and raised one eyebrow. He crossed his arms as if to say, "I dare you to tell me I'll be safe as a baby in its momma's arms."

"Better'n that," Lazarus said.

"I'm listenin'," Hogg said.

"Here's how it goes—"

"Uh, pardon the disruption, Lazarus, but did you happen to bring along anything to eat?"

Lazarus sighed and walked over to his horse. He reached into a saddlebag and pulled out some biscuits wrapped in cloth. He handed them to James Lee, who tore into them like a vulture on carrion.

"Mokay, go 'head wif da plan," James Lee said with his mouth stuffed full of the doughy biscuits.

Lazarus watched James Lee's disgusting eating habits with considerable disdain. At least *he'd* been brought up by a mother who taught him not to stuff your whole meal in your mouth at once. Obviously, James Lee Hogg had not been blessed with the same good fortune.

"Sanborn says I'm to sneak you back into town late tonight. We'll slip up the back stairs to the hotel and you can go to my room to hide out. No one will ever suspect you'd be brazen enough to saunter back into a town that's brimmin' with cowboys that'd like nothing better than to castrate you before hangin' you up to either choke or bleed to death, whichever came first."

"Uhgm," James Lee grunted, struggling to swallow that which he'd turned into a mass akin to wallpaper paste.

"Then, in two days, at the hour of Sanborn's choosing, you'll walk out onto the street and call out the sheriff. You'll be hollerin' somethin' like 'the sheriff is a murderer, a wanted man,' and then you'll say you've been sent to haul his sorry ass off to jail. Or shoot him down like a rabid dog if he don't come along peaceful-like."

"'N jus' where'll you be? Sittin' in the shade watchin' the fireworks?"

"You watch what you say to me. I'm likely the only person keepin' you alive. I'll be in Sanborn's room, behind his curtain with my Sharps. There ain't a chance in the world that the sheriff can resist the opportunity to face down the man who has accosted his filly not once but twice. With you already set for the confrontation, he'll be forced to come to you. He'll walk right into my sights. At the split second the sheriff goes for his gun, I shoot him through the heart. You'll take your shot a split second after I hit him, so naturally you'll miss. No one will even question whether you killed Cotton Burke. You'll get the credit all over the territory. Probably get quite a reputation for your feat of bravery."

"Wha' wif you're shlow in takin' yer shot? I could get killed." James Lee looked around for his canteen.

"Quit whinin'. You aren't goin' to get killed. You gotta trust me. I been doin' this for Sanborn for years. That stupid son of his called out some of the best shootists in Texas, and I never let him down, did I? If I'd had an inkling of what he'd done to the sheriff's sister, I'd have been there to stop the killin' of Lucky Bill. But I wasn't. So I reckon he wasn't so lucky after all, was he?" Lazarus said with a chuckle.

"Mokay," Hogg mumbled, stuffing the last biscuit in his mouth whole.

"With no moon tonight, it'll be dark enough to leave here in about an hour."

Hogg nodded his acceptance of the timetable. His nods weren't enough to convince Lazarus that the big, dumb oaf wouldn't manage to screw up the plan one more time. He could only hope he wasn't in the line of fire when it happened. He was imagining Hogg getting restless halfway through the day and deciding to take a stroll over to the saloon and risk ordering a whiskey in front of a bunch of cowboys who'd taken quite a liking to Miss Lucy. In such a case, he could see Sanborn completely losing control and ordering him to shoot everybody in sight, including Hogg, a feat better left to someone with something less limiting than a single-shot rifle.

A few minutes before midnight, Lazarus kicked a loudly snoring Hogg's bootless foot.

"Get up. It's time to shove off."

"Oww!"

"Oh, sorry. Didn't know that was your bum foot."

"Huh? What the hell . . . ? Ohh, it's you. O-okay." Hogg slowly stumbled to his feet, stretched and yawned, then shuffled over to where he'd picketed his horse. Lazarus led out, with Hogg sleepily wobbling from side to side in his saddle. Lazarus had mapped out a route back to town that would avoid contact with any ranch houses. He didn't want to bring attention to two riders traveling in the dead of night, something that would surely arouse the suspicions of a community already nervous since Lucy's violent death.

Lazarus had, from the beginning, been unable to understand why a man with Sanborn's cunning would saddle himself with a disreputable oaf like James Lee Hogg. Hogg had a reputation for being unruly, unreliable, and a poor shot. If Sandorn had picked a gunslinger of some note, the whole plan would have made sense, and likely progressed smoothly. Of his own volition, James Lee Hogg had caused havoc and brought too much attention to himself, and thus to any who might appear to be associated with him.

As they neared the town limits, only two or three windows had lamps lit. There were no signs of life on the streets, not even a stray dog to nip at their heels. The coast looked clear. Lazarus motioned for Hogg to follow him in. When they got to the back of the hotel, Lazarus dismounted, whispered for Hogg to do the same, and then tied the horses to a railing. James Lee followed Lazarus up the back stairs to the third-floor room where he was to be ensconced for a day and a half.

Lazarus unlocked his room and went in, then closed and

locked it behind Hogg. He struck a lucifer and lit an oil
lamp, turning the wick up only enough to make out what
little furniture there was. While he hated sharing a bed with
the unkempt Hogg, Lazarus had no choice. If the plan was to
work, he knew he must stick to the every detail as worked
out by the judge. It looked as though things had gone perfectly. No one had seen them, of that he was certain. He
could rest easy in the knowledge he'd followed his part to the
letter.

"Why is the judge wantin' to wait an extra day?" Hogg
asked.

"He wants the sheriff to stew a bit longer, maybe worry
himself into a frenzy," Lazarus said.

He smiled as he turned down the lamp.

At the back of the alley, a walnut-skinned man squatted
against a stockade fence in the shadow of a lone cotton-
wood, a Spencer rifle resting across his knees. He watched
and waited. The information he had gathered that evening
would prove invaluable to a certain man of the law. Of that,
he was sure.

Chapter 45

When the posse returned to Apache Springs well after midnight, having seen neither hide nor hair of the elusive James Lee Hogg, a disgruntled group of men bent on revenge disbanded in front of the sheriff's office and staggered off to their homes for some much-needed rest. Jack, never one to let conversation get in the way of his sleep, merely gave Cotton a half-assed salute and wandered across to Melody's saloon and her bed.

He staggered up the stairs, opened the door gingerly, and slipped inside. He pulled off his shirt, gun belt, and boots, and eased into bed beside Melody. He left his pants on. Too much trouble to remove them as sleepy as he was. He was snoring within a minute.

It felt as if he had no more than drifted off when he was quickly awakened by being punched and pummeled by a frantic, naked woman. Melody. And she seemed to have finally lost her mind.

"Jack! Jack! Jack!"

"Melody, stop! I need my sleep. Wake me later, please . . ." And he rolled over to bury his head in his pillow.

"No, Jack, get up! This is a matter of life and death. Please, wake up!"

"Uh-huh, life . . . and . . . deafp . . ." he muttered, his voice muffled by the deep folds of the down pillow.

"I'm not kidding, Jack. If you don't wake up and listen to me, you could be lying out there on the street as cold and dead as Cotton Burke."

Jack suddenly came awake. He pushed himself up on one elbow and met her face-to-face. What he saw was fear.

"Wh-what did you say? Cotton . . . what?"

"I had a visitor today while you were gallivanting all over looking for Lucy's killer. He made it a point to drop by and let me know about the danger you are in."

"What danger and what visitor, Melody?"

"Seems there's a gang of lowlifes on their way to Apache Springs. They intend to see Cotton Burke dead in the dust. This man very kindly warned me to keep you off the street so you don't end up like Cotton. He said these men are so evil they'd stop at nothing to get their quarry and anyone nearby wearing a badge. That'd be you."

"This visitor. Who was he?"

"Said he was a new judge—Sanborn, I think he said— and that he is privy to information plain folk don't know. Sounded like he knew what he was talking about."

"Sanborn, huh?" Jack mulled that over a couple of times, swung his legs off the bed, and pulled on his boots. He grabbed his holster, gun belt, and Remington .44. As he was finishing getting ready to leave, Melody's expression changed from despair to shock.

"Wh-what are you doing? Didn't you hear me? I said you are in *danger*."

"I heard you. Did this judge happen to mention when this was all goin' down?"

"I, er, think he said something about tomorrow . . . at noon. I . . . think."

"Good." Jack leaned over and gave Melody a kiss on the cheek. "I'll be back in a little while. Keep the bed warm."

When he opened the door, Melody put her hand to her mouth.

"I-I can't believe you'd take a chance on going out on the street when you know there's trouble brewing. What if those men get here early? What if the old judge got his day wrong? All sorts of things could happen that make it dangerous for you to leave this room. Haven't you been listening? Don't you understand?"

"Oh, I understand, all right. And I'll explain later, but in the meantime, don't fret your pretty face about me. Why, you might cause wrinkles to set in," Jack said with a laugh and closed the door behind him. The last he saw of her she was sitting up in bed with the sheet pulled up to her chin to cover her nakedness, wearing nothing but a frown that could burn a hole in shoe leather.

"Cotton, it appears the old judge has put his next move into motion," Memphis Jack said, as he walked through the open door to the jail at first light. The heat from the past few days meant windows were left open all day and all night, along with doors at least kept ajar by a rock or a chair.

Cotton, in early because of a restless night, looked up from pushing a cleaning rod with a piece of cloth soaked in cleaner through the barrel of his six-shooter. The desk was covered with various parts from rifles and shotguns, in addition to the sheriff's Colt .45. He didn't stop attending to the task at hand as Jack continued.

"Anyway, it seems Sanborn stopped over to Melody's while we were out with the posse. It sounds like you were right, much as I hate to admit it. He indicated to her that some *owlhoots* are on their way to town to gun you down. He let her know in no uncertain terms that I should stay out of the way and I wouldn't get hurt."

"Nice to know he's concerned over *your* welfare."

"Kinda what I thought, too. Why, the more I think about

it, I could grow to like the old buzzard." Jack laughed. Even Cotton found that humorous.

"Time to prepare for Sanborn's version of Armageddon." Cotton stopped what he was doing and leaned back in his captain's chair. "Strange as it sounds, I'm lookin' forward to gettin' the whole thing behind me."

"Unless, of course, it all turns sour and it happens he had planned farther ahead than we figure."

"There's that possibility. But I kinda doubt it."

"Why's that?"

"Sanborn has always been a man to take his time conjurin' up some evil doin's and never wavering from 'em. He doesn't seem to favor last-minute changes."

"Hmm. I reckon I see what you mean. James Lee Hogg's crazy antics would have put most normal-thinkin' men to scrub the plan and come up with another. Or leave town altogether."

"Exactly. Jack, I do believe there's hope for you yet."

"So, you still expect to be meetin' Hogg all by himself?"

"Not really 'all by himself.' There's that other element I told you about."

"Oh, yeah, Lazarus Bellwood."

"Unless I'm way off the trail, he's in it up to his neck. The very same neck we'll hang him by if he goes through with Sanborn's orders."

"You seem pretty confident you have it all figured out. I hope to hell you're right. I'd hate to become sheriff by an unfortunate accident," Jack said, turning to step back outside.

"Where you goin'?" Cotton asked.

"I didn't get a chance to eat anything. I need a little something to wake me up."

As Jack was leaving, Henry Coyote strolled in.

"I'm glad you're here, Henry. You get what I asked for?" Cotton said.

The wily old Mescalero smiled as only he could.

"You got coffee? Trade for information," he said with a chuckle.

Chapter 46

James Lee Hogg awoke before dawn. His mouth was dry, and he had the jitters. He hadn't had a drink of whiskey since the day he'd lost control and smashed Lucy's head in with the butt of his gun. His stomach was turning over from lack of food, too. *I can't stay cooped up in this dismal room for another twenty-four hours, no matter what that jackass Sanborn says. I gotta get me somethin' to eat and a bottle of whiskey to wash it down.*

With that thought in mind, he stood up, a little wobbly at first, then started across the room. Four steps from the bed he stumbled and fell. Hard. Hitting his head on the floor.

"Wh-what the hell!!" Lazarus sat up. James Lee was lying across his legs, trying to sit up as he rubbed his forehead. "What're you doin' up wanderin' around, James Lee? Damn you anyway."

"I didn't know you was lyin' on the damned floor. What're you doin' there, you idjit?"

"Just what I'm bein' paid to do, watch over you to make

sure you don't go doin' somethin' stupid . . . again. Now, get off me and go back to bed."

James Lee's face was flushed with anger at the dressing down by someone he considered his inferior. Hadn't Sanborn originally told him *he* was the man in charge? If so, why was he taking orders from this scrawny, rifle-toting nobody? After all, at least in his mind, he was a gunslinger, bounty hunter, and marshal, even if his badge *was* a fake. He did enjoy puffing out his chest and playing the tough guy. He sat back on the edge of the squeaky bed to ponder the possible ramifications of any disobeying of Lazarus's command he might be tempted to consider.

"I, uh, need to go out back. Duty calls," he muttered.

"Oh, all right. Go down the back stairs and don't let no one see you. I'll be watchin' from the window. Get back soon's you're done."

"I'm hungry, too. A man's got to eat."

"When you're back in the room, all safe and sound, I'll go down and get us some victuals."

James Lee didn't like being cooped up. He knew he'd screwed up seriously by getting drunk and killing that prostitute, but he was about to crawl out of his skin waiting for some action, the kind Sanborn was paying him for. He wanted to get it over with, collect his money, and move out of this dismal part of the country.

"All right." James Lee pulled up his suspenders and boots and stomped to the door.

"Uh, don't forget, James Lee, I'll be watchin'."

Lazarus's stern warning just about pushed James Lee over the edge. He held on, staring at the wood grain of the pine door, gripping the handle hard enough to squeeze water out of it, then flung the door open and stormed down the hall and down the back stairs. *Maybe I'll come back and maybe I won't, you little weasel. That'd teach you a thing or two.*

"Okay, Henry, what have you seen?" Cotton leaned on the desktop, clutching a hot cup of coffee in both hands. He hadn't slept well for the last several nights, and the only way he could cope with the circumstances of Judge Sanborn being so close was to guzzle coffee pretty much all day long.

"Man with fancy rifle sneak other man into hotel in dark. They go up back way."

"Could you tell for sure it was James Lee Hogg?"

"No mistake bad foot."

"Anything else you can tell me?"

"Need coffee. Remember better."

Cotton laughed out loud. "Grab a cup off the counter and fill 'er up. Drink all you want."

Henry was all smiles as he was, probably for the first time, allowed to serve himself.

"Could you tell which room they went to?" Cotton asked, sitting back.

"Make only small light. But saw them move about in room at back."

Cotton thought about that. Such a position would give Lazarus no chance at all for a shot at him. Then it hit him. "Which floor?"

Henry looked at him quizzically. "Floor?"

"Where was room located in building? Up high, in middle, down low?"

"Ahh," Henry said, grasping the concept of floors. "Up high."

Just then Jack came back to the jail, gnawing on a thin piece of steak between two pieces of bread, took off his hat, wiped his brow, and sat on the edge of the desk.

"Whew, it's already building up to be a scorcher. Just checking with shop owners on my way to the restaurant for any more break-ins 'bout sapped me."

"Have some coffee, Jack."

"Coffee? Are you crazy? Didn't you hear what I said? It's hotter than Billy-be-damned out there. Hot coffee isn't the solution I'm lookin' for." Jack shook his head as if Cotton had lost his mind. Cotton just smiled and turned back to Henry.

"I'm goin' over to the saloon for a beer. It may not be

cold, but it sure won't burn my lips," Jack said. He spun around and sauntered back outside, his sandwich half eaten.

"Now that we got that settled, I think I got Sanborn's plot figured out, Henry. I talked to the desk clerk at the hotel, and he said he'd put Sanborn in the second-floor room, front corner. That would give someone a perfect shot at the street out front of the hotel. A sharpshooter couldn't miss his target from there."

"You think that his plan?"

"Indeed I do. In fact the very thought of it has brought several incidents to mind that no one had ever given any thought to."

"What that?"

"Every time Lucky Bill Sanborn faced a man down, it was in the street, in front of the hotel, right out in the open. Every time his opponent drew, he was instantly blown to hell. It looked to everyone like Bill had done the killin'. It was never questioned. Besides, who was goin' to question a judge's son?"

"You think other man doing shooting?"

"I'm afraid so. Even though no one ever saw anyone else. Lookin' back, the whole thing makes a lot of sense."

"You think it man with rifle?"

"I never met the man, but if it was him, I figure *that* was his message when he went out to Emily's ranch to show her how good he was with a rifle. He probably had orders to throw a scare into me."

"Teddy say he very good."

"Yep, and I need you to continue keepin' an eye on him. Just don't let him see you. He might get spooked and do somethin' we aren't expectin'."

"I watch good. He no see. I get more coffee now." Henry scooted his chair back and went to fill his cup.

Cotton interlaced his fingers behind his head and sat back with a satisfied grin.

Looks like for once I'm ahead of you, you scheming old buzzard.

Chapter 47

Thorn McCann sat across from his friend, Army Captain Berwick, pouring each of them a glass of the finest Kentucky bourbon they could find. The bartender guaranteed it was the real thing, and he demonstrated that point by showing them the wax seal around the cork. That was good enough for Thorn, who loved a good whiskey, but truth be known, he couldn't tell if it came from Kentucky, Scotland, or someone's backyard still. Their glasses clinked and were raised in a toast, then quickly consumed. Thorn hastened to pour another round.

"Good whiskey, Thorn, thanks. But you haven't told me yet about that favor," Captain Berwick said, one eyebrow raised in curiosity, mixed with a touch of cynicism. He'd known Thorn McCann from when they both served in the army at the beginning of the Indian Wars. That was before Thorn discovered how little money he got paid, even as a lieutenant, for risking his life in extremely rough conditions. Thorn resigned his commission and began wandering all over looking for opportunities for easier money with fewer risks. Being a bounty hunter had only marginally met his requirements.

"It isn't exactly for me. A friend is in some danger, and this favor could be a matter of life or death." Thorn took another swig from his glass.

"Well, you better get on with it or the governor will start thinking I've been gone from my post too long and figure to bust me back to lieutenant," Berwick said with a smirk.

"Oh, yeah, sorry. Well, here's the way it lays out. A man named Arthur Sanborn blew into Apache Springs—the town where I'm currently livin'—claimin' to be a newly minted circuit judge. Told everyone who'd listen that Governor Wallace gave him the appointment. Happened real recent. You know anything about this?"

Berwick leaned back with a burst of laughter. He shook his head.

"Hell, Thorn, someone's been yanking your leg. That old fool sat in the waiting room outside the governor's office for damned near a whole day expecting me to talk the governor into bestowing a judgeship to him, and him without any credentials whatsoever."

"None?"

"Not a whit. What an idjit."

"So do you mean the governor flat turned him down?"

"Several times. Yep. Governor Wallace is a shrewd man, and you don't pull the wool over his eyes easily. The governor would be more likely to make *you* a judge than that old scalawag."

Thorn leaned back and smiled. Satisfied he'd found what he needed, he reached over and poured another round for them both. He held his glass up.

"Don't suppose you'd be willin' to put that in writin' for me, would you?"

"Why not? Can't have men like that misrepresenting themselves in the governor's name, now, can we? I'll make sure folks'll know it's official because it'll have the governor's seal on it."

Each man downed his glass and started back for the

captain's office. The captain pulled an important-looking piece of stationery from a drawer, took a pen, and dipped it in the inkwell on his desk. He then wrote out all that he'd told McCann, folded the paper, stamped it with the seal, and handed it to him.

"Here's to a governor with integrity," Thorn said, as he put the paper in his pocket. He reached out to shake the captain's hand. "And to an old friend."

"Thanks. Oh, since you've been hanging around Apache Springs *and* Silver City, Thorn, maybe you could make a couple inquiries about something the governor is interested in."

"What would that be?"

"There've been rumors floating around that someone has been spreading some counterfeit money. See if you can put the rumor to rest, or maybe ferret out the culprit, if there is one."

"I—uh, will do my best, Captain. Is there any reward if I can find out?"

"It's my considered opinion that Governor Wallace would be sufficiently appreciative of putting a stop to such activity to approve a reward."

"Got any idea just how big a reward that might amount to?" Thorn asked, leaning forward and narrowing one eye.

"It hasn't been discussed in much detail, but I wouldn't be surprised to see something like a couple thousand dollars change hands. Let me know if it interests you, Thorn."

"Oh, it interests me. I don't have to think on it. You can bet your britches it does. I'll do some askin' around and see what I can come up with," Thorn said, eagerly. He stuck out his hand. Berwick took it and they shook.

"Wish I could stay and jaw with you a bit, Thorn, but duty calls. I'm sure you see this pile of papers that need attending to before the governor gets back to town. Keep in contact." Berwick quickly returned his attention to the papers on his desk.

"Good to see you, too, Captain, and thanks for your help," Thorn called out as he left the office.

* * *

Shortly after nightfall, Lazarus tapped lightly on Sanborn's door. He heard someone moving about inside, then the door eased open a crack. He could see little more than one sleepy eye peering out at him.

"Who is it and what do you want?" Sanborn said with a grumpy whisper.

"It's me, sir, Lazarus, and I got a problem."

"Come in and be quick about it."

Inside, the judge struck a sulfur and touched it to an oil lamp. He blew out the flame and sat back on the edge of his bed.

"All right now, what's this big problem? Hogg didn't get away from you, did he?"

"Not yet, but that don't mean he ain't been tryin' his damnedest."

Sanborn let out a deep sigh. He began muttering under his breath. There was just enough light in the room for Lazarus to make out a reflection of the lamp's flame flickering in Sanborn's eyes, as if the devil himself was inside, working his evil magic straight from hell. The whole thing made Lazarus shiver.

"Then there's only one thing to do, strike before that bumbling fool ruins everything."

"What do you suggest, sir?"

"We'll move our plan up earlier in the day. Instead of waiting till afternoon, we'll do it in the morning, first thing. The light should be sufficient for your shot. Go get Hogg and bring him down here. I've got to make him see the plan clear as day, which for his dimwitted mind may be asking too much. But we don't have time to find someone else to take his place. I've waited far too long for my revenge to wait longer on account of some fool that can't control his urges."

Lazarus didn't move. The look on his face suggested he wanted more.

"What's eating you, Lazarus? Spit it out."

"I was just wonderin' why you needed to be a judge if you just intended to shoot Burke from the start."

"Being a judge carries with it a certain unquestionable power. When James Lee goes out there on my orders to confront the sheriff, it makes it all legitimate. And it makes our getaway easier. I won't have to explain anything to anyone. Besides, I want Burke shot down in the same manner as we did it every time that Bill got himself in over his head. Does that clear it all up for you?"

"Yessir, it does."

Lazarus slipped out the door and raced up the back stairs. When he got to his room, he found the door ajar. "Hogg. You awake? Hogg!"

When he got no response, he lit a lamp, and made the sudden chilling realization that James Lee Hogg was not in the room. Lazarus went to the window to see if he could spot Hogg on his way somewhere. He knew he had to stop him before another catastrophe occurred from James Lee's crazed impulses. Seeing no trace of him, Lazarus ran down the stairs to the front desk. The night clerk was sitting on a stool, chin held in his hands, nodding. He came fully awake at the sound of Lazarus's stumbling approach.

"H-have you seen a large man with a limp come through the lobby?"

The surprised clerk shook his head.

In a near panic, Lazarus ran out the front door, into the street, then around the side to the alley. *What the hell am I goin' to do now? Sanborn's gonna make my life hell for lettin' Hogg slip away.* As he stood there, shaking and grumbling to himself, a dark figure ambled up behind him.

"What're you doin' in the alley, Lazarus? Lost somethin'?"

The sound of Hogg's voice both scared and relieved him.

"Where the hell you been, you son of a bitch? You nearly took ten years off my life."

"I had to visit the outhouse."

"You already went out there once today."

"So what? That was this mornin'. When a man has to

go, he has to go. Ya can't take it back. I a'ready done did it."
Hogg gave Lazarus a big grin. "What'd you need me for,
anyway?"

"Sanborn needs to see you right away. C'mon." Lazarus
grabbed Hogg by the sleeve and started to tug him toward
the back stairs. Hogg pulled away with a growl.

"Don't never lay a hand on me again, Lazarus; I don't
like it one damned bit. Besides, what could be so important
he can't wait till tomorrow?"

"Oh, quit your fussin'. Sanborn's awaitin', and he don't
like to have to twiddle his thumbs for nobody. Neither those
he likes or those he don't like. And right now, you ain't his
favorite person." Lazarus started to lead off, thought better
of it, and waved Hogg in front of him. "And if I was you, I
wouldn't bring up the whys or wherefores of Sanborn's
thinkin'. He may not carry a gun, but that don't mean he ain't
dangerous."

"I appreciate your lookin' out for me, Lazarus, I truly
do." Hogg put his hand on his revolver, eased it from the
holster, cocked it, and aimed it at Lazarus. "But I think it's
time you quit treating me like your ignorant half brother.
Understand? Or that fancy rifle of yours will be lookin' for a
new owner. And I'm just the one to help it on its way."

Chapter 48

———◆◆◆———

When Jack walked in later in the evening, after checking the town for vagrants or break-ins, Cotton was busy drawing some sort of diagram on the back of a wanted dodger with barely more than a stub of a pencil. Jack walked up to the sheriff, leaned over, and said, "You're better at drawin' flies than you seem to be at drawin' pictures."

Cotton ignored his sharp-tongued deputy.

Unfazed by his opinion's rejection, Jack took up a seat across from the desk and continued a steely-eyed perusal of Cotton's attempts at artistry. He didn't say anything, content to watch for several minutes before curiosity got the best of him.

"All right, you can't just ignore me forever! What the hell are you doin'?"

"Makin' a map."

"Map? You goin' somewhere?"

"Nope. You are."

"Whoa! What's that mean? I got no plans to leave here."

Cotton leaned back, turned the paper around, and said, "Lean closer and learn your fate."

Jack did just that. He frowned for a couple seconds, then, realizing what he was looking at, he smiled.

"Ahh, I understand now. You've mapped out your movements and where you plan to stand when James Lee Hogg calls you out, right? Right there where that 'X' is?"

"Close. Except it won't be *me* facin' Hogg. What reason could you conjure up for me to draw a map of movements for myself? I think I can remember where the hotel is."

"Well, who then?"

"Come on, Jack, you're not stupid. Think about it."

"I'm thinkin' you've lost your mind. But I still don't get it."

"All right. Listen up. We have to figure Sanborn will make Hogg appear in the street hollerin' somethin' or other about me bein' a murderer and that he's got to put me under arrest. Right?"

"Sounds right. But Hogg, himself, is wanted for murder. And he knows it."

"Yep. And now Sanborn knows it, too. All the more reason to send Hogg out there to call me out. He knows I'll show up."

"I see your reasonin'."

"We also know Sanborn is a creature of habit. He makes plans and doesn't let anything stand in his way. He has had this confrontation planned down to the second, and you can bet he'll be right up there in his room watchin' every move. He'll take no chances on missin' the sight of his enemy gettin' plugged. His sharpshooter will be beside him taking a bead on my chest. You still with me on this?"

"Every step. So why the map?"

"If we're to beat this evil old man at his game, we have to be a step ahead and throw a brandin' iron into his spokes. And it's a game Sanborn has played many times before."

"That's where you're losin' me. How do we do that?"

"We don't. You do."

Jack's eyes shot open wide with surprise. He began to sputter.

"W-what d-d'you mean? Me? Do what?"

"How do you think you'll look wearin' one of my shirts, my Stetson, and my gun belt?"

"Like I'm swimmin' in someone else's castoffs, that's how I think I'd look."

"Hmm, I might get Emily to do a little needlework. You'll look fine."

"Let me get this straight. You're sendin' me out to brace that asshole Hogg, wearin' your clothes. Do I have this correct?"

"You do."

"Are you suggestin' I have to beat Hogg to the draw or go down in the street? While you're doin' . . . what? And how am I supposed to be the brandin' iron in the spokes?"

"Jack, quit your bellyachin'. *Emily* could beat Hogg to the draw. While you're toyin' with that oaf, I'm goin' to be puttin' a halt to the *real* shooter in this devilish scheme."

"You ain't figurin' that person to be Arthur Sanborn, are you?"

"Hell, no! You're forgetting about the man who's been hangin' back in the shadows all along, Lazarus Bellwood, a true sharpshooter and a cold-blooded murderer of the first degree."

"I still don't understand why you made a map."

"Because I want you to memorize the *exact* route and the *exact* place you are to stand in the street. It's very important for you not to be exposed to Bellwood's rifle before everything is ready. Can you do that?"

"Yeah, I suppose."

"Good. Now, let's go over it and I'll explain why every detail must be followed *exactly* as I've laid it out."

After changing shirts and buckling up the cartridge belt, Jack kept shifting around, changing positions, practicing

reaching across his stomach, trying to get used to wearing
Cotton's cross-draw gun belt and holster. He wasn't finding
the transition an easy one. Also, the Colt .45 felt more than
a little awkward to a man used to a Remington. He hefted
each as if to determine a difference in weight. Cotton could
see his deputy's discomfort at the differences and decided
to change his mind about the gun. Everything had to appear
natural. Nothing to give away the switch before he was
ready.

"It appears you don't seem that all-fired eager to try out
my Colt. So while there isn't one chance in hell that James
Lee Hogg could outdraw you even if you were buried in
sand up to your chin, I'm goin' to let you use your Remington instead. I don't know how, but I suppose somethin'
could happen to come along and muddy the water. Besides,
Sanborn hasn't seen enough of either of us to notice we
carry our guns differently."

"Thanks, Cotton. I'll feel better with a smoke wagon
I'm familiar with." Jack removed Cotton's rig and grabbed
his own off the desk.

"Hogg'll be so damned nervous about his big chance to
get at me, he'll never notice what gun you got on anyway.
Besides, by the time you get to within twenty feet of him,
he'll realize you aren't me. That's when his tough-guy act
will crumble like the walls of Jericho."

"So just where do you figure to be while I'm savin' you
from bein' cut down like a clump of ragweed?"

"Flickin' a pesky gnat off my food."

Jack leaned over the map and at least acted as if he was
studying it.

"Now, just to make sure we got the thing worked out,
let's go over it once more. We can't afford a misstep. It
makes sense that Hogg will show himself right in front of
the hotel, standing where he's directly below Sanborn's
window. If you walk down the middle of the street, you'd
be a perfect target almost the whole way. That's why I want
you stayin' under the porticoes over the boardwalk all the
way to here," Cotton stressed, pointing to the last storefront

on the block. "That way, you're not exposed to whatever Lazarus Bellwood has in mind. Sanborn will want him to hold off his shot until the person he thinks is me is where he can get a good view of the takedown. He'll want to savor the moment. He'll probably hold Lazarus off until the very last second, just before Hogg makes his move to put me under arrest. That's why I say, when he discovers it's you instead of me, he'll lose whatever nerve he started with."

"I see where you're comin' from, but what if Hogg doesn't wait for Sanborn's signal or whatever it is—"

"Damn!"

"What?"

"I hadn't thought about that."

"About what?"

"Sanborn's signal. He can't signal to Hogg or anyone else without givin' himself away. He can't let anyone know he's waitin' in a hotel room with a sharpshooter to blow my insides all over the street. What kind of judge would do that? He'd lose whatever credibility he has."

"So how does Hogg pick his time to draw?"

"Only thing I can figure is it might not make any difference. Sanborn probably doesn't figure on Hogg livin' long enough to be of any further use to him. He's likely told Lazarus to shoot as soon as I, you, make a move to draw. If Hogg goes down before Lazarus shoots, so be it."

"Then you're sayin' if I don't go for my gun, nothing will happen?"

"Sanborn's likely made Hogg understand that he has to keep pushing until I get so angry I'll lose control and pull on him. He's countin' on me drawin' on Hogg."

"Knowin' you, I'd say he's got a right good plan."

"Uh-huh." Cotton screwed up his mouth in response. He looked at the floor, then the ceiling, then all around the room. He was pensive, lost in thought.

"When do you figure it's all goin' down?"

"Sanborn has to know we won't give up lookin' for Hogg for that girl's murder until we catch him. Sooner or later, that idiot will screw up and show himself. If that happens, Sanborn's goose is cooked. Hogg'll spill his guts like a fresh-killed buffalo. It's comin', and comin' soon. I can smell it hangin' heavy in the air. Could even be tomorrow."

"I guess I'd better get some shut-eye, then," Jack said with toss of his hand.

Chapter 49

O ne more of your stupid moves, Hogg, and I'll make sure they hang you after Burke is lying in the dirt. Since there is no doubt you killed that poor whore, all I'd have to do is turn the town's men loose. I'm sure they would make short work of it," Sanborn said, waving a bony finger in his face. "You'll have no defense. From now on, one misstep and you can count on being the second victim of a righteous shooting."

Lazarus was leaning against the far wall, his Sharps cradled across his chest. Hogg couldn't help but notice that the hammer was cocked. He was trapped, and he knew it. His nerves couldn't take much more of being shut up in a tiny room with Lazarus Bellwood, but he had apparently run out of options. All he had really wanted when he took the deal in the first place was enough money to get far away from the dirty, blistering desert. He'd figured he'd find a way to get paid before he had to face Cotton Burke, a man he knew damned well he couldn't beat.

I wonder if that old fool has all my money in that leather valise he's got sittin' on the bed, James Lee thought.

That's when his mind began conjuring a plan to grab the money and light a shuck for California or Canada. He'd have to get far away from both Sanborn and Bellwood. Ideas started floating around in his muddled brain like leaves in a whirlpool. He hadn't eaten for a while and he was in serious need of a drink, maybe a whole bottle of whiskey. *Maybe by the time Sanborn is ready for me, I'll be ready to make my escape.*

He was puzzling how he might accomplish his goal when a voice interrupted the silence. He was brought back by the realization that Sanborn was yelling at him. Screaming. Just then he felt like an earthquake had opened up the ground and he'd been thrown, tumbling, into a deep chasm at light speed, racing toward the center of the earth—a hellish prospect. He couldn't believe he was hearing what was being said.

"Hogg, because of your foolish, drunken tirade, I have to move the plan to tomorrow morning! Now, sit down and listen real good! If you mess up one more time, and once again become an impediment to a successful conclusion of my desire to see Sheriff Burke dead, Mr. Bellwood has been instructed to solve my problem. You *do* understand, do you not?"

"Hell, Judge, I don't understand half them fancy words of yours. If you're sayin' I'm in trouble if you don't get what you want, don't worry about it. I'll make it look like I dusted Burke, as planned, so your sharpshooter can take him. You just be sure you got my money ready. I can bite, too, you know. Just ask that whore Lucy." Hogg had gotten up to leave, when Sanborn made him understand who had the last word.

"Mr. Hogg, have you ever seen what a hunk of lead from a fifty-caliber Sharps can do to a man? It goes in about the size of your thumb. Coming out, and I assure you it will come out, the hole would be impossible to cover with a fist, even *your* big fat one."

Hogg stared at him with hatred in his eyes. "I'm goin' down and get something to eat."

"You most assuredly are not! Mr. Bellwood will bring food up here. Sit down, Mr. Hogg, and make yourself comfortable. I'll not say it again. You aren't going anywhere until I say so." Sanborn was forceful. James Lee found it hard to believe such a powerful, commanding voice could come out of that shriveled, emaciated body.

As angry as he was, Hogg obeyed. He couldn't explain why, exactly. Lazarus left the room to bring back food. Sanborn smiled with devilish satisfaction.

The next morning, well before first light, Sanborn lit a lamp and nudged Lazarus, who responded instantly.

"It's time we make our preparations. I'll get Hogg up. You go down and bring back some coffee. We need to be ready by dawn. I plan to see this stinking town wake up with a rebel yell and an announcement that will shake it to its core. I'll teach these belly-crawling snakes to elect a murderer for a sheriff." The look on Sanborn's face could have frightened a grizzly at that moment. The fury in his eyes was in full bloom as he prepared for his day of glory. Soon, his war would be over and he could sit in the shade of a big oak, sipping cider and reveling in his finest hour.

"On my way, Judge." Lazarus slipped on his boots, pulled up his suspenders, and eased out of the room and down the hall.

When Lazarus was gone, the old man kicked James Lee to wake him up. Being but a splinter of a man, his kick was more like a gentle nudge to a man the size of Hogg. The gunman merely groaned, mumbled something incoherent, and rolled over. Sanborn took this to mean he was being ignored, and no one ignored the great Judge Arthur J. Sanborn.

He reached over to where Hogg had put his six-shooter when he took it off. Sanborn pulled the .45 from the holster and aimed it directly at Hogg's head. Not a man familiar with guns, Sanborn was unaware of the differences in weight, balance, and trigger pulls of various models. His weak, palsied hands could do no better than bring the hammer back to half-cock. So he was surprised when he pulled the trigger and it failed to go off. He cursed so loudly that James Lee was at once awake, startled by the ferocity of the old man. As he opened his eyes and saw the .45 pointed his way, he nearly jumped out of bed.

He couldn't believe his eyes. Sanborn was prepared to kill him. Hogg jumped straight up with fire in his eyes, fists clenched, spluttering profanities and looking for someone to throttle. He charged the old man, grabbing him by the throat. Just as he was about to beat him senseless, Lazarus opened the door and barged in, rifle at the ready. He dropped the cups and coffeepot that he carried on a tray with a crash of steaming brew and shards of cheap chinaware.

"You lay one more hand on the judge and I'll blow you to hell, Hogg! Now, let him go and back off! Do it now or so help me the next bullet to exit this rifle will be the one that seals your doom." For a man with a steely quiet presence, Bellwood had an incredible ability to rise to the occasion. His forceful defense of the judge rocked Hogg back on his heels. He was in a bad situation and was now awake enough to recognize it. Sanborn had one of his revolvers, and Lazarus was aiming the Sharps squarely at his head. His choices were limited to say the least. He sat down on the bed in an effort to shake the sleep from his muddled head.

Sanborn placed the revolver back in its holster and turned to Lazarus.

"Thank you, Mr. Bellwood. As usual, you are the soul of timeliness," Sanborn said, then turned to Hogg. "Now, Mr. Hogg, shall we prepare for the opening of our little one-act play?"

Hogg was at the mercy of the old man calling the shots, as well as a man with a powerful weapon and an eagle eye. He nodded his acquiescence to Sanborn's request.

"You will start downstairs one hour after dawn, thus giving folks an opportunity to begin milling about, opening stores and such, and you will apprise the town's citizenry of its greatest liability: Sheriff Cotton Burke. Once outside, you will shout loud enough for the whole town to hear. Your declaration of the unspeakable crimes of Sheriff Burke must be made clear. Do you have any questions, Mr. Hogg?"

"None. Uh, sorry about that mess lyin' there. Reckon I don't like to be woke up suddenly."

"Mr. Lazarus will replenish the tray so you'll be refreshed and ready for your appearance on the street." He nodded to Lazarus, who responded by picking up the tray and once again retreating down the hall. "One last time: any questions, Mr. Hogg? Now's the time to ask."

"Uh, no sir, reckon I'm ready as I'm ever gonna be," he grumped.

Chapter 50

———❖———

A half hour before dawn, the door to Cotton's house opened and the sheriff stepped into the doorway, yawning and stretching. Henry, refusing to stay inside for the night, as usual, had insisted he remain there to keep watch. He gave the sheriff a nod. Cotton knew what that meant. Lazarus Bellwood, James Lee Hogg, and Arthur Sanborn were all still in the hotel.

"Well, old friend, if it turns out that today is Sanborn's choice, I reckon it could get mighty interesting before it's over. Want some coffee?"

"Coffee is good. You think three men ready to cause big trouble?"

"Come inside and we'll talk. I'd like your help."

Cotton went into the kitchen, stuck some wrinkled newspapers, old wanted dodgers, and wood shavings into the belly of the iron stove, added a couple of split logs, and lit it all. He filled the coffeepot with water from the well, opened a bag of Arbuckles' coffee, and poured some in. He put the pot on the burner and went into the other room to await the smell of the only thing that could wake him from his drowsiness, the result of lying awake half the night worrying whether he'd figured out Sanborn's scheme correctly. If he hadn't, Jack's life could be on the line. He was grateful to have Henry Coyote watching his friend's back.

The pot began to spew out the sweet smells of coffee brewing and then ready. He poured a cup for each of them. Cotton had to blow on his to cool it before sipping. For some reason, which the bewildered sheriff had never figured out, Henry simply lifted the tin cup to his lips and drank as if the steaming liquid was no more than a scoop of cool water from the stream. Cotton shook his head as Henry grinned in satisfaction. Finally, Henry put his cup down, as if to say, "Is there any more?" which, of course, there almost always was.

"How Henry help?"

Getting up to refill the Mescalero's cup, Cotton frowned as he said, "I think I know Sanborn well enough to have his scheme pretty well figured out. But as with most things where evil is concerned, something could go wrong. If he does what I expect, we'll be okay. If not, I'm going to need another pair of eyes ready to take action."

"What you think he do?"

Cotton went on to spell out in detail his version of Sanborn's likely plan. Henry sat in silence, listening intently, waiting to see a flaw in the sheriff's way of thinking. He saw nothing.

"You have good plan. I still keep watch on back. Man with fancy rifle slippery, like snake. I be ready if needed. You no see me."

"That's what I was hoping you'd say, my friend. The first thing I want you to do is cover me as I slip into the hotel from the alley entrance. Then stay and watch to make sure no one comes out that might present a danger to Jack. I fear more for him than myself. We don't need any back-shooters greasin' the wheels."

Henry nodded. He might not always understand Cotton's words, but he clearly understood their intent.

At this point, all Cotton knew to do was bide his time

until Sanborn made his move, that is to say enabling Hogg's
theatrical debut. It was exactly what Sanborn had done
many times before in making sure his son would always be
the last man standing. And he'd made certain the whole
town was aware of the coming storm. From past experience, Cotton knew what was coming; he just had no way of
knowing when. *That* was the unknown. He just knew he
had to be ready. He had prepared Jack for *his* role in the
drama and felt reasonably certain his deputy would pull it
off correctly. As for Henry, there was no doubt he was the
best man in the county to cover both of their backs. The
remaining unknowns were simple: Would Sanborn or either
of his cohorts change their well-practiced tactics at the last
minute and try to pull off something completely unexpected? Would Jack stick religiously to the instructions Cotton had laid out or bow to Melody's demands that he put a
bullet in Hogg as soon as he saw him? Were there any wild
cards, as there had been so many times before, when a plan
went awry?

Jack had gotten up well before dawn, trying his best to slip
out of bed without Melody awakening. He came close, but
not quite close enough. As he was pulling on his pants, he
heard a small voice coming from beneath the covers, asking where he was going.

"Just to the outhouse," he whispered. That turned out to
be the wrong answer. Melody came out of bed like a shot.

"What's the matter with the chamber pot I sent all the
way to New York for? All that hand-painted porcelain too
damned delicate for your ass? And since when do you need
to strap on your gun belt to go to the potty? What're you
trying to pull?" Melody was wide awake at that point. She
was stark naked as she stood, hands on hips, staring a hole
in him. Although it was still dark out, enough light snuck
beneath the door from the many lamps scattered all over the
saloon—which was open for business twenty-four hours a

day—to allow her to see exactly what was going on, and she didn't like it one bit.

"I, uh, told Cotton I'd be in early to attend to the needs of our one prisoner. Last time I saw him he wasn't lookin' too good, and—"

"What prisoner? You didn't say one damned thing about a prisoner when you came in last night. Who is he? What'd he do to get himself hauled into your iron hotel?"

"Nothin' serious, just drunk and disorderly. At least, I figured he was drunk. Maybe he was sick, or somethin'. That's why I best look in on him." Jack continued to buckle his gun belt. He figured Melody would understand and return to bed. He thought wrong.

"If the man's sick, I'll send Arlo to fetch the doc and check him over." She started to holler for the bartender, but Jack clamped a hand over her mouth before she could let out a sound.

"*Mmfph*," she mumbled, then grabbed his thumb and yanked down on it. He let out a yelp as she protested, "What's the big idea tryin' to shut me up? I'm only trying to help."

"I-I know, but there's no need to bother the doctor over something this unimportant. I'll just check him myself, and if he's all right, which I'm sure he is, we would have just upset Doc Winters by rousting him out of a sound sleep. If I find there is a problem, I promise I'll get help. Now, go back to bed and let me take care of this."

Melody narrowed her eyes and glared at him. Jack leaned over to pull on his boots. He could tell by the way she was moving her mouth from one side to another that she wasn't through with this. If she did something rash, Cotton's plan to take down James Lee Hogg and Judge Sanborn might be in jeopardy. His *own* life could be on the line, as well. He quickly slipped out of the room as she glared a hole in his back.

Chapter 51

In preparation for the possibility that today was the day of Sanborn's retribution, Jack was shrugging into Cotton's familiar blue cotton shirt, the one with the hole sewn up where a bullet had found its way into his side. The fit was fairly good, although Cotton was two inches taller and ten pounds heavier. Jack placed his own hat on the desk and had just put on Cotton's when he heard her voice from behind him.

"Jack! Why in the hell are you wearing Cotton's shirt? I'd know it anywhere. You better 'fess up. Something stinks mightily of skunk in here," Melody shouted.

"Melody! I thought you were going back to bed," Jack muttered meekly.

Melody was swishing about the sheriff's office in her flowing robe with pink feathers all the way from the floor to her neck. She hadn't bothered to put anything on under it, and had just tied it with a satin belt in front. She went over to the room that contained the cells. Glancing in, she stomped her foot and spun around.

"Where's that poor sick man you told me about? Did he suddenly die? I'm sick of your lies, Jack. I want some answers and I want them now. Why are you wearin'—oh, my god. What that judge said was true. There's some men coming to kill the sheriff and you're going out in his place to face them down! He's too big a coward to do his own dirty work."

"No, no, no, Melody. This is part of a plan we put together to trap that old man. He's the evil one here. There aren't any hombres comin' to Apache Springs intendin' to kill anybody. You were lied to."

"I don't believe you. Why would a judge lie to me? Huh? Tell me that."

"Because he is a crooked, vengeful, rotten old bastard that can't let go of his desire for revenge."

"Revenge for what?"

"Uh . . . I can't discuss that right now. Maybe at a later date." Jack was feeling trapped by her barrage of questions, and time was running out for him to be ready for Hogg's expected appearance.

"Now! I want to know now! And I'm not leaving until you tell me. Everything!" Melody's face had turned three shades of pink in her fury. She gritted her teeth.

Frustrated beyond control, Jack reached for her arm to usher her back out the door and set her on a course straight for her bawdy house. Just then she did something quite unexpected. She reached into her robe pocket and pulled out her Remington double-derringer. She pointed it at Jack, her hand shaking as she pulled back the hammer.

"Don't think you can just walk me out that door, either!" she said, her voice full of anger. She stuck the derringer in his chest.

"What the hell, Melody! *You* gonna shoot me? Why? You figure to keep me from getting shot by shooting me yourself? That musta took some real cogitatin'."

"I, uh, no . . ." Her eyes seemed to be searching for some elusive answer to his questions.

As she was muttering incoherently, Jack took the opportunity to grab her gun away from her. Her expression was

one of shock and waning fury. He knew she wasn't going to
go away quietly. He had to do something, and he didn't have
a lot of time to think about it. He did the only thing he could
under the circumstances: he whirled her around and shoved
her into one of the empty jail cells. When she realized what
had just happened, she burst into her terrible rant all over
again, stomping her feet and cursing a blue streak. A couple
of the words that came out of her mouth he could swear he'd
never even heard before. He gave her an "I'm sorry" grimace
and a shrug as he locked her in and hung the keys on the
hook next to the gun rack. He went back to finishing the job
of making himself appear as close as possible to the sheriff,
Cotton Burke. He checked his Remington and sat on the
edge of the desk to wait for whatever was to come. He tried
to shut out Melody's string of curses and keep it from reaching everybody in town. The closest he could come was to
close both the window and the door.

Cotton and Henry watched the street in front of the hotel
from behind the curtains of Cotton's house. They could see
out, but no one could see in. Just as Cotton was beginning
to believe he'd been wrong about how Sanborn's scheme
would unfold, the hotel door opened and out stepped James
Lee Hogg. The man looked as if he'd slept in his clothes.
He hiked up his gun belt and looked around nervously. He
walked to the front of the porch and stepped into the street.

"Time for me to go, Henry. I'm taking the alley out back
and crossing the street at the west end of town. No one will
pay any attention to me if I act as if I'm just out for a casual
stroll. You know what you need to do. Keep to the rear of
the buildings to the east before you cut over behind the jail
and up to the hotel. Keep a keen eye out for Jack. Go ahead."

Henry nodded and left by the rear door. Cotton was right
behind him as he turned in the opposite direction. When he
stopped after a few steps and looked around, Henry had
already disappeared. The sheriff bolted down the alleyway,
reaching in a couple of minutes the point where he intended

to cross the street. He slowed and looked around the corner of the gunsmith's storefront before heading across to the other side. With the possible exception of a woman sweeping the boardwalk in front of the dressmaker's shop, he went unnoticed as he sauntered casually across the dusty street on a trajectory that kept him out of Hogg's sight.

When he reached the back stairs to the hotel, he looked down the alley to find Henry already in position to watch the rear door while also keeping an eye on Jack and anyone who might try getting behind him. Cotton opened the rear door and slipped inside. There was no one in either the hall or on the stairs. He took them two at a time as he raced up to the second floor. He slowed as he approached Sanborn's room, from where he figured Lazarus would take his shot. As he neared the room, he leaned close so he could hear anything that might be said between them. At first there was no sound, but after a minute or so, he heard Sanborn giving a last-minute order.

"Don't shoot until he goes for his gun, remember that. It has to look like Hogg killed him in self-defense with a clean shot."

"Don't you worry, Judge, I'll have him dead to rights the moment he gets out of the shadow of the building next door."

Cotton smiled to himself. That's when he heard Hogg's first shouted declaration.

"Citizens of Apache Springs, I, Deputy U.S. Marshal James Lee Hogg, have here in my hand a warrant for the arrest of one Sheriff Cotton Burke for murder, worthy of a hangin' by all that's holy. This vicious killer has, uh, pulled the wool over your eyes far too long, and I aim to end his reign of power over the good people here who thought they had an honest and honorable man as their sheriff. Yes, the guilty man is none other than Sheriff Cotton Burke, the man who murdered an innocent young man in Texas. It's time he got dealt with properly. I'm here on orders of the Honorable Judge Arthur Sanborn. Come on out, Sheriff!"

Chapter 52

James Lee Hogg puffed up his chest in self-importance as people began slowly to step outside their places of business and venture onto the boardwalks that lined the main street through the center of Apache Springs, to see what the commotion was about. They were smart enough to know to stay a safe distance from the boastful Hogg, for his words were certain to bring a swift reaction from the sheriff. Should a confrontation ensue, and bullets begin to fly, none wished to be the unlucky recipient of a stray hunk of lead.

"I'm callin' you out, Sheriff Burke! Step out and face me, if you dare!"

All eyes turned as Jack emerged from the jail, staying close to the buildings and keeping in the shadows of the porticoes that popped up intermittently along the way to the hotel. His hand rested on the butt of his Remington .44 as he strolled along at a leisurely pace, obviously in no hurry, even though Hogg was demanding he do just that.

Hogg was becoming more and more impatient for the sheriff to appear before him instantly. He began wringing his hands, shifting from one foot to the other, looking generally disconcerted. He shifted his glance from the street to buildings on the other side, to windows that overlooked the road. That's when he must have noticed the onlookers shift their gaze from him to somewhere down the street toward the jail. His nervousness seemed to increase by the second, as perspiration began to trickle down his forehead.

"Where the hell are you, Burke? I can't wait all day for you to show up so I can either put you in irons or plug you where you stand! There's a circuit judge waitin' to take you to trial, and he's anxious to get on with it."

Hearing the racket outside, Mayor Orwell Plume stepped from his door and took up a position next to the town's clerk. They looked at each other for a moment before Plume spoke up.

"So that's why the old judge wanted to hold court in the street. He was out to get the sheriff all along. I knew there was something wrong with that man from the beginning. I don't like what I'm watching."

"You figure we should round up some folks to back the sheriff? There's no damned way he could have done what that fool's claimin'." The clerk looked at Plume, awaiting an answer. Plume said nothing. He seemed frozen in place.

Just then Jack stepped out from beneath the cover of an overhanging portico and onto the street. He was no more than twenty feet from Hogg. The phony marshal instantly recognized Jack and grew flustered. He clearly didn't know what to make of this development. He twisted to look up at Sanborn's window for some sign, some direction.

Listening at Sanborn's door, Cotton heard the distinct sound of a hammer being cocked. That was his cue to make his move. He took one step back from the door and slammed into it with all the force he could muster. The door was ripped from its flimsy hinges, crashing to the floor to the complete astonishment of Lazarus and Sanborn. Suddenly seeing his nemesis standing a mere three feet from him, the wide-eyed old man began screaming at the top of his lungs.

"Kill him! Kill him, you fool! Kill him before he shoots me!"

Unnerved by Sanborn's crazed yelling, Lazarus tried his damnedest to turn the Sharps rifle around in Cotton's direction before the sheriff could take aim, but the barrel first banged against the windowsill, then caught in the wafting curtains, causing him to hesitate that one split second too long. Cotton's Colt bucked as it roared, spewing fire and smoke to send a lethal hunk of spinning lead straight for Lazarus's forehead. The Sharps flew from his hands at the impact, crashing to the floor in front of Sanborn, who looked at it like it was a snake. Lazarus's death was instantaneous, as his body was hurled through the open window, taking pieces of curtain, window frame, and glass with him and landing with a dusty *whump* on the street below. Having come to rest, sprawled behind a startled James Lee Hogg like a discarded bag of laundry, the body of the late Lazarus Bellwood didn't even twitch as the dust from his untimely demise slowly dissipated in the slight breeze. The whole thing had transpired in the blink of an eye.

Hogg's eyes were wide as a barn owl's. He swallowed hard, then spun back to face Jack. He had yet to complete his part of the bargain. He was suddenly face-to-face with a scowling deputy sheriff with a cocked Remington .44 aimed directly at his head. Hogg's hand was shaking so badly, he couldn't even find his still-holstered weapon. Finally, resigned to his fate, he could think of nothing to do but slump his shoulders in defeat.

"Unbuckle that gun belt, Hogg, and take off the badge we both know you somehow got illegally. There's no marshal on earth that would pin a badge on you. You and I are going to revisit the jail. Your last visit there didn't last long enough. This time I'll venture to guess you'll be there for a month, which is when a real circuit judge will be here to pronounce you guilty of murder and set a date for a hangin'. I personally will be on hand to enjoy that moment."

Hogg hung his head and slowly began the trek to the jail, defeated and shamed in front of the whole town.

* * *

In the hotel room, Arthur Sanborn was spitting angry curses over what he saw as a violation of his privacy. He wasn't through seeking his vendetta against this pompous sheriff, not by a long shot.

"You've done it again! You just shot an innocent man down for no cause whatsoever. He was simply in my employ to assure there'd be no shenanigans when Marshal Hogg tried to arrest you. I'll see you swing from a limb for this, you bastard; you mark my words!"

"Oh, I'll mark them all right, Sanborn, but I doubt it'll get you anywhere."

"We'll see about that when I bring charges against you for cheating a man out of his life by your callous act."

"Well, in the meantime, I think you and I will saunter down to the jail and continue our little chat there as we await a telegram I'm expecting."

"Telegram? Telegram from whom? Is this another of your tricks, Burke?"

"No trick, Sanborn. Now, get going. You might as well bring along your belongings, too. I have a feeling you'll not be comin' back."

As they left the hotel, the mayor, the clerk, and several of the citizenry crowded around the two of them. Their curiosity was palpable. Questions came thick as flies to manure.

"What's going on, Sheriff? Who is that man lying in the street? Did you shoot him? Why'd your deputy arrest that marshal?" Mayor Plume bombarded him with inquiry after inquiry, as did several other people who shouted their own queries.

Cotton held up his hand to stem the tide of anxiety surrounding the town's citizens.

"Folks, if you'll let me get this man down to the jail, I'll explain to everyone's satisfaction as soon as *I* have all the answers myself." The sheriff pushed Sanborn ahead of him and made his way toward the boardwalk in order to pinch off much of the crowd. Only a few people at a time could be accommodated by the plank walkway. Many dropped by the wayside, choosing to return to their shops and businesses. But Mayor Plume doggedly followed the sheriff's footsteps, chin held out as if to say *he* would not be denied answers.

When they reached the jail door, Sanborn was nearly knocked on his rump when Melody burst out like a buffalo stampeding, arms flailing to clear the way. She was sputtering some gibberish about a fine thing for a gentleman to do, humiliating a lady, or at least that was Cotton's assessment of her words, unintelligible as they were.

"What the hell was that all about, Jack? Why was Melody here?"

"I had to lock her up because she demanded I stay out of your business with Sanborn. She held a gun on me. Didn't give me any choice."

Cotton smiled and snorted. "You're learning, my friend, you're learning. Lock this snake up, will you. Better not put him in the same cell as Hogg. I'm not sure they'll be gettin' along after how well their plan went."

Jack shoved the hesitant Arthur Sanborn into the cell and closed and locked the door. Sanborn was still fuming as Hogg sat morosely on his cot. Cotton sent Jack to fetch the undertaker.

"While you're out, bring Henry here from the alley behind the hotel.

"What's he doin' there?"

"Coverin' both our butts."

Chapter 53

———◆———

Cotton hadn't seen Mayor Plume since he sent him off in a huff with no answers to his myriad of questions. He'd picked up a horse from the livery and sent Henry back to the Wagner ranch with an acknowledgment of his appreciation for all his help. No word had passed between them concerning Henry's insistence that Cotton was in grave danger, as Cotton hadn't really seen things that way. He'd felt he knew Arthur Sanborn well enough to stay at least one step ahead of him. Lazarus Bellwood had been a wild card, but he never doubted the eventual outcome. He'd figured out early on that there had to be someone else involved in shooting down all those men who'd opposed Lucky Bill Sanborn, and when it appeared Lazarus was that person, things seemed to fall into place rather nicely.

"What're you plannin' on doin' with those two owl-hoots we got locked up, Sheriff?" Jack asked, leaning back in a chair with his boots on Cotton's desk.

"I plan to wait."

"Wait? On what?"

* * *

When Jack came back later in the afternoon, he found Cotton sitting on the edge of the desk with a big grin on his face. He was reading a telegram, likely delivered by the telegraph operator Jack had seen racing down the street just as he pushed through the batwing doors of the saloon. Cotton chuckled at what he was reading when Jack entered the jailhouse door.

"You're lookin' darned chipper for a man with a dead body on display just down the street in front of the undertaker's," Jack said as he began searching around for his coffee cup.

"Uh-huh."

"So what's on that paper there that's got you lookin' like you just discovered a gold nugget the size of your fist?"

"Huh?"

"I said, what's got you lookin' so pleased?"

"Oh. That confirmation I told you about."

"Confirmation of what?"

"What I figured all along. There is a *weasel* in the woodpile. And it's time to show him up for the liar he is right now."

"What in tarnation are you talkin' about?"

"It's all right here on this paper. And in spades."

"So now we're talkin' about a poker game?"

"No, no, we're talkin' about makin' sure a certain rattler gets what's comin' to him, or maybe even . . ."

"You mean Sanborn? That who's got you all smiles?"

"In a manner of speakin'. Yep."

"So what's it say?"

"Solid gold evidence and it could prove deadly to someone."

"Who? You, me, Emily?"

"Nope. None of us . . . now."

"The judge?"

"Yep. It's time to bring him down to earth."

"How do you figure on doin' that? And what the hell's in that telegram?"

"Proof."

"Of . . . ?"

"Proof that the no-good son of a bitch is a liar and a murderer. And it's goin' to get him put away for the rest of his worthless life. That is if he doesn't hang first."

"Who's that telegram from?"

"Our own cagey bounty hunter, Thorn McCann."

"Why would he send you a telegram? Isn't he holed up at the hotel with Delilah Jones?"

"Nope, not anymore. He's been out of town for four days. Gone to see the governor. I'm amazed you didn't notice, since Delilah has been seen around town without Thorn at her side. He volunteered for a mission and I accepted his offer."

"So what's on that paper, or are you gonna make me guess?"

"Says here we got ourselves a genuine counterfeit judge. And you were right in your assessment of James Lee Hogg—he's no marshal, either."

"So, if the judge ain't a judge and Hogg ain't a marshal, we got them dead to rights?"

"Yep."

"We damn sure got the goods on Hogg for killin' Lucy, but how do you plan on provin' Sanborn killed anyone? I've not even seen him with a gun," Jack said with a quiz-zical look.

"I agree that may be difficult, since the man he hired to shoot a number of men is dead."

"Yeah, thanks to you."

Since he still hadn't confided in Mayor Plume about the reason for the shooting of Lazarus Bellwood and the events leading up to it, Cotton asked Jack to bring the mayor down to the jail before he confronted Sanborn. Cotton had always thought Plume was a rather shallow man, easily pumped up by flattery and constantly requiring a boost to his ego. But the sheriff was also aware that there were times when he needed the mayor's cooperation. This he figured to be one of those times.

"Well, Sheriff Burke, I'm here," the mayor said, as he stormed into the jail. "Are you finally ready to take me into your confidence about the occurrences of yesterday and the claims made by that Hogg fellow?"

"Yes, I am, Mayor. I hope you'll forgive my reluctance to discuss the whole thing in front of a lot of folks who really didn't need to know what was goin' on. Perhaps you could see your way to excuse my secretiveness."

Plume loosened up and said, "Yeah, I reckon a sheriff has to have a few things he don't blab to just anyone. Apology accepted."

"Thank you, Mayor. Now, about the two men being held in our jail, we have a messy situation, particularly over that man claimin' to be a judge. First of all, he isn't."

"He isn't what?"

"He isn't a judge. I have here in my hand a telegram from a friend at the capitol in Santa Fe proving that Arthur Sanborn is no more a judge than me or Jack. The word is straight from the governor." Cotton handed the telegram to Mayor Plume, who read it with eyes growing wider by the second.

"Well, I'll be damned. That sniveling highbinder pulled one over on me. Why, if it was up to me, I'd say hang him now and be done with it."

"How about you and me confront him together," Cotton said.

Chapter 54

The pounding on Cotton's front door did not come as a pleasant wakeup call. The yelling wasn't much help, either. He swung his legs off the bed, pulled on his pants, and lumbered, barefoot, to the door. He swung it open to find Memphis Jack Stump in a lather, hollering loudly enough to wake the whole town.

"Cotton! Thank heavens you're here instead of out at the Wagner place. We got ourselves a problem. A *big* problem."

Cotton stepped aside sleepily, yawned, and waved Jack to sit on the small couch.

"I'll make some coffee. I'm goin' to need it to wake up enough to understand what you're blatherin' about." He had started to the kitchen, when Jack's next words stopped him in his tracks.

"You won't need any coffee once I tell you what's up. You'll damn sure be awake."

"Uh-huh."

"First off, you *do* remember tellin' me to go back over

and make up with Melody as soon as I got them two owl-hoots tucked in, don't you?"

"Yeah, that's what I said. And I assume that's what you did."

"Correct, amigo. Left about eleven o'clock, after the prisoners were fed and had a chance at the outhouse one last time. Then I went to the saloon to find Melody. She was all smiles when I walked into the place. It was almost as if nothing ever happened between us."

"Jack, you're tellin' me things I either know or don't care about. My head is full of cobwebs because I need coffee. So, be quick about it or I'm brewin' up some Arbuckles'."

"Just wanted to make sure we both remembered last night's instructions, that's all."

"You're covered. I remember."

"Well, then we got two problems. The first one is the old man, Sanborn. He's deader'n a picket fence. And the second one is: James Lee Hogg is nowhere to be found. Busted out! Lit a shuck for who knows where."

"What the . . . ! Why didn't you tell me?"

"What the hell you figure I'm doin'?"

Cotton grabbed his shirt off the chair beside his bed, pulled on a pair of socks and his boots, then ran his fingers through his tousled hair before putting on his Stetson. He picked up his gun belt on the way out, buckling it as he busted through the door. Jack was having trouble keeping up as Cotton charged down the street toward the jail like a raging bull. When he threw open the door, he rushed inside, aiming straight to the cells. What Jack had said was certainly true, and completely unexplainable, by Cotton, at least.

"This just the way you found things when you came in, Jack?"

"Exactly the way. And in case you're interested, I got no explanation, either."

"Run down and get Doc Winters. We're goin' to need to know how ol' Sanborn died. Maybe Hogg killed him, maybe not."

Jack left in a hurry. Cotton went into Hogg's cell looking for an explanation. There was no indication that Hogg had been able to find something to *pry* open the lock—no scratches, no bent pieces. Everything was completely intact. It appeared that the door had been opened with a key. Cotton went back out to where the keys to the cells were kept. The one to James Lee's cell was still there on the ring with the other. He had to unlock Sanborn's cell to go inside.

If someone came in the middle of the night to free James Lee, why didn't he cut Sanborn loose, too? He checked the man's pockets for anything that might explain his sudden demise. That's when he noticed Sanborn's valise. He'd let the old man keep it when he put him in his cell. He'd checked first to make sure there wasn't a gun or a knife in there, or anything else that might make escape possible. The only thing in it was a bundle of papers and about a hundred dollars in greenbacks.

The whole thing made no sense. He had gone back out to his desk when Doc Winters came in.

"Understand you got yourself a corpse, Sheriff."

"Yep, and I need to know how he slipped off into the world of the dead without showin' any indication he was sick or somethin'. He's in there, cell's open." Cotton motioned the doc toward the back room.

"This isn't a decent place to make a proper determination of death. Especially when there's no evidence, like blood or holes in the body. Help me get him down to my examining room and I'll do what I can to solve your mystery."

Jack and Cotton lifted the emaciated corpse of Arthur J. Sanborn and toted it down the street to the doctor's office. Once inside, they placed him on the table on which both Thorn and Henry had been treated recently.

"You two may want to go back to the jail and wait. Things can get a little gruesome when you're trying to find a cause of death. I'll let you know as soon as I have some answers."

*   *   *

"Winters is a good doc, Cotton, at least when he's sober; he'll figure it out," Jack said, watching the sheriff pace back and forth across the room. "Anyway, you can't be all that tore up over Sanborn's death, can you? After all, wasn't he the one who wanted to see *you* sprawled out there on the street, all cold and stiff?" Jack had seated himself comfortably in the sheriff's swivel chair, tenting his fingers while Cotton kept the air in the stuffy office moving nicely.

"Yeah, it's not really Sanborn I'm concerned about. The important thing is where the hell is James Lee Hogg and how did he escape? *That's* what's botherin' me."

"Yeah, well, I been figurin' on it, myself, and haven't come to any satisfactory solution," Jack answered.

"If someone came in to break James Lee out of jail, why didn't they set Sanborn loose, also? Or was Sanborn already dead?"

"Yep, that's a real puzzlement." Jack got up, walked over to the stove, and stuffed some kindling in to start a fire for coffee. He went out back and brought back a pot full of cold water and set it on the top of the stove. He was fishing around for the Arbuckles' when Cotton stopped pacing and began staring at Jack. "What're you lookin' at me like that for?"

"It just occurred to me you're takin' all this pretty casual-like. You know somethin' I don't?"

"Of course not. What would make you say such a thing? You think I had something to do with James Lee's escape and Sanborn's death?"

Just then Doc Winters strode in through the open door. Overhearing Jack's words, he jumped into the conversation.

"In case you're wondering, Cotton, and since your deputy brought it up, I can say for certain Jack had nothing to do with Sanborn's death, nor did anyone else. The old man's ticker just up and quit. It was worn out. He was in pretty bad health anyway, and I suspect the thought of spending the rest of his life behind bars was more than he could take.

Didn't help none that a man was shot right in front of him, either. No one's to blame, except maybe Sanborn himself."

"His frustration at not gettin' me likely took its toll, too. I reckon that makes it easier on all of us, then." Cotton stopped pacing for a moment. "Of course, that doesn't explain Hogg's disappearance," he said, more to himself than anyone.

The doctor left, and Jack asked if it would be all right if he went over to the saloon and had a brandy. The sheriff just waved him off and took over the swivel chair Jack had been using. He frowned as various scenarios blew through his head. *How the hell does someone escape an iron-barred cage without leaving any evidence behind? He doesn't, and that's all there is to it.*

That's when the idea hit him. He got up and meandered over to Melody's Golden Palace of Pleasure. Not in any hurry, since the town's latest threat had passed. In fact, he was feeling more relaxed than he had in months. When he pushed through the batwing doors, he spotted Jack at the end of the bar laughing with Arlo, the bartender. Cotton walked up and stood next to Jack, jerked his head to one side, then turned and walked off to an empty table. Jack got the message and picked up his glass of brandy and followed.

"Jack, when you and Melody were makin' up, did she happen to ask if I had stayed in town or gone to the Wagner ranch?"

"She asked if you were through puttin' me in danger for the night. I did mention you were exhausted and had left me in charge while you went home and hit the sack."

"So, she figured *you'd* be stayin' at the jail to watch the prisoners?"

"Naw. I told her you had been generous and said I should get a little shut-eye, too."

"What was her response to that?"

"She grabbed my arm and sorta dragged me upstairs. In case you're wonderin', I didn't resist."

"Did she leave the bed before you started sawin' logs?"

"Yeah, once to do her business. She was only gone a few minutes. Why?"

"And when you first came into the saloon after beddin' down the prisoners at the jail, were there any customers still here?"

"Yeah, a few cowboys were sittin' around, playin' cards, and chattin'. Mostly, it was them that joined our posse when we went lookin' for James Lee the first time. Why all these questions?"

"No reason. Just that I'm a curious soul. I'll see you later."

As Cotton walked out onto the porch, he saw several cowboys riding into town. They dismounted in front of the saloon and walked right by him without a word other than a barely audible greeting from one of them. As he passed their horses, he noticed something unusual, at least for cowboys.

He noticed two shovels tied on behind the cantle of one of the saddles. He smiled to himself.

Sometimes, justice does manage to take care of itself in proper fashion, he mused as he crossed the street and thought, *I hope they buried him deep.*

Chapter 55

———————◆———————

When Thorn McCann arrived back in town, he could
sense that something was different. The streets seemed
alive with people coming and going, doing business and
getting on with their lives just as if there were no threat
from a phony judge and a crazed gunslinger. He stopped
and dismounted in front of the jail. When he went inside, he
found the sheriff with his feet up on his desk, cleaning his
fingernails with a penknife and whistling to himself.

"Mornin', Sheriff. You appear chipper. Thought I'd stop
by and see if that information I sent you was helpful. Looks
like it mighta been."

"Well, McCann, I must say it was, indeed. Thanks for
sending it. I reckon we're even now."

"Since you appear to be pretty calm about the whole
Sanborn situation, I'm assuming he got wind of you finding out he was a liar and charlatan. Probably hit the road
before you threw him in the pokey."

"You assume wrong. Sanborn's dead, Hogg's dead, and
Lazarus Bellwood, Sanborn's hired killer, is likewise

deceased. Sorry you missed all the action." Cotton closed his penknife and stuck it back in his pocket. "Got pretty lively around here for a while, though."

"*You* killed Sanborn?" McCann asked.

"Nope. He did himself in with a heart that was so full of bitterness and hatred it just naturally burst. He died like he lived, angry and alone."

"Good. Saved the town a trial. But at least you gunned down James Lee Hogg, huh?"

"Nope, wrong again, McCann. He was, uh, apparently the unfortunate victim of some righteous fellows lookin' to teach him some manners as to the proper treatment of a fallen angel."

"And that Bellwood character? He commit suicide?"

"Well, no. I reckon I *do* have to take credit for him fallin' out a window."

"As a result of a little push from our erstwhile sheriff, I presume?"

"More like him walking in front of a hunk of lead from a forty-five."

Thorn snorted and shook his head. "Three dead rattlers. My, my, sounds like you have your town back all nice and peaceable and you hardly had to lift a finger, other than your trigger finger, of course."

"Just the way I like it." Cotton stood up, stretched, and stepped out from around the desk. "Now, if you'll excuse me, Mr. McCann, I'm going to go to the hotel and look in on that Denby Biddle fella. Haven't seen him around. Kinda wonder if he's too afraid to come out of his room after nearly being murdered by redskins."

"He did seem a little pale last I saw, if I remember correctly," Thorn said.

"Indeed. I must admit I'm also rather curious about what he was carryin' around in that wooden box he clung to like it was a matter of life or death."

"Mind if I walk along? I'm kinda anxious to lay these appreciative eyes on one Delilah Jones. I'm certain you understand."

Cotton snickered. "Reckon I do at that. C'mon."

When they walked into the hotel, Cotton went straight for the check-in counter.

"Howdy, Sheriff. Lookin' for anyone in particular?" the desk clerk asked.

"That little fella, Denby Biddle. He around?"

"Why, no. The day you brought him to town, he came down asking for Bart Havens. I told him Mr. Havens was dead. He flew into a rage; slammed his fist down on the counter, uttering things I dare not repeat. Not if I want to keep my job, at least."

"He *did* take a room, though, didn't he?" Cotton asked.

"Oh, no. He rushed out of here with a small wooden box tucked under his arm and headed straight for the Butterfield office. No more'n an hour later I saw him board the stage for Las Cruces or Lordsburg, don't know which."

"Damn!" Cotton muttered. "There were some things I needed to ask him."

As he started to leave the hotel, he noticed Thorn hurrying up the stairs toward Delilah's room without a word. Since he knew Thorn was looking forward to seeing his dark-eyed beauty, he could easily forgive the slight. Jack was sitting on the bench out front when Cotton got back to the jail.

"Where'd you go?" Jack asked.

"I'd been intendin' on checkin' on that little fella, Denby. Wanted to be sure he'd recovered from his experience with the Indians."

"You find him?"

"Nope. Looks like I missed him by several days. Took the stage and skedaddled out of here like a frightened rabbit. That little skirmish with the Indians musta spooked him. Too bad. We'll probably never know what was in that polished walnut box he never let leave his sight."

As Cotton took a seat next to him, Jack motioned toward the hotel.

"Looks like Thorn and Delilah are doin' the same. He say anything to you about goin' somewhere?"

Cotton turned in the direction Jack was pointing and rubbed his chin, deep in thought, as he saw Thorn McCann and Delilah Jones board the Butterfield stage headed south.

"Almost looks like they suddenly bumped up against some unfinished business," Cotton mused. "Curious, real curious."

"Like what? You think it had to do with the box?"

"Can't say for sure, but I think it's likely," Cotton said. "*And* I got a strange feelin' we haven't heard the last of them two."